TH ON A BRANCH LINE

DEATH ON A BRANCH LINE

ANDREW MARTIN

ISIS
LARGE PRINT
Oxford

First published in Great Britain 2008
by
Faber and Faber Ltd.

Published in Large Print 2013 by ISIS Publishing Ltd.,
7 Centremead, Osney Mead, Oxford OX2 0ES
by arrangement with
Faber and Faber Ltd.

CIP data is available for this title from the British Library

ISBN 978–0–7531–9196–5 (hb)
ISBN 978–0–7531–9197–2 (pb)

Printed and bound in Great Britain by
T. J. International Ltd., Padstow, Cornwall

I would like to thank, in no special order: Colonel Parkinson of Sandhurst Protocol and Media; Mike Ellison of the North Eastern Railway Association; Phillip Davies of the Armoury of St James; the staff of the Porthcurno Telegraph Museum, and my fellow members of The Railway Club (www.therailwayclub.org). All departures from fact are my responsibility.

Author's note

Death on *a Branch Line* is a work of fiction. It does not seek to depict anyone who might have lived in 1911, or indeed anyone who lives today.

PART ONE

Friday, 21 July, 1911

CHAPTER
ONE

"Palace Hotel," said the voice from Scarborough.

"Have you any rooms for tonight and tomorrow?" I asked.

"Sorry, sir," said the voice, "but we're quite full up."

"Any good?" asked Wright, and he propped open the police office door to let in fresh air, or what passed for it in York station.

I put the receiver back on its cradle and shook my head.

"Pity," said Wright. "It's a good one is that. Bang on the front."

Old man Wright, the police office clerk, already had his weekend by the sea booked so he'd been pretty cheerful all that Friday — and pretty annoying with it. Just now, we were the only two in the office and he was giving me the benefit of his full attention. He stepped forward to wind the handle again.

"How about trying the Grand?" he said.

"I can't run to that," I said.

"Eh?" he said, for he was connected to the station operator again, and had only one ear cocked in my direction.

3

The office clock said three twenty-two. I still hadn't eaten my dinner, and it sat on the desk in front of me: bread and cheese and a bottle of warmish tea — an engineman's snap.

By propping open the door, Wright had only changed the quality of the stifling heat, not reduced it. It now came with a smoke smell and a rising roar. On some distant platform, a porter or guard was shouting "This is York!" as if he'd only just discovered the fact.

"Scarborough Grand, please," Wright said to the operator and then, turning to me: "Whatever price they quote you, just say, 'I'll pay half.'"

"Come off it."

"It's what's expected," said Wright, as he handed me the receiver once again, saying, "You're connected."

He then stood back with folded arms to watch.

"Is that Scarborough Grand?" I said into the receiver.

"I've just *told* you it is," said a man.

"It's a different person speaking now," I said.

"Must I repeat everything I've already said?" asked the man in a peevish tone.

"I don't know," I said, "since I didn't hear it."

Some muttering from down the line, which I broke in on with: "This is Detective Sergeant Stringer of the York Railway Police," for that would put some folk on their mettle. But this fellow just gave a sigh.

I asked him: "Do you have any rooms for over the week-end?"

"For how many people?"

"Two."

"Double bed?"

4

"Aye."

The line went half-dead. It was like suddenly going deaf. Looking through the door I could see clear across Platform Four to where a little saddle-tank engine had rolled into view.

"What's going off?" asked Wright, who was forever nosing into other blokes' business in a way that would have been somehow more tolerable if he'd been a younger man.

"Fellow's hunting up a double room for me," I said.

I knew very well that the man at the Grand would only be looking in a ledger, but I pictured him (a small, bald man in my mind's eye) wiping the sweat off his brow as he climbed the mighty staircases of the great hotel in search of an unoccupied room. He'd be a little bloke in a stand-up cellulose collar that chafed at his neck, and all the well-spoken chatter and swanky clothes of the guests would make him furious.

Cradling the receiver between neck and chin, I took off my suit coat and hung it over the back of the chair. Then I looked again through the door. On the footplate of the tank engine there was no driver but just a pawky-looking kid, going ten-to-the-dozen with his coal shovel. I thought: *What's that daft little bugger about? He's over-stoking; the engine'll blow off in a minute if he doesn't look out.* Of course it just would happen that, at the very instant the man at the Scarborough Grand came back to the telephone, the safety valves on the tank engine lifted and the excess steam began screaming through them.

"Hello?" I bawled down the line to the man at the Scarborough Grand. "Could you just hold on a tick?"

Wright was pacing about the office, shaking his head.

The kid on the footplate had finally left off shovelling and was climbing carefully down from the engine looking guiltily to left and right as he did so. I thought for a minute he was going to run away from it, for it was bad practice to make an engine blow off, what with all the wastage of water and steam and the horrible racket.

"Hello there?" I yelled again into the receiver.

I motioned to Wright to shut the police office door, but before he could do so, the stream of din ended, at which precise moment I heard the click of the line to Scarborough going dead.

"What happened?" said Wright as I replaced the receiver.

"Bloke hung up," I said.

"Pity is that," said Wright, who was pulling at his collar to ventilate his scrawny self.

I glanced down at the black steel box that supported the receiver and its cradle — it always put me in mind of a little tomb, somehow.

"You should try again," said Wright, from behind the pages of the *Yorkshire Evening Press*, for he was now back at his desk and looking over the pages of that paper. "Every room at the Grand boasts a sea view, you know. Why have you left it so late, any road?"

"Just . . . forgot," I said.

"You'll be in lumber with your missus over that," he said from behind the paper. "Likes flower gardens, doesn't she, your missus?"

The heading on the back page of Wright's paper was "The Crisis At Hand".

Wright put down the paper.

"The blooms in the Valley Gardens'll be absolutely glorious at this time of year — absolutely bloody glorious."

Wright stood up, pitched the *Press* across his desk and quit the office, leaving the door open behind him, having no doubt thought of another way of avoiding doing any work. I read the heading now uppermost on the *Press*: "The German Move in Morocco".

It was holiday time, but all the papers were full of war talk.

I was now alone in the police office, and I watched through the door as the saddle-tank engine moved away. I then looked around the green walls — at the Chief's half-a-dozen shields won for shooting that rested on the mantel-shelf. (There was no railway police team as such, so the Chief shot for the Wagon Works.) I glanced at the photograph of Constables Whittaker and Ward competing in the tug-of-war at the North Eastern Railway Police Southern Division Athletics, which had been held at Doncaster racecourse in pelting rain two years since. The picture showed them in the process of *losing* at tug-of-war, but nobody was to know that since the other team was cut out of the picture.

Then there was the photograph by the armoury cupboard, which showed some big men in shorts making a pyramid by standing on each other's shoulders and supporting, at the very pinnacle, a slightly smaller man. These men were soldiers, and this pyramid was an achievement of the Chief's days in the York and Lancashire Regiment, which was not named after York, the city in whose railway station I presently sat, but after the *Duke* of York, whose lands were somewhere else altogether — although still within Yorkshire, of course. The Chief had been a sergeant major, and mad keen on fitness.

I looked at the dead dust of the fireplace: a poker lay in it, left over from the last time the fire had been stirred. That was three months since. It was said that the temperature had lately touched 99 degrees in the shade in London, and an artist at the *Press* had taken to drawing a fat, sweating face in the middle of the flaming sun that appeared above the weather bulletin.

I sat down at the chair of the desk that Constables Whittaker, Ward and Flower spent most of the day arguing over. The noises of the station beyond gave way to the ticking of the office clock, and I looked at the time: 3.30p.m. The clock chimed — you never thought it was going to, but it always did — and the significance of that chime to me just then was that I had two hours forty-five minutes left in which to book accommodation for the week-end away I'd promised the wife (for I would be meeting her at our usual spot in the middle of the footbridge at 6.15 p.m.).

Looking back later on, though, it seemed to me that the three-thirty chime marked the start of one of the most sensational periods ever to pass in York station.

It all began at three thirty-one, when the telephone rang in the police office, the sound clashing with that of running feet from beyond the office door and the cry: "The gun . . . There's a gun in his hand!"

CHAPTER
TWO

It wasn't logical, but I arrested my dash towards the door to answer the phone.

"You are not, repeat not . . ." I heard the voice on the line saying before I replaced the receiver with a crash. It had been Dewhurst, governor of the York station exchange. Evidently he'd got wind that I'd been using a company telephone for private business.

I was through the office door in the next instant — out into the muffled sunlight, and the black sharpness of the station atmosphere, the smell that makes you want to travel. Everywhere people were running and screaming. The very trains seemed to have scattered, for I couldn't see a single one.

Only three people were not moving and they stood on the main "down" platform — number five — amid abandoned portmanteaus and baggage trolleys. I stood on the main "up" — number four. One of the three held a gun out before him and the other two faced him; it was plain that not one of them knew what the gun would do next.

The new footbridge stretched between the main "up" and the main "down", and a steeplechase was being run over it, what with everyone fleeing the gun.

But one bowler-hatted man was running the opposite way, and battling through the on-rushing crowd: the Chief. I knew he'd been knocking about the station somewhere.

I bolted for the footbridge, and began fighting my way through the crowds in the wake of the Chief. A succession of ladies in summer muslin seemed to be pitched at me, and some wide-brimmed hats were scattered as I fought my way to the main "down" where the Chief was closing on the three blokes.

As soon as we made the platform, the Chief slowed to a walk, gesturing me to stay well behind him. The gunman swung his revolver towards the Chief, saying, "Are you another of them?"

"Another of what?" asked the Chief.

"Another of these bastards," he said, indicating the two roughs facing him.

This was not the common run of shootist. For a start, he wore spectacles. He was also decently spoken and smartly turned out — and alongside his polished boots rested a good-quality leather valise. The two standing before him — blokes of a lower class — neither moved nor spoke, but watched the gun, which was a revolver of the American type.

"We're all staying right here until the police come," said the man with the gun.

"I *am* a policeman, you fucking idiot," said the Chief, and that was him all over — rough and ready.

"Well, you don't look like one," said the man with the gun.

"I happen to be in a plain suit," said the Chief, and I wondered why he did not hold up his warrant card. I would have come forward and shown my own, but it was in the pocket of my suit coat in the police office.

"Plain suit?" said the gunman, eyeing the Chief. "*Dirty* suit, more like."

The Chief, as usual, looked like nothing on earth. His trousers did not match his top-coat, and they were both of a winter weight — it almost made you faint with heat sickness to look at them. In York, people were jumping into the river off Lendal Bridge to get cool, but the Chief didn't give tuppence about the weather. He'd been in the Sudan, where 95 degrees was counted a rather chilly spell, and he'd worn a thick red coat throughout that show, which was perhaps why he wore his winter coat now. His bowler was greasy and dinted, and stray lengths of orange hair came out from underneath it so that a stranger might have been fascinated to lift the hat off his head and see the way things stood with the *rest* of the Chief's hair. A man who'd served in the colours ought to have been smarter, I always thought.

But you knew the Chief had been a soldier by other signs.

In the greenhouse heat of the station, he was moving towards the man with the gun. I watched the Chief make his advance — and then a noise made me turn around. The great mix-up of lines and signals beyond the south end wavered in the heat, and a train was there in the hot, shimmering air. *Here's trouble*, I thought.

The train bent like a flame or a fever vision as it came on and, as I watched, it slid to the right with a high whine, so that it was heading for our platform.

The Chief, still advancing on the gunman, was making great windmilling movements with his right arm. He meant to wave the train through, as if it was a horse and trap approaching a partial blockage in a country lane (and the Chief *did* walk with a farmer's plod).

The engine driver could see that something was up, and he hung off the side of his cab to get a better look — one tiny scrap of humanity clinging onto thirty tons of roaring machine. The train seemed to frighten the gunman, for he yelled, "I'll shoot, I'll shoot!" The Chief was roaring too, and waving as the train came rolling alongside us. I imagined the riot among the passengers on board. Their train was giving the go-by to York, principal junction of the north!

As the train rolled away, I heard the Chief say to the gunman:

"Now give it over."

No reply from the gunman, and no movement from him either.

The five of us stood amid the abandoned bags and the posters for "Sailor Suits — Young Boys Will Appreciate Them This Weather" and "Ebor Lemonade — The Drink That Refreshes".

A half-minute passed.

"I said give it over," repeated the Chief, and his voice echoed about the brick arches, the fourteen platforms and the like number of lines. I heard a distant clunk, and, looking towards the great signal gantry beyond the north end, I saw that all the levers had been set at stop. To my knowledge, they had never all said the same thing before, and it meant word had reached the mighty signal box that controlled the station and hung suspended over the main "up". The signallers would all be in there, but moving about on their knees, below the line of the windows.

I looked again beyond the station end. The signals resembled so many soldiers with shouldered arms. Out there in the great unroofed world, passing trains were setting cornfields ablaze, signal boxes were catching fire for no good reason and all kind of trouble was brewing: the miners were out, the dockers were out and the great heat had been given as the cause of many suicides. The ancient city of York itself had become a kind of Turkish bath.

The gunman was in fits now, pointing and repointing the revolver at the Chief. He looked the part of an ink-spiller — it ought to have been a fountain pen and not a revolver that rested there in his hand. The Chief stood three feet before him, one ruffian to either side of him.

The Chief repeated his request:

"Hand it over."

The gunman shook his head, and sweat flew. The stuff was rolling down from underneath his hat all the time.

One of the ruffians spoke up:

"He reckons you're after his bag."

The Chief turned around and looked at the fellow for a while.

The Chief's face . . . well, it was a bit of a jumble: little brown eyes that lurked behind slanting cracks in his head like those sea creatures that live inside stones; big, no-shape nose. The only orderly feature was the well-balanced brown moustache, which looked twenty years younger than the rest of him.

The Chief turned back to the gunman.

"I don't want your bag, only the gun."

The gunman kept silence.

"Can I tempt you to a glass of ale?" the Chief suddenly asked him.

No reply from the gunman.

"Strikes me you might *prefer* a glass of ale to twenty years' hard labour," said the Chief.

The gunman said, "If I give you the gun, there'll be nothing to stop you taking the bag."

"Look, I keep forgetting about this fucking bag," said the Chief. "That's on account of the fact I've no interest in it and do not bloody want it."

"You're one of them," the gunman said, addressing the Chief, but nodding towards the two roughs. "They know you. When you came up, they said, 'It's Weatherill.'"

"And did they look pleased about it?" asked the Chief.

The Chief took two steps towards the gunman, and there was now not more than a yard's distance between him and the revolver.

"So now then," the Chief said, and he advanced again.

The gunman looked down at his bag, then up at the Chief.

"One more step and I'll fire," he said.

The Chief took one more step; he removed the revolver from the hand of the gunman, who stared at the Chief amazed.

"That was painless, wasn't it?" said the Chief, smiling, and I winced at that for I knew what was coming: the fast blow that sent the man to the ground.

It was then that the two roughs made their breakaway. I turned and scarpered over the bridge after them. In the middle of the bridge, I was ten feet behind the slower of the pair; then seven feet, five, closing . . . But the five became seven again, and he had ten yards on me by the time he reached the ticket barrier, where he went out through the "in" gate, clattering against the pole that supported the sign: "Please show your own ticket".

I nearly gave up the pursuit just then, but I saw that the second one had crocked himself on that pole, and that I was gaining on him again as we pounded through the cab shelter.

We came out from under the glass roof of the shelter and ran on hard under the great heat of the blaring sun, but we were both slowed by it, as was the man in the lead, who was also back in my sights now.

I was separated from the first bloke by seventy yards' distance, from the second by thirty. As we went along by the dying gardens of the Royal Station Hotel,

16

pink-cheeked, bewildered women in white dresses came and went; black-suited, sweltering railway clerks were presented to us in a steady stream, and were pushed aside or dodged if lucky. To my left, I saw Leeman Road, and the central post office of York, with a dozen vans queuing up before it to deliver the letters that people would insist on writing in spite of the suffocating heat.

Under the arch of the Bar Walls, and the headquarters of the North Eastern Railway came up. Beyond the offices was the Cocoa Factory, hard by the river, and I was now running under the raying sun and the smell of burning chocolate combined. At the river's edge, the first man ran right, heading along the road that ran between the two towering buildings of the cocoa works, while the second man ran straight — gaining Lendal Bridge ten seconds before me. I was keeping on the tail of this second man, since I knew that he was in the same state as me: half-dead. Under the bridge, the river was low and dirty, over-crowded with pleasure cruisers that puffed out bad-tempered black smoke. In Museum Street, the man dodged right. Was he in the doorway of the Conservative Club? Half-fainting, I stopped and verified that he was not . . . and I gave up the chase.

When I returned to the station and to Platform Five, with my shirt sweat-soaked and the whole place re-awakening, the man who'd held the gun was only just righting himself.

The chief was holding the man's valise — which was locked.

"What's in here, then?" the Chief asked the bloke.

"Specie," he muttered, as he sadly collected up the wreckage of his spectacles.

CHAPTER
THREE

Four twenty-two by my silver watch.

The Chief sat at his desk, and I sat on the chair opposite with my suit coat on my knee. The gas hissed like a jungle snake, for the Chief's office — which was an enclosed part of the police office — was windowless. On the green wall behind him was a plan of the whole of the territories of the North Eastern Railway. The station beyond was still quieter than normal.

"It'll be like this when the strike comes, sir," I said.

Everyone knew the railwaymen would be the next lot to be out. They wanted recognition for their union. Could I count myself a railwayman? I had certainly been one once, in my days firing on the footplate, and I could still find myself checked by the beauty of a locomotive, but I was a copper now, a passenger not a pilot on the iron road, and I would not be coming out even if the true railwaymen did. The Chief did not normally speak about politics but he had once said of the strikers that it was "our job to keep those fellows down". I'd kept silence at that.

The Chief was side-on to me, hardly listening but smoking a cigar and fretting about the gunman. He'd taken him into the holding cell and given him a bit of a braying, while I'd stood outside the cell door feeling spare — and guilty with it. I'd put a stop to the rough-house by rapping on the door, and asking the Chief if he wanted a cup of tea. I'd brought one for the prisoner as well, and taken a good look at his face. He'd come off lightly compared to some, and I handed him a bottle of carbolic and a cloth as the Chief stepped back into the office.

"You'll stand witness to this," the bloke had said, pointing to his cuts and bruises.

"Pipe down, mate," I'd said, "and you'll be out of here directly."

After coming out of the cell, the Chief had consulted his filing system, and had for once turned up the right paper. There was the bloke, set down in cold print as an employee of the Yorkshire Penny Bank, certificated to carry arms when transporting specie — and there'd been over five hundred pounds' worth of sovereigns in the valise: the week's wages for Backhouse's nurseries, the York General Draperies and half a dozen other places.

"I half-recognised the fellow," said the Chief, putting his boots on his desk. "But why did he not come out and say he was running cash for the bank?"

The Chief's neck was red where his collar rubbed, but that collar could rub his head right off before he'd notice anything amiss.

"Because he thought you were out to rob him, sir."

Train smoke floating in from outside, cigar smoke inside; the strikes; the scrap that was brewing with the Kaiser . . . A fellow wanted to get away and *breathe*.

But I knew I'd lost my chance to make a late booking in Scarborough.

"He was in a funk, sir, not thinking straight."

I liked the Chief and didn't like to see him worried — not that he was ever really worried about anything. If you read the Police Manual, it was all very careful: "In exercising the power of arrest, officers must use the greatest caution and discretion . . ." But the Chief never *had* read the Police Manual, and it was too late for him to do so now that he was just a few months short of his retirement. I would have said that getting on for half the things he did were unlawful, but it seemed to me that he always had the right *end* in view. I thought of him as being at once modern and old-fashioned: modern in that he fostered "initiative" in his men, old-fashioned in that he didn't hold with paperwork and would clout a ruffian as soon as look at him. I supposed that I covered up for him too often in this. I knew I'd got a name in the office for being the Chief's favourite, and despite being less than half his age (twenty-seven to his sixty-four), I was the only one he'd take a pint with.

"You might have shown him your warrant card," I said, and the moment I let fall the words, I regretted them. The Chief could be set off at a touch, so I put in a belated ". . . sir".

The Chief turned towards me and blew smoke. He'd tramped for hundreds of miles across the boiling deserts of Africa; he had a slash mark from a dervish spear across his chest. A newspaper report existed of an army boxing match of about '79 in which the Chief had been described as a useful heavyweight of the "rushing" type, which was a polite way of saying that he went nuts in a scrap.

"Come again?" he said, by which he meant, "Let's see if you've got the brass neck to repeat those words."

"The thing of it is, sir . . . How do you let folk know who you are if you don't show your warrant card?"

A beat of silence.

"That's their look-out," said the Chief.

He ought not to have given the bank's man a pasting. Banks were rich and powerful. They could fund legal actions for assault.

"If that bugger does put up a complaint," said the Chief, who seemed to have read my mind just at that moment, "I'll bloody mill him."

By which the Chief meant that he would see him gaoled, but I wondered on what charge. The company solicitors might be able to dream something up. Had the bank's man not impeded the Chief in the execution of his duty? And had his actions not allowed the escape of the two York roughs who'd been eyeing the money bag?

My next question was designed to get points with the Chief.

"How did you know the fellow wouldn't fire on you?"

The Chief threw open his desk drawer and pitched the weapon — which he'd confiscated — onto his desk top.

"Pick it up," he ordered, and I did so. Guns were always heavier than you expected.

22

"It's a Luger," he said. "Single action."

"Right-o," I said. "So that when you pull the trigger . . ."

". . . Nothing happens," said the Chief, taking back the gun. "You must cock the hammer first."

"And the bloke hadn't done that?"

The Chief shook his head.

"What if he *had* done, sir?"

The Chief stood up.

"I dare say I'd have been a little more cordial. Fancy a pint, lad?"

On Platform Four, I gave good evening to the Chief. We'd just returned from the Station Hotel, where we'd put the peg in after a quick two pints. It was the Chief's wife's birthday, and he had to get off.

I looked up at the great clock: five to five. I thought about wandering over to the booking office, where they kept some sea-side brochures. It might be worth pitching up in Scarborough and calling in on a few places in hopes of a vacancy. The heat had barely abated, but the station light was yellow, signifying the start of evening — yellow with floating specks of soot plainly visible.

A fair quantity of passengers stood on the platform, and they were not excursionists but business types, for a London train was about due.

I turned to my right, and the train was approaching under the far gantry where the signals were once again various, looking like a rabble rather than a disciplined army. But it was a "down" train coming in across the way that held my attention. The oncoming engine was one of the Great Northern company's 0-6-0s, and its fire was for some reason not in good nick, so that thick black smoke was brought towards the platforms by such little breeze as existed.

I watched the stuff roll past the open door of the First Class Tea Rooms, where ladies ate strawberries and cream with long-handled spoons and pretended they were in a nicer place. The smoke came on, and was now combined with a few drops of moisture from the chimney of the engine, so that it seemed as though we were in for an electrical storm. There seemed to be an epidemic of bad firing that day. The firebox must be fairly smothered in coal to give that much smoke.

I walked over the footbridge to Platform Nine where the engine came to rest — and where the driver was down from his cab, and talking to the platform guard, who looked agitated. The guard then broke away and came dashing past me as I approached.

"What's up?" I said.

"I'm to fetch an ambulance team," he called out, and he began bounding up the stairs of the footbridge.

"Railway police," I said to the driver, as I gained the engine.

"It's my mate," said the driver. He held a rag in his hand, and he used it to draw sweat and coal dust from one side of his face to another.

I swung myself up on the footplate, and the fireman seemed curled up asleep in front of the fire door — just like any cat on a tab rug before the hearth. Only he was lying in half an inch of coal dust.

The fellow stirred as I stepped up, and the driver said, "Heat sickness."

I could quite credit it, what with the great heat of the day, and the white, rolling fire of the engine.

"We're up from London," he said. "Passed Retford in very fair time," he said, "but I knew summat was up. He hadn't said a word since Peterborough, and he's normally a great one for nattering, is Bob."

I leant over the fireman, and shut the fire door to save him from a roasting — at which he rolled over a little, and looked up at me, saying, "No, no, the fire needs air. Must keep up the steam, you see."

". . . Fired her in myself," said the driver.

I didn't like to see the man lolling down there in the dust, so I said, "Let's have you up, mate."

The driver gave a hand, and we sat him on the sandbox, and he sat there rocking, and looking too white. An inkling of trouble told me to step back just as the great wave of stuff came out of his mouth. Half a minute later, the driver was playing the water hose over the footplate, and the fireman was saying, "Reckon I've shovelled ten ton of coal today . . . and it's not the bloody weather for it."

The spray of boiling water was moving the last of the stuff off the footplate. It wasn't a very manly colour, being yellow and bright pink.

As the stuff rolled away, the fireman said, "I don't know what that is," just as though he was trying to disown it. "I en't eaten all day," he said.

"Bob forgot his snap," said the driver, and he turned a lever to stop the hose, which caused the whole engine to judder. "Bloody cursed, is this run," he said, looping the hose and setting it back on its hook.

I looked down, and there was a whole press of blokes on the platform by the engine. First, there was the ambulance team — four blokes in queer hats. I stepped aside, and they came pouring up. One of them began questioning the fireman, and it was more like an interrogation than a medical examination. The driver stepped down to make room, and I followed him. He began talking to two men in dark suits. They'd evidently just climbed down from one of the carriages.

"Will we be held here, or what?" asked one of the two blokes.

"We'll need a relief," said the driver.

"I'll send a lad over to the firemen's mess," I said. "Should turn one up in no time."

As I spoke I raised my eye to the small clock that hung above the team rooms on Platform Nine. It was dead on five. The clocks would be clanging all over York.

"And who are you?" asked the first of the blokes.

"Railway police," I said.

He was being short with me, and he'd get likewise in return.

"We're Met boys," said the second of the two blokes, meaning the Metropolitan Police. He had boggly eyes, which made him look as if he was trying to burst out of himself.

Beyond this pair, I saw a man step down from one of the carriages, and another came down after him, or more like *with* him. They were too close. The first wore an official-looking moustache; the second had long hair, and had not lately shaved. Well, I knew what was going off all right.

"Prisoner under escort," I said.

The first of the two blokes standing directly before me gave me the evil eye. He would've denied it if he could.

"Who is he?" I said, indicating the prisoner, who was now being fairly dragged towards us by his guard.

The boggly-eyed man looked at me, and I watched his eyes. It was like waiting for Bob the fireman to chuck up his guts.

"Now that", he said, indicating the man under escort, "is what you might call perishable goods."

CHAPTER
FOUR

Pending the arrival of a new fireman, the prisoner was stowed in the holding cell of the station police office. The hard-looking Met man stood smoking on Platform Thirteen along with the guard who'd brought the prisoner down from the train. They both stood within hailing distance of the boggle-eyed man, who was evidently junior to both of them. He stood in the doorway of the police office, which Wright had now vacated.

I was the only man in the office, and I sat at my desk looking at the bread and cheese. It was a quarter after five. The question of the time seemed to press on me rather; had done all day. The hot weather was like a clock ticking.

"His name's Lambert," said the boggle-eyed man, turning in the doorway and entering the police office. "Hugh."

He meant the prisoner, of course.

"From the quality he is," he went on. "Brought up in a country mansion — old man lord of the bloody manor. Adenwold. Heard of it?"

I nodded.

"Went to all the best schools, Cambridge University — nothing wanting at all, and then what does he go and do?"

He took out a leathern wallet and began making a cigarette out of the stuff inside it.

"Shoots his old man."

He eyed me over the top of a cigarette paper.

"Ungrateful," he said.

"He's for the drop, then," I said.

"Monday morning," said the boggle-eyed bloke. "Eight o'clock sharp."

Holding up the baccy pouch, he looked a question at me.

". . . Obliged to you," I said, and he lobbed the whole thing over, whereas I'd been banking on him rolling me one.

As I caught it, I said, "Hold on — this is the Moorby Murder."

Moorby was immediately south of the Yorkshire Moors, and a place just waiting for a murder to happen so that all the papers could speak of "The Moorby Murder", which rolled so easily off the tongue, and looked eye-catching in print. But Adenwold, which was near to Moorby, was where it had actually happened. I had read of the trial, which had been held about three months since, down in London — a regular Old Bailey sensation. But I could not recall the details of the case beyond the striking fact that a son had killed his father.

"I don't understand why you're shifting him," I said, as I set to work with the baccy. "It en't regular to move a condemned man."

(*It's adding insult to injury*, I thought, *that's what it is.*)

"Well now," said the boggle-eyed man, "we're taking him to Durham. Reason being, the scaffold at Wandsworth nick's busted. The drop mechanism . . ."

And he violently mimed the pulling of what might have been a signal lever.

". . . It's packed up, and there's no prospect of fixing it in time."

"Is it on account of the heat?" I asked.

He folded his arms.

"Why would it be on account of the heat?"

"Well, it's playing bloody murder with everything else," I said.

He shook his head, while unfolding his arms.

"No," he said, "it's just busted. They need to get a blacksmith to it. Gas torch. But that ain't the only reason we're shifting him," he ran on, blowing smoke. "There's another, more important."

And now he really started boggling at me.

"What's that, then?" I said.

More boggling.

"It's confidential, mind," he said.

I nodded, and struck a Vesta for my cigarette.

"Governor at Wandsworth," he said, "he don't think he did it. Won't hang him."

I took this in, smoking.

"Won't have it on his conscience," said the bloke.

"But the gallows either *is* bust or it en't?" I said.

"Well then," said the boggle-eyed bloke, "it's not."

30

Through the opened door, I could hear trains coming and going, and it all seemed so vulgar and unmannerly with a bloke in the holding cell having only one week-end left to live.

"Did he not appeal?" I asked the boggle-eyed man. He shook his head, and I thought about the time I'd seen a fellow hung at Durham gaol . . .

The execution had not arisen from a railway police case, but from a stabbing in the Durham workhouse. It was just after I'd had my promotion that the Chief had taken me north, and he'd eyed me throughout the proceedings. He'd said, "It'll *fix* you, lad. A copper who's not seen it happen is floating about in a dream world."

But the business itself had *been* like a dream — both fast and slow like a dream. The prisoner had been marched through thick fog across the yard, and this had happened in a sort of relay. He'd set off in company with four wardens, the governor, the vicar and the doctor — all blokes who might have been looking out for him, who might in some way have been on his side; but they gave him over to the hangman and his assistant, who definitely weren't. The Chief and I had waited in the shed that held the gallows, and which normally contained the prison van. We'd stood alongside the High Sheriff of Durham or some such gentry.

The place smelt of oil and horse droppings, and the absence of the van was the most terrible thing about it. When the prisoner came in, it was all movement and no words. The High Sheriff had whipped off his top hat at

31

the exact moment of the drop, and I thought he should have done it sooner.

The man was left hanging in what seemed to be a great weight of silence, and it came to me only then that the whole thing had happened in the time it took the prison clock to strike eight.

And that silence, and the fog, had seemed to stay about us for the rest of the day.

The boggle-eyed man was now looking at the photographs in the police office; his suit coat was over his arm.

"He'll be roasted in that cell, you know," I said.

"Bring him in here if you like," he said. "He's not the sort to attempt a breakaway."

CHAPTER
FIVE

The condemned man had on a good-quality flannel suit, and a loose white necker that was rather bandage-like. He'd been permitted to carry a roll of papers, and these he stuffed into his suit-coat pocket as I opened the cell door and said, "You can wait up in the office if you'd rather."

"It *is* a little close in here," he said.

He was well-spoken, and my own accent was a little "out" when next I addressed him, as it usually is when I try to accommodate to upper-class pronunciation.

"You can sit here," I said, indicating my own desk.

Boggle-eyes was not giving us the benefit of his distinctive expression but lounging in the doorway with his back to us. He'd collected up his baccy, I noticed. As we entered the room, he gave us only a brief backward glance before stepping out onto the platform and falling in with his two confederates.

Lambert nodded at me as he sat down, and then looked all about the room. It was a young man's curiosity and he *was* young — about of an age with me: late twenties, not more. He had very wide dark eyes, and he looked like an author. Not just any author, but a particular one: the fellow that wrote *Treasure Island*.

I'd seen his photograph on the first page of a copy of that book, but I couldn't just then lay hold of his name.

Hugh Lambert blew gently upwards, and his long hair lifted.

"What do you think?" he said. "Is it a hundred?"

"Ninety-six here in York," I said. "They say it'll break come . . ."

I tailed off. Thunderstorms had been predicted for Monday, by which time the man before me would be well beyond their reach. Boggle-eyes was still talking to his mates about ten feet away from the office door. I heard him say, "I've lost my golf swing, and do you know, it's haunting me — fairly *haunting* me, it is."

His place at the doorway had been taken by a sparrow. Hugh Lambert caught sight of it, and at first swivelled in his chair to get a better view; he then very gently picked up the chair and settled down again facing the bird. He looked up at me and, indicating the bread left on my desk, said, "Mind if I . . .?"

"Not a bit," I said, and he rolled a pellet of bread, and pitched it over towards the bird.

"You've fed her before," said Hugh Lambert, as the bird took the bread. "She wouldn't be there otherwise."

"She?"

Lambert nodded.

"A male sparrow has a grey crest."

"Well, you wouldn't necessarily know," I said. "I mean, anything that comes in here ends up more or less black. There's a robin that pitches up pretty regularly. He stands there and sort of demands to be fed . . . Makes me laugh — the sheer brass neck of it."

34

"The robin is the most English of birds," Lambert said in a dreamy sort of voice.

Was this a good thing or bad as far as he was concerned? After all, it was England that would shortly be hanging him. He threw another bit of bread for the sparrow.

"I saw a robin once at line-side," I said. "He was sitting on a "WHISTLE" board."

"And was he whistling?" asked Lambert, half-turning towards me.

"He was."

Lambert grinned. In fact, it was more like a short laugh, and it showed pluck to laugh in his situation.

"It was by Grosmont," I said. "Up on the moors yonder."

A beat of silence. Lambert threw another pellet.

"You were with the railway up there?"

"Porter," I said. "That's how I got my start."

"Are you keen on railways *per se*? Or is it just a job for you?"

Perhaps this was his way of taking his mind off what was coming . . . by examining the minds of others? But before I could reply, he said:

"My brother reads timetables for amusement. Can you beat that?"

"Well, I'm a bit that way myself," I said, "or was as a lad, anyhow."

"I always liked the adverts in the Bradshaw," he said, and it was very worrying to hear him speak as if he was already dead.

"Eux-e-sis Shaving Cream," I said, "and then the picture of the two men shaving: '"Eux-e-sis versus Soap', and the man using soap is bleeding half to death."

I ought not to have used that last word, of course, but Lambert gave a grin, before saying, "I always liked the adverts for hotels at the back — to know that all those places would be happy to accommodate you. I found that very welcoming. You were at Grosmont, you say?"

"That's it," I said. "*Your* part of the world."

I wanted to get onto him. I felt I ought to give him a chance to say something because I had the notion that he *wanted* to speak up. He turned towards me but kept silence.

I said, "Adenwold's a pretty spot, I believe."

"Just now," he said, eyeing me levelly, "the hedges will be full of thrushes."

I nodded once.

"Skullcap, tufted vetch, alder," he continued, in a tone now severe. His face was black and white: white skin, black eyes, black beard, His clothes were worn anyhow, but still with a rightness about them.

"Have you been there?" he asked.

"I don't believe so," I replied, slowly.

"Do you mean to go?"

I looked towards the doorway, but the sparrow had made off. I was on the point of replying to Hugh Lambert when he asked, with great emphasis, "Could you see your way *clear* to going?"

My boots creaked, and the wooden floor also creaked in the unbreathable heat as I moved towards the police office door. The three guards were talking by the platform edge. A high screeching of wheel flange on rail came from some far-off platform, and a single green locomotive was running light through the station, going fast and seeming to enjoy its freedom, like a child running home from school. I pushed the door until it was on the jar. I turned to Hugh Lambert.

"What's at Adenwold?"

"My brother John," he said.

"Will he not come up to Durham to see you?"

Lambert shook his head, shook his hair, I supposed it was the privilege of the condemned man to be allowed to grow it.

"My brother is a very intelligent man," he said, "but in this business he's too partisan."

I didn't take his meaning, and I told him so.

"Well . . ." said Lambert, "he believes me to be innocent, and he means to secure my release."

"How? Will he bring forward some new evidence?"

Lambert moved his hair with his hands.

"I can't say, but he has told me that he means to make a stand or *take* a stand this week-end."

"But again," I said, "*how?*"

"I don't know how, I don't know *why*. My father always said I should be hanged, and the governor of Durham gaol will shortly oblige him. That is to be considered an accomplished fact."

I'd got more than I'd bargained for there, but I was spared the need to reply by the office clock chiming the half-hour. I was embarrassed by that clock. It seemed to fairly whiz.

"Look," I said to Lambert, "*did* you do it?"

"I don't know," he said, and he met my gaze for a moment before looking sidelong, towards the door. "It's certainly possible," he continued, "otherwise why would they be hanging me?"

A beat of silence.

"In trying to secure my release, my brother puts himself in considerable danger from people who . . . want to stop him."

"How do you know?"

"He has told me that much, and you see there ought not to be any more deaths over this. Two is enough. Will you open the door again?"

I did so, and the sparrow was there once more. It looked ridiculously small. The three guards were beyond the bird at the platform edge.

"The idea is that I save your brother?"

Lambert nodded, side-on to me again and lobbing pellets at the sparrow.

"And not you?"

"I'm past saving."

"As a consequence of your brother being saved, you might be saved."

"Two for the price of one," he said, and he folded his arms, and nearly smiled. "Now I doubt that."

The men on the platform were stirring. They'd finished their talk, and were coming towards the police office.

"These people who mean to stop him speaking out," I said, "who are they?"

The Met men approached the open door.

Lambert said, "I don't know . . . Only that they are . . ."

"What?" I said, indicating the guards. "Is it *these* men?"

He shook his head very violently at the suggestion, and I must have been mad to make it. The London blokes were all quite above board: I'd seen all their warrant cards.

"These people you mention," I said, "are they in Adenwold?"

The fellow who'd been short with me was the first through the door and into the room.

"They will be there this week-end," said Lambert.

And the Met men were now close about him, a new fireman evidently having been found.

CHAPTER
SIX

A minute after they'd gone — during which time I'd sat stunned on my desk — Old Man Wright pitched up again.

"Anything doing?" he said.

"Not much," I said.

There was something about Wright. You didn't want to tell him things.

"I've found you a hotel room," he said.

"Oh aye?" I said.

"Well, a word of thanks wouldn't come amiss," he said, "seeing as how I've just spent half an hour telephoning from the Institute."

Don Shearsmith, the manager of the York Railway Institute, would vouch that any personal calls you made were in fact made on North Eastern Railway Company business. In theory, these favours were given gratis and with no expectation of return, but with Shearsmith there was always a price to pay at some later date.

"It's Jernigan's Hotel," Wright said. "Not one of the premier ones, granted. There's no sea view, but that would be asking the earth at this late stage. It's above the Marine Drive on the north side. It faces sort of *side-on* to the sea, so if you leaned out of your window, and kind of craned your . . ."

I said to Wright: "Pitch us over a Bradshaw, will you?"

In the police office, we had the use of all the working timetables, but for ordinary business we used the monthly Bradshaw just like any ordinary tripper. Wright chucked over the one that sat on his own desk, saying, "There's a train for Scarborough at six. *We've* booked, but you and your missus would have to stand."

I looked up Adenwold, and folded the corner of the page.

I stood up, and walked through to the Chief's part of the office.

"Do you want this bloody room or not?" Wright called after me. "You've to confirm directly if so."

"I'll think on," I said.

A map of the network hung behind the Chief's desk. I climbed onto his desk chair, so that I was at eye level with Adenwold.

It lay twenty miles north of York on a quiet branch running west to east between the market towns of Pilmoor and Malton. Pilmoor was on the North Eastern main line and Malton was a regular destination from York, and the branch ran between them like a filament in an electric light bulb — something delicate and slight.

From west to east the stations on it, beginning after Pilmoor, were Husthwaite Gate, Moorby, West Adenwold, Adenwold, East Adenwold, Slingsby, Barton-le-Street, Amotherby. These were all villages, and

Adenwold, I knew, was smaller than both West Adenwold and East Adenwold, which was rum because their names would lead you to think it was bigger.

They would be there *this week-end*. Adenwold was small, but it still might have a population running to hundreds, or a hundred at any rate, and the station was like a valve, periodically letting in more.

I looked again at the map.

Another singular' point: there were bigger gaps between Adenwold and *West* and *East* Adenwold than between any other two stations on the branch. The three Adenwolds sounded like a family, but in fact they were not.

"What the bloody hell are you playing at?" asked Wright, who was watching me from the doorway of the Chief's office.

Pilmoor to Malton was the "down" direction; Malton to Pilmoor was "up". Farm produce and machinery, timber, limestone and gravel (for there were plenty of quarries up there) would be carried by the pick-up goods trains, and there'd not be above one of these each way every week-day. As for the passenger trains ... I took up the Bradshaw, sat down in the Chief's chair and put my boots on the desk as he often did.

"You'll catch it if he walks in," said Wright, who was evidently unaware of the Chief's wife's birthday.

I turned to the page I'd marked in the Bradshaw. A down-line train from Pilmoor would arrive at Adenwold at 8.41p.m., but there was an earlier "up" train from Malton, marked with a "B" symbol in the timetable. This service only stopped at the principal

42

stations on the branch, and Adenwold was not counted one of these. But the "B" meant that it would set down at any station if advance notice was given to the guard. Why "B" meant that in a Bradshaw I never knew. Anyhow, this service was scheduled to call at East Adenwold at 7.45p.m., which meant it would pass through Adenwold itself about ten minutes after, or stop there if requested.

On the *Saturday*, three trains were scheduled to call at Adenwold: an "up" service from Malton arrived at 8.51a.m., a "down" from Pilmoor arrived at 12.27p.m. and another "up" arrived at 8.35p.m. One train arrived in Adenwold on the Sunday — a "down" at 10.05 a.m.

The best bet would be to go to Adenwold, find Lambert's brother directly and have the whole tale from him.

"Ever been to Adenwold?" I called across to Wright.

"Now hold on a minute," he said, "your missus is in hopes of the beach and sea air. You can't take her to bloody Adenwold!"

"The inn there," I said, stepping back into the main office, "what's it called, do you know?"

Wright shrugged, having fallen into a sulk. He was so dead set on getting me fixed up with a hotel in Scarborough — preferably one slightly more inconveniently placed than his own — that he wouldn't be party to any plan that took me in a different direction.

"Your missus!" he called, as I stepped out into the hot gloom of the station light. "She'll be in fits!"

CHAPTER
SEVEN

I walked through the ticket barrier, past the booking office and cab stand, and turned right under the glare of the sun. Two minutes later, I was breathing the dusty air of the Railway Institute reading room. The clock said twenty to six, and it ticked away the life of the super-annuated railwayman sleeping in the one armchair. The rest of the room was mostly hard wood: tall stools, and tall, sloping desks. At these, you read the paper of your choice from the selection ranged on the long table by the window.

The back numbers were stowed underneath. I hauled out a bundle of *Yorkshire Posts*, and leafed backwards through them until I found the account, in the paper dated Thursday, 27 April, 1911.

There was a woodcut of Hugh Lambert in the dock, and the name of the writer came to me in a flash. Stevenson. Hugh Lambert looked like Robert Louis Stevenson. The article was headed "The Moorby Murder — The Killing of Sir George Lambert", then "The trial in summary by Our London Correspondent". It began: "For the past week, the crowded court has listened closely to the sad and painful story of how a son perpetually at odds with his father finally resorted to murder."

The killing had occurred in the early evening of Wednesday, 8 November, 1909. Hugh Lambert had made off immediately afterwards, and had eventually been arrested in London after living for more than a year abroad. It had happened during a "rough rabbit shoot" in the woods close to the Hall at Adenwold, family seat of the Lamberts. Present at the shoot were Sir George Lambert, his friend the Reverend Martin Ridley, parish priest of Adenwold, and Hugh Lambert. Two villagers had also been employed to "walk-up" the rabbits, but these were not named.

Hugh Lambert did not go in for country sports, and he described the shoot as "a debauch", in which he had been forced to participate by his father. He had admitted that he had earlier quarrelled with his father, and that they were both drunk on the ginger liquor that his father habitually consumed before walking nightly through the coverts with his guns, of which he kept a good many. The three men on the shoot had become separated in the woods. Hugh Lambert's account was that he had fallen down in a drunken swoon. When he returned to consciousness, an extra shotgun was beside him. He picked it up, and found that he was standing over his father's body, A policeman called Anderson ("Constable of the Three Adenwolds") was just then walking through the woods with his spaniel. He had hailed Hugh, who had then run off, making his way to Paris and later Italy. The gun was later found to be one of Sir George Lambert's, and to be covered with the finger marks of Hugh.

I read that "The Reverend Martin Ridley, vicar of Adenwold, spoke as to the frequent disagreements between father and son" while John Lambert — eldest son of Sir George — had spoken for the defence about his brother's gentle disposition and kindly nature. These pieces of evidence, however, were not detailed in the report. John Lambert had been in London on business at the time of the killing.

A doctor of Wandsworth Prison had given medical evidence that the prisoner was of sound mind — and the end of the article came as though the newspaper had suddenly realised it was running short of space. There was the heading "VERDICT" in bold black type, and below it, "The jury's verdict was guilty and the prisoner was sentenced to death."

I looked up from the *Post* as the reading room clock tolled six with a horrible clanging. It was not enough to wake the elderly sleeper, though, and when the clock reverted to ticking it did so (it seemed to me) with a kind of weary sulkiness.

As I returned to the different heat of the railway station, a "down" service trailed away north-east from Platform Eleven — half a dozen old six-wheeled rattlers. That would be the Scarborough excursion, taking Old Man Wright and his missus away. The train at the next platform was exceptionally short: just one carriage hooked up to a Class S. The train was a special. I walked towards it, and Hugh Lambert, the condemned man, was sitting in a corner seat of the carriage. I'd thought him long gone.

He looked like a man in shock, which it seems to me that people in train compartments very frequently do, especially the ones sitting in the corner seats. The three Met men were in there, too.

I moved to a position alongside the compartment, and one of the Met men stood up and turned his back to me, as if to block my view. Lambert kept his white face side-on. I did not believe that he had seen me. From somewhere a whistle blew, a shout went up and the S Class, barking furiously, dragged away this vision of death-in-waiting.

The special was out from under the station roof, and was approaching the "down" signal gantry, when the irregular thing occurred. What I at first thought of as a short white stick was poked out through one of the windows. It then fell and divided: white sheets of paper floating in the hot hair — some swooping under the moving carriage and into the path of its bogies, others carrying on a little way pressed against the carriage sides, others again descending directly to the sooty ballast between the tracks. I knew immediately what had happened. Lambert had risen to his feet, and posted his papers through the compartment window.

I dashed along to the end of Platform Ten, and down the slope into the black gravel. As I ran along the tracks, I could feel the weight of the gazes from the station upon me. Some loony, driven crackers by the heat, was trying to run to the sea-side! In the forbidden area under the great signal gantry, I began to collect up the papers. Some creaking of the mechanism above me told me to beware; I looked up and a signal fell with a great thud, so that I first thought it was going to drop all the way onto my head. I looked into the station, and a filthy goods engine was coming through it, pulling an eternity of empty, lime-washed cattle trucks. This again was irregular. The train ought to have been using the servants' entrance so to speak, going around the outside of the station on its way north. At any rate, it was soon alongside me, and the endless shuddering wagons gave the spilt papers another mix-up, and a few more of them were carried away. I caught up another twenty or so papers from off, or in-between, the tracks. I had seen prison-issue paper, and this was not it, which made me think that Lambert must have written these notes before being arrested, and that he'd then been allowed to keep them. I tried to make out a bit of the writing, but it wasn't easy. "It is the printer that I feel sorry for — the compositor," I read, and then again: "It comes down, like most things, to mathematics."

Standing on the tracks, oblivious to on-coming trains, I shuffled the papers and read: "He says that the work is Euclidian, and this he means as a commendation of it!"

I had taken too long to puzzle out that word "Euclidian". I looked at my silver watch: six fifteen. The wife would be waiting on the footbridge, with her bag packed for Scarborough.

CHAPTER
EIGHT

I slept right through to Malton, with the wife reading on the seat over-opposite. After our change at Malton — which did smell of malt, as though the dizzying heat brought out the true character of the place — we were over-whelmed by fields. At Amotherby station, two wood pigeons cooed somewhere out of sight. At Barton, a man and a bicycle boarded.

In-between were vast golden fields with the telegraph poles standing calmly in the corn, each with its regulation shadow made by the low sun. As we approached each station, the poles would move closer together, bringing the wires up to the signal boxes or small station houses.

And it was that bloody *hot* . . .

The harvest had already begun, and there were corn stooks in some fields, the bushels arranged in a cross — hundreds of crosses to a field, like an over-toppled crucifix or a mistake made over and over again. In one field, men were still hard at it, following the harvester which rolled forward like a moving factory. In another, men were going about some late hay-making: six fellows around a stack on a cart, tossing up the stuff with pitchforks. Up and up flew the hay, ascending always to the very top of the stack. It was like seeing the force of gravity reversed. Two ragged-looking horses had the next field to themselves, and the sun gave them a golden outline.

We had practically the whole three-carriage train to ourselves. A couple of others had boarded at Malton, and the bicyclist from Barton was aboard somewhere. It was Friday evening, and most people who were going to do something for the week-end in this great swelter were already about it. I had not yet seen the train guard in order to ask for the stop at Adenwold.

The wife was reading, going between the *Yorkshire Post* and the *Freewoman*, a paper taken on subscription by the place at which she worked part time: the Co-operative Women's Guild, York branch. It was all about the women's struggle, and what was wrong with men.

She'd said practically nothing since train time at York, when I had explained that, since Scarborough was full up, Adenwold might do just as well. She'd just sighed, and said, "I don't want to go to Adenwold."

But she'd climbed up into the train all the same.

She wore her new light, white dress with the wide belt and the short skirt that showed off her pretty new calfskin boots. It was one of two new summer dresses, and the second was in her bag. Her new, highly polished straw boater with the blue silk ribbon was beside her on the seat. It had been bought especially for Scarborough. Lydia had a very simple connection with the sun: it turned her brown in May, and that way she stayed until October. It made her dark eyes darker and brighter too; and the whites of them whiter.

I'd decided that the full explanation of what I was about ought not to follow too closely on the news that we were not bound for Scarborough. I was ready for her response to the story of Hugh Lambert: "It's too daft for words!"

Well, it was her fault that I'd get caught up in these tangles from time to time. She'd wanted me off the footplate and into the railway police, it being a more respectable sort of profession, but police work bored her, or at any rate my accounts of it did.

"Is this oats or barley?" said the wife, all of a sudden putting down her paper.

I looked out at the wide, golden fields.

"Well, it's *corn*, at any rate," I said.

"I know *that*," she said.

She put the paper up again, but I knew I'd been forgiven.

She was glad of a holiday of any sort, and the beauty of the scene beyond the window was winning her over. I fished in my bag for the beer bottle I knew was in there. I found it wrapped inside the blue and green sporting cap I'd bought for the week-end from Walton and Reed's of York. At Adenwold I would wear it in place of my bowler. I thought the cap went well with my new blue twill summer suit, but the wife did not approve of Walton and Reed's. She held that it had been all right as Walton's, but had gone off with the arrival of Reed. Their rig-outs were now too raffish. But this cap had been marked down from five bob to two, and, as I'd explained to the wife, it was specially tailored so that it could be folded up very flat and placed in an inside coat pocket.

"Good," she'd said. "You can put it in your pocket and keep it there."

There was a bit more rummaging — and a bit of a panic — until I could put my hands on the clasp knife with its bottle opener attachment. The stuff was warm as tea, but I'll take my beer anyhow. I then fished out of my kitbag the book that Lydia had brought home for me a few weeks before: *The Student's Guide to Railway Law* by M. E. Chapman, MA, LLD Cambridge — this in hopes that I might leave the railway police and train up as a solicitor. I read the familiar first sentence: "This book is intended to present in ordinary language, and as clearly as possible free from technical terms, a general view of the main features of the subject."

That was a laugh.

I turned to the page about the Railway Fires Act, 1905. There were at least sixty-eight sections in that Act, and it was a sight too many. I put away the book, and took out the sheaf of papers that Hugh Lambert had dropped from the carriage window. There were about forty in all, not numbered, and I reckoned I was missing a dozen from the original bundle. The writing was tiny. I could make it out, but it was very hard going. I read:

The fire was never sufficiently banked for her.
The housemaid, who had been perfectly good at

making fires, was all of a sudden deemed incompetent. Not that mother would ever tell her so, of course. Instead, she called Ponder or I in to put on more fuel while she sat shivering on a mild afternoon in her cardigan. I would have been eight or nine, not yet a schoolboy. The blanket was on her knees in the morning room in summer, and then still there in the summer.

This was the time that Ponder and I became "my boys", to be spoken of as such at every opportunity, and that certainly did alarm me. It was gushing, and that was not mother. Ponder knew it too, of course, and so he burrowed deeper into his books.

I looked up.

Who was "Ponder"? Must be the brother: John.

I wondered whether the papers held one especially important bit of information; at the moment they seemed a sort of rag-bag of memories. I thought of the scene in the carriage, after Lambert had slipped the papers through the window. The guards would have come down hard upon him for that, but what could they do? You couldn't hang a man twice.

The wife was looking directly back at me.

"What's that?" she said, indicating the bundle.

"Just some papers."

"Work papers?"

"I found them under the tracks, just under the north signal gantry."

"Hard up for reading matter, are you? Because you ought not to be . . ."

She was referring to *The Student's Guide to Railway Law*.

She caught up her paper again, and I looked at the headings on the back page: "The Question of Non-Union Men — Demonstration in York"; "Insurance Bill — Friendly Societies Alienated"; "Plan for Reform of the House of Lords — Prime Minister to See The King"; "Ballot in Favour of a Strike"; "Riots in Liverpool"; "Giant Leeds Blaze — Firemen Run for Their Lives"; "The Moroccan Sensation — Reports of a Further Grave Incident".

"Mr Balfour's gone on holiday," said the wife from behind the paper. "He left Victoria this morning for Gastein. When he returns to Britain, he's off to Scotland to play golf."

Mr Balfour was not in government. Therefore he was unable to do anything to bring about women's suffrage, not that he would if he could. The Women's Movement had no time for Mr Balfour, but their principal hatred was directed at Mr Asquith who, being the prime minister, *could* do something about votes for women but didn't seem inclined to. "Today," the wife was saying as she lowered the paper, "Harry asked me, 'Why have the Germans sent a panther to Agadir?'"

Harry was our boy. He was nigh-on seven years old, and a lovely lad, but the reason the wife had been looking forward to this week-end most particularly was that her friend Lillian Backhouse had agreed to take him in until Monday dinner-time.

"He thought it was a real panther?" I enquired.

"I told him it was a boat, of course."

"A *gunboat*, I hope you said."

The wife looked out of the window, watching the rolling fields, and keeping silence. Then she said, "What do you think I told him? That it was a flipping canoe?"

"Well, I hope you told him all about the Moroccan crisis," I said.

"What I can't make out", said the wife, who did not keep up with the foreign news, "is why Agadir?"

"Because it's a port in Morocco, and this is all the Moroccan Crisis."

"So you keep saying."

"It's the *second* Moroccan Crisis as a matter of fact."

"When was the last one?"

"About five years since."

The wife frowned.

"It crops up periodically," I said, taking a pull on my beer. "You see, the French and the Spanish run Morocco. We let them do that . . ."

"That's not like us."

"Well, there's nothing there — just sand and terrific heat. But Germany's always wanted to get a leg in as well."

"Are there soldiers on this boat, then?"

"There's believed to be a brass band on it, I know that."

"And are they threatening to strike up?" the wife said, picking up the paper again.

We stopped at Slingsby in order for nothing to happen. A lad porter was cleaning the waiting-room windows, and signs running half-way along the platform read: "Do Not Alight Here". I called to the lad and asked if he wouldn't mind nipping along to the guard's van to ask for the Adenwold stop. He said he would do, and disappeared from view.

We rolled on, and I might have slept again. I looked out just as the great dark sail of a windmill came close to the compartment window, and we were into a tunnel of trees. Two screams on the whistle as we ran through the woods; then the carriage gave a jolt as an application of the brake came, and we were going slowly through a clearing. In the centre of it stood a great steam saw with stacks of logs near by. Around the saw, the trees had been felled at all angles, and it looked as though they'd collapsed into a dead faint at the sight of the machine. The dark wood came in on us again as we closed on the station.

"Adenwold," I said to the wife as a platform came into view.

CHAPTER
NINE

We'd come in amid a slow hurricane of dust. I opened
the door of the compartment, and we climbed down.
The place was not as I had expected: somebody had
picked up the village of my imagination, turned it
around, removed some houses, added a lot of trees and
made the air hotter, thicker and more orange-coloured.
For a moment, the two of us stood still on the platform,
watching a single cloud from the locomotive unwind
through the stagnant air. There wasn't much *to*
Adenwold, or to the little station. There was no station
canopy, and even though it was eight o'clock at night I
had to shield my eyes against the glare of the low sun.

I was about to make my itinerary of this silent place
when a door crashed open in the next carriage along. A
man in a green sporting suit climbed down. It was the
fellow who'd boarded at Barton. He immediately faced
about, and took his bicycle down. He'd carried it with
him in the compartment. The bell clanged as with an
effort the man set the machine on the platform boards,
and when the handlebar became entangled with the
leathern valise he carried, no porter came to his aid.

The train began to move off, each of its three
carriages complaining in a different manner. No-one

gave it the "right-away" — it had arrived and now left of its own accord. As the guard's van clattered past, I craned to see if there was anyone in there, but could make no-one out. Our tickets had not been checked; no-one had prevented the bicyclist from carrying his machine in the compartment instead of placing it in the guard's van . . . and yet there *had* to be a guard riding up somewhere, and the bicyclist *must* have asked him for the stop at Adenwold.

The train had left us on the longer of the two platforms, which was the "up". Here stood the station house — a cottage in yellow stone on which a single advertisement was pasted: "Smoke Churchman's Number One Cigarettes". Outside it were two cut-down barrels pressed into service as flower containers, but they held only a few poor blooms parched half to death. A waiting room and booking office were attached to the station house, and an iron bench stood outside these — a great flowing thing like a stationary bath chair or tricycle. The booking office door was on the jar, but I could make out nothing of its shadowy interior. A little way beyond it stood a wooden urinal, which was little more than a screen, being just four low walls and no roof.

After the platform, the "down" line divided, one track running into a three-road siding with a stack of general railway rubbish piled between the tracks — baulks of timber, rusted track shoes and the like. There was a small goods warehouse, not much larger than the station house, with a weighbridge outside it.

58

The "down" platform over-opposite contained nothing but a single bench, with more cornfields beyond.

The bicyclist, wheeling his machine, advanced upon us and gave not so much as a nod as he passed on his way. Was he off to silence John Lambert? His machine made the whirring sound of a dragonfly. I was wondering whether I ought to pursue and question him when a sudden bark of laughter came from the woods ahead of us.

At first, I thought this came from the signal box, which was half in the woods, and raised one storey off the ground on stone arches. (This, I supposed, so as to give the signalman a clear view of the trains arriving and departing through the trees.) The signalman stood at the top of the wooden staircase that led to the high door of the box. He did not look like one of the usual solid sorts employed in signalling: he was thin with a straggly beard, no cap and a uniform worn anyhow.

But when the laughter came again, I knew it had not come from his lips, but from those of another lounger on a level with him but on the other side of the tracks. This scrawny youth I took to be the lad porter at Adenwold. He sat like a crow on the little iron platform built onto the top of the pole that held the signals controlling the station. He was on a level with the treetops, yet slightly in advance of the trees, giving him a view of the whole station and the village hard by. And he was smoking.

He called across to his partner the signalman: "Reckon this pair are thinking, 'Crikey, where've *we* pitched up?'"

"Reckon so," the signalman called back.

"Who's that?" asked the wife, screening her eyes and looking up towards the signal gantry.

"He ought to be down here giving a hand with our bags," I said, "not cackling in the bloody trees."

There was a movement from the direction of the booking office, and I saw a fat man turning in the doorway. I made towards him, passing the open doorway of the waiting room where stood one giant black bench with horsehair bursting through holes in the seat cover.

The complications of light (too much of it outside, too little of it inside) meant I could make out little more than a silhouette in the booking office, but I knew the man for the station master by the glint of brass buttons on his tunic.

"Your porter's not up to much," I called across to him, but there was no answer, only a sort of rumble and whistle from within the dark room. I set down my bag and walked over.

"I say, mate," I began, "I've never seen the like of . . ."

The words died on my lips as I looked inside the booking office.

It was a sort of wood-smelling hovel. There was a counter with an ABC telegraph machine on it. But there was so much clutter on the floor in front of the counter that I supposed most passengers had their tickets served out through the doorway. There was a wide cabinet fixed to the wall, and a clock beside it. A tall sloping desk held many papers and tattered books, but a good many more books lay on the floor: *Wagon Book, Transfer Order Book, Delivery Book, Goods Not Reserved Book* — all of these were on the dusty floorboards, and it was all wrong. It was like seeing a Bible on the floor of a church.

The fat man stood guiltily in amongst this wreckage, as well he might do. One visit from a company auditor and he'd be stood down on the spot. He was no smarter in appearance than his two juniors in the trees, but in manner he was the opposite. The sweat rolled off him, and he looked scared. He was standing beside a small table, and here was the queerest thing of all, for on the table top (which was covered over with a green cloth) were perhaps sixty or seventy tiny leaden soldiers set out in a battle scene. I looked at the man, and his eyes flickered towards me, then away. We were both struck dumb, save for the fact that a kind of regular, desperate whistle escaped from the man's throat as he laboured to breathe in the heat.

I said, "Your lad porter, Mister . . ." at which he gave a start and a small cry of "Oh yes?"

He looked at me with great anxiety, practically trembling.

"You ought to know that he's sitting at the top of the signal pole and cheeking the passengers," I said.

"Leave off, Jim," came the voice of the wife from the platform. "Could you just ask the gentleman where we might get a bed for the night?"

"I sent the boy up to oil the lamps," said the station master. "He's . . . he's still up there, is he?"

He had a high-pitched voice, and was better spoken than I had expected.

"He's nattering away to the signalman, who's also fifteen foot up," I said.

"Well," said the station master, "they like to keep a look-out, you know."

"What for?"

"Well . . . trains."

"So they can ignore them when they come in?"

"We've just one more through this evening," said the station master, and you'd have thought from his tone that every one that came by was a torture to him. He looked strained all to pieces — to the point where I felt it wrong to keep on at him about the slackness at his station.

"Do you know if there's an inn with beds roundabout?" I asked him in a kindlier tone.

"Oh," said the fat official, and he began wiping his forehead with the fluttery fingers of his right hand. "The Angel," he said. "They'll do you pretty well there."

"Is it the only inn?"

"It is."

I looked again at the books on the floor, and saw again the anxiety in the man's face as I did so. I felt I ought to account for the clutter in some way.

"Having a bit of a clearout, are you?"

"Oh," the station master said again, and it came out as a sort of surprised hoot, ". . . no."

The wife was at the door now; "If you don't mind — where is The Angel exactly?"

"Just up the way there," said the SM, giving us a look that so plainly said "Please go away now" that we both turned, collected our bags and did so.

We walked out of the station under the eyes of the lad porter and the signalman. They were both still on their perches but now kept silence as they watched, and it struck me for the first time that I might have put the wife in the way of danger.

I held open for her the wicket gate that separated the station proper from the station yard, and there was a notice pinned to it: "Adenwold Christmas Club Summer Outing. Friday 21 July to Monday 24 July. To Scarborough, Premier Watering Hole of the North & Queen of Spas. Tickets from Mrs Taylor at the Post Office."

The wife was reading it over my shoulder.

"Some folks are all luck," she said.

The station yard was a dusty white triangle. Beyond it was another triangle, this one green, or at any rate yellowish, for the grass was all burnt by the sun. There were several shops around this green. One was a brick block of a building with a sign reading: "A. AINSTY: SHOEING AND GENERAL SMITHS (MOTORS REPAIRED)". The double doors at the front were closed, an iron bar fixed across. A great heap of old horseshoes was stacked against one side wall, together with a bench seat from what might have been a carriage or motor-car propped on trestles.

A little way along from the smithy was a flimsy clapperboard shop, which was also closed and blank-looking. On the signboard was painted a word that had faded almost to nothing, and that I could not read. It was followed by the word "Provisions", and then came another unreadable one for good measure. Before the shop stood a sort of wide step-ladder meant for displaying goods, but it was quite bare. There was also a cottage under a thatch that was laughably thick — put me in mind of a sheep that needed shearing. A tiny tin sign dangled from the front of it, reading "Post Office", and it was hardly bigger than a post*card*. Fixed into the side wall was a posting-box, and I wouldn't have fancied dropping a letter in there. It looked as if it hadn't been emptied in years.

Scarborough seemed to have claimed the whole village. I thought of the way a school yard is cleared for a fight, and I thought again of the bicyclist. It was Friday evening. Could he be said to have arrived *during the week-end?* What exactly did the word "week-end" mean?

Three dusty roads led away from the square. One went more or less the way the station master had indicated.

As we approached this one, I asked the wife:

"When does a week-end begin?"

"That's just what *I'm* wondering," she said.

CHAPTER
TEN

On the right side of the road were trees; on the left side a row of white, bent cottages which declined in the middle like a line of washing. Two old women stood before the houses, and looked like they belonged to them, for they too were old and bent. Then came high hedges in which many kinds of wildflower were entangled. These in turn gave way to fields of cut corn, and The Angel.

It was on the left side, a taller white-painted house than the others. A long trestle table had been placed before it, and three people sat there. It was like an exhibition of country life. At one end sat a man in late middle-age. His face was all colours: white and grey beard mingled with red and grey skin. His eyes were half-closed and he sipped ale from a pewter. In the centre sat a plump, brown woman surrounded by lemons. She was slicing them on a board with a great knife and squeezing them into a pail. A lad of about twelve years sat with his knees pressed up against the table end. At first I thought it was a small dog that was tied by a string to his chair, but on second glance it turned out to be a ferret or polecat. Behind the table, a bicycle — the machine belonging to the man who'd lately climbed down from the train — was propped against the front wall of the pub.

As we approached, the wife looked at the front of the inn and, giving a sort of gasp, said "wisteria". She was trying to get a plant of that name to grow over the front of our terraced house at Thorpe-on-Ouse, outside York, but it would not take. This one had taken all right. Its black branches and purple flowers quite covered the windows on the upper left-hand side so that The Angel seemed to have a patched eye.

Touching my hat, I gave the three good evening, at which the man and the boy stirred a little, but only the woman went so far as to return the greeting.

"Do you have rooms?" I asked her, but my question was answered by the words painted in large black letters half under the wisteria: "The Angel Inn — Beers and Wines — Rooms for Travellers."

"Yes, dear," said the woman, shading her eyes against the low sun.

"Do you have a room for two for tonight?" put in the wife.

"We do, love," said the woman — and yet she made no move.

"Looks like most of the village has gone to Scarborough," I said.

"Most *has*," she said.

Lydia was looking down at the ferret or polecat.

"He's very pretty," she said.

"Don't stroke 'im whatever yer do," said the lad.

Lydia stepped back.

66

I introduced myself to the woman — though not as a policeman. It would pay dividends, I had decided, to observe this village as an ordinary tripper.

One magpie sat on the roof of The Angel. It was black and white, like the inn, and looked made of leftovers from it.

Why did I think Lambert was innocent? Because he had fed the bird outside the police office. And I was in good company: the governor of Wandsworth gaol had thought the same.

The woman was at last rising, giving her name as "Mrs Handley" and wiping her hands on her pinafore.

Lydia, still looking at the polecat, was saying to the boy:

"He'd have my finger off, I suppose."

"He wouldn't have your finger *off*," said the boy, evidently thinking hard. "It'd be left on . . ."

"Would you like to follow me up?" the woman was saying.

". . . Only it'd be *danglin'*," the boy ran on.

The lad was also rising to his feet. Where his mother was tawny, he was a brighter brown. He seemed smallish for his age, but he had a great wave of black hair, which must have been oiled naturally, for he was not the sort of boy to be brilliantined. The kid reminded me of one of the over-thatched cottages. He wore a suit of rough purplish corduroy, and balanced what seemed like a very small cap on top of his great quantity of hair.

The sign above the front door read: "Mr P. Handley, licensed retailer of foreign wines, spirituous liquor, ales, porters and tobacco". We stepped beneath it into the hot dimness of the inn's tiny hallway. There was a door on either side. One said "Saloon", the other "Public".

"Lovely wisteria," Lydia said, as we climbed the stairs.

The landlady smiled but it was the lad who answered.

"Threatens to 'ave the 'ole front down, that does," he called up the staircase.

The lad, who'd seemed stand-offish at first, was now eager to be included in the conversation; he was certainly the brightest spark we'd struck so far in Adenwold. He carried my bag — he'd insisted on doing so, while his mother carried Lydia's. The landlord himself had remained at the table outside with his ale.

The staircase walls were decorated with wallpaper — white with red roses — and this continued along the narrow landing and into the room we now entered, so that the whole of the interior of The Angel seemed to have a bad case of measles.

The room was small and buckled, with a single tab rug on a polished wooden floor. Beside the high bed stood a rickety washstand, a dresser, a cane chair and a small wardrobe. I whisked off my topcoat, and put my warrant card in the top left drawer of the dresser. There was one picture on the wall, showing two fish facing different directions, each marked "Pearch" — the old-fashioned spelling. Between them were drawings of four hooks, and these were marked "Lob worm", "Minnow", "Brandling" and "Marsh Worm". The room was clean and light — this even though we were, so to

68

say, *inside* the wisteria, for its purple flowers fluttered at the window.

Lydia complimented the woman on the prettiness of the room, and I gave the boy a penny for carting my bag up the stairs. I asked his name, and he answered, "Mervyn."

"Who's the fellow on the bicycle?" I enquired.

"Him?" he said. "He's a bicyclist."

I could see that he knew his answer to have been a little lacking, but before he could make any further remark his mother had bundled him out of the room. She turned about in the doorway, saying, "There's a cold supper laid on in the saloon from just after nine. Yorkshire ham and salad — will that do you?"

"Just the ticket," I said.

As she quit the room, the wife sat on the bed.

"Why is there any need to call it a 'Yorkshire' ham?" she said when the door was closed. "That talk's all for the benefit of trippers. Doesn't she see that we *are* Yorkshire?"

It was a strange thing for the wife to say, for she herself was *not* Yorkshire. She'd been born in London, and had lived there until we'd married. She was now looking down at her dress, as if trying to make out her knees through the muslin.

"Well, I'm torn about the landlady," I said. "She's sort of half-friendly, isn't she?"

"It's quite obvious that her husband never does a hand's turn," said Lydia. "Why is it his name over the door, and not hers?"

It seemed to me that the wife always fell back on her hobby horse, the sex war, when in a bad mood.

"I liked the lad, though," I said, and the wife made no reply to that.

"Still hot, en't it?" I said, removing my collar and moving over to the washstand. "You could cut it with a bloody knife."

I lifted up the jug of water that stood beneath the washstand and began giving myself a sluice down. The washstand was too small, and, although I wasn't looking towards the wife, I knew that she was eyeing me and thinking: *Why must he slosh about so?*

"What was she doing with the lemons?" the wife asked, as I dried my face.

"Making lemonade," I said.

The wife, who was no great hand in the kitchen, seemed irritated that I knew this. She was browned off again, and the little headway I'd gained with her on the train since Malton was now lost. The Angel Inn, although clean and bright, was not up to the mark, being too cottage-like and countrified. The wife liked wildflowers and she was a good walker, but Thorpe-on-Ouse (where we lived, and which was just three miles outside York) was village enough for her. For all her Liberal-Labour leanings, the wife aspired to society, and that was not to be had in a remote spot like this.

As I put on a clean shirt, she walked over to the window, which gave onto the kitchen garden of the inn. I stood behind Lydia, towelling my face, for it was not just then safe to touch her. The garden was pretty well-kept, but lonely-looking somehow. The raspberries, growing along twines stretched between canes, put me in mind of telegraph poles and wires. Cut cornfields lay beyond, and beyond them the dark green wall of the woods. There was something not right about the woods. Shadows of trees fell upon the trees at the edge of it — and yet where were the ones that *made* those shadows?

Just then there came a clattering noise from close-by, and Mrs Handley came out of the back door of the inn and walked across the garden into the outhouse. She returned after a moment carrying a ham. The Yorkshire Ham. The call of a nightjar came from the yellow cut field, and it stopped Mrs Handley in her tracks.

"Is she crying?" I said, looking over the wife's shoulder.

Lydia sat down on the bed again.

"I wouldn't be in the least surprised," she said.

I heard the clatter of the door from directly below, signifying that Mrs Handley had re-entered the inn.

"What are you thinking about, love?" I asked the wife, as I fixed what I thought of as my holiday neckerchief in place. It was green to match the sporting cap, but I reserved that for the present on account of the wife's mood.

"Scarborough," she said.

I should've known not to ask.

". . . The Italian band on the pier," she ran on, ". . . a lemon tea at the Grand . . . the Chinese lanterns at dusk in the Esplanade Gardens."

If we'd gone, I thought, *she wouldn't have been so keen on it all.*

"We *will* go to Scarborough," I said, transferring the bundle of papers from my kitbag to the inside pocket of my suit-coat, which lay on the bed. "I've another leave in August, and we'll go then. Meantime, shall I tell you how we've come to fetch up here?"

I had been eyeing the place next to the wife on the bed, but I thought it better to tell the tale while standing.

I gave Lydia the story I'd had from Hugh Lambert, and told her of my plan of campaign. I didn't say whether I believed the story to be true. When I'd finished, I stood waiting for her to say, "Well, it's all too daft for words." Instead there came through the open window a beating of air. It was the fire-breathing of the iron intruder: the 8.41 "down".

"I'm off to meet that in," I said, and I snatched up my suit-coat and new cap and quit the room. Let the wife digest the story at her leisure — it was a lot to take in.

Spilling out through the front door of The Angel, I saw that the long table now stood empty, and that Mervyn Handley's ferret had been untied and removed. The train gave two screams as it approached through the trees, and I began running along the dusty downhill road, which brought the sweat pricking under my shirt. The floating sharpness of engine smoke mingled with the dizzying country-side scents of hay, cut corn, hedge flowers and meadow flowers — and all for my benefit alone, for there was no-one else about. It was unnatural for an evening to be so close. A man deserved a rest

72

after six, but this bugger of a sun would never let up. Seemed set on proving a point, it did: I can keep this up for ever, you know!

I ran past the triangle of dying grass that marked what seemed to be the centre of Adenwold, and across the station yard, where I had to step aside to let a man in a long white dust-coat come through. He was hatless, and with silver hair, and the coat came out behind him like wings. Behind him, the train was just coming to a stand. Had he come down early from it? He'd have risked a broken ankle if so. I turned about and watched him tear across the station yard, and then away in the opposite direction to The Angel.

He might or might not have arrived by train. My priority was to observe those who certainly had done.

I gained the "down" platform, and stood level with the tail light of the guard's van, which blazed away needlessly in the golden evening. A man was walking away from a third-class carriage. He was a clerkly sort, sweating in tall collar, black shiny suit and a cheap, high-crowned brown bowler that clashed. He carried a portmanteau and a Gladstone bag. The lad porter was on the platform, watching the man. He'd made no move to assist him.

The clerkly sort kept turning about as he walked, as if to make sure that nobody else had climbed down from the train — which nobody else had. He stopped as I watched him and gave me a steady stare for a second or two before striking out for the barrow boards and Adenwold.

As he crossed the station yard, he passed a man approaching the simmering train: a parson in a light white suit. He carried a small suitcase.

Was this the Reverend Martin Ridley, the vicar who'd been in the woods at the time of the killing? He stepped onto the platform and came past me without a glance. The porter closed on him. They exchanged a word, and the porter took the suitcase. The vicar wore a white straw hat with a red ribbon around the crown that pulled at the brim, making it wavy and flower-like. His face was redder than a vicar's ought to be. I did not care for his looks, but he was evidently deemed worth money by the porter, who now opened a door marked "First" for him. The vicar climbed up, passed down a coin or two and the porter slammed the door.

So that was one less to worry about.

The engine gave a whistle, and I watched the train move away, the reflected sun burning in the blank carriage windows. When it had gone, the lad porter turned and faced me — giving me a stare that had in it a sort of steady defiance. Maybe he'd been given a rating by the station master after my complaint, but I doubted that.

I doubled back over the barrow boards just in time to see the lately alighted fellow in the bowler skirt the triangular green. From the station yard, I watched him take the dusty uphill road. He must be heading for The Angel. After all, it was that or a ten-mile tramp to the next village.

The man appeared to be having bother with the catch on his Gladstone bag, and kept pausing to secure it. A female form was advancing on him from the part of the road that was bounded by the hedges. It was the wife in her high-waisted holiday dress. As the two crossed, the clasp on the man's bag gave way, and the goods inside spilled out onto the road. Four heavy-looking items in green cloth bags tumbled down, and a quantity of papers floated up and a little way away in the hot evening air. The wife closed on the man, and I was a little jealous of him for the speed with which she came to his aid. She almost knelt in the road to help collect up the papers. By the time I was level with them, everything was back in the bag.

"You for The Angel?" I asked, lifting my sporting cap.

"I'm for the *inn*, anyhow," said the man.

His accent was London.

"It's called The Angel," I said.

The man removed his bowler to mop his brow. His hair was divided perfectly into two halves from neck to forehead as though he was just up from a swim.

"It's a lovely evening," said the wife.

"Well, it is extremely oppressive," said the man, before remembering himself and adding, "but yes, it is lovely."

There was something artificial about his speech, as though he wanted to be better than he was.

I said, "You've come up from . . . ?"

"Oh you know," he said, "London way . . . Norwood area," and then, in a kind of panic, he looked up at the sky, saying, "Not a cloud!"

He had us down as people who could be fobbed off with talk of the weather. He nodded to us, turned on his heel, and marched on, but after a second he stopped again, and called to me: "I say, you ain't Franklin, by any chance, are you?"

"Name's Stringer," I called up to him, "Jim Stringer."

He nodded and turned on his heel. He had not given out his own name. I ought not to have given him mine. Lydia stood next to me, and close enough for me to know that our late argument was at an end.

"Why did you not say you were a policeman?" she asked, when the man was out of earshot.

"I don't want him to bolt," I said.

"You think he's here to make mischief for this John Lambert?"

"Well, he's not here for a ramble in the woods, is he?"

"I don't suppose you've found out where this man Lambert is?"

"He's at the Hall."

"Which way is that?"

"Don't know just yet."

"Why not ask someone?"

I looked at my silver watch: quarter to nine.

"I don't know who to trust. You don't know who might be in with the bad blokes."

Lydia was grinning at me. I might almost have thought she'd taken a drink at The Angel, only she never touched a drop.

"Fairly drowning in mysteries, aren't we?" she said.

"What's up?" I said.

"*Him*," she said, taking hold of my sleeve, and pointing up the road after the clerk.

"Well," I said, "what about him?"

"The papers he's just dropped," she said. "Half were quite blank, and half were written in German."

"*German?*"

"Your face, Jim Stringer," she said, grinning.

CHAPTER
ELEVEN

We were taking a turn through the woods, the wife occasionally giving a glance at my cap, and frowning. I had half an eye out for the Hall, but I was above all trying to develop a plan.

The low sun seemed to track us through the trees, always keeping a wary distance. I revolved in my mind the events of the evening, while the wife talked fast. She was in good spirits in spite of my cap, and she picked wildflowers as she walked. She'd fallen into conversation with Mrs Handley, the landlady at The Angel, and taken a liking to her. "She's a feminist, if she but knew it," Lydia said. "She's perfectly well aware that she ought not to do as much work as she does, but she says that her mind runs on so if she doesn't, and she'd rather have the work than the worry."

"Why was she crying in the garden?"

"I'm sure that was on account of the work," said the wife.

"Not the *worry*, you don't suppose?"

She gave me a quick glance, but made no answer.

The wife had also been galvanised by a quick cold bath, and a glass of Mrs Handley's lemonade. "It's nectar, Jim," she said. "Do you suppose that man from

Norwood is connected to the Moroccan business?" she went on.

"Well . . ." I said, for the question knocked me.

"He's up to devil knows what," said the wife. "Do you suppose it's too late for violets?" she said, as we came out into a clearing.

We looked about, and I said, "That fellow's made you sit up, hasn't he? Do I take it you believe something's going on?"

"No," said the wife, "I don't for one minute."

I put my hands in my trouser pockets, and eyed her coolly.

I said, "But it's true about the German papers?"

She nodded once, briefly.

"There are fixed agents," the wife said cheerfully, "and there are travelling agents. The Germans have a brigade of spies in Britain . . . I'm just thinking of all the lies I've read in the newspapers . . . Honestly, it's all such rubbish. Why shouldn't a man have German documents about him? He might be half-German for all we know."

"Yes," I said, "but given what I told you at the inn . . ."

She was shaking her head, wouldn't have it. She had chosen her side in Britain's battles. The folk who talked up the German menace were the ones who talked down the women's movement, and you couldn't believe in both.

I saw by the presence of telegraph poles that we were hard by the railway line. Swallows flew fast through the evening air, making a high, singing noise as they swooped over the wires. I might once have taken this for the sound of the wires themselves, for I had been told in my early days on the railways that it was possible to hear the electrical signals as they flew from pole to pole. But this was not true. You could not hear the signals however close you stood.

Just then, two sharp cracks came from the wood; a cloud of birds rose up from it, and moved away to the left like smoke.

"It's fucking *happened*," I said.

"You will *not* . . ." said the wife, but I was straight back into the woods and crashing through the branches as a third shot came.

"You there!" I called out. "Police! Stop firing!"

I felt panic as I clashed through the trees, but my curiosity was stronger than my fear.

"Give over, mister!" came a high voice through the trees — a boy's voice. "It's only t' rabbits I'm after."

It was Mervyn Handley, the kid from the inn, but I had to march on for a good half-minute more until I clapped eyes on him. He stood amid fallen trees in the woodsman's clearing I'd seen from the train, and he held a double-barrelled shotgun pointed down. His powder flasks and shot pouches were too near the fire that bent the warm air behind him. His ferret — which was tied to the skeleton frame of a steam saw — was too near the terrier that was tied to the thickest branch of a fallen log, the result being that the dog was barking fit to bust, and the ferret was giving a constant thin scream. In the clearing, patches of ferns grew, and there were two dead-straight rows of sunflowers. Some of the timbers had been used to make a low shelter with a tarpaulin slung over the top. At the entrance, I saw a dead rabbit, a woodsman's bill-hook, a funny paper for boys and a sack.

The boy was calming the dog — and so also the ferret — as I spoke up.

"Do you know of a John Lambert?" I asked him.

The boy nodded.

"Stops up at . . ."

"Where?"

"Up at t' all."

"The Hall? Is he the squire, so to speak?"

Mervyn Handley frowned.

"Well . . . there's t' *new* man."

But surely, I thought, *John Lambert — being the eldest son — would have inherited the house? He* would be the new man. But this might be a rather complicated matter. I tried a different tack.

"John Lambert's father died, didn't he?"

"Aye, mister," the boy said, and he looked at me levelly. After an interval, and still eyeing me, he said, "Shot to death."

"And who shot him?"

Silence for a space. Then the boy said:

"His son. Master Hugh."

"He's about to swing, en't he?"

The lad nodded.

"Why did it take so long to come to a hanging?"

"Master Hugh made off. France, and all over."

"When did they lay hands on him?"

"Last back end."

"And you knew the man accused — Master Hugh?"

A long beat of silence.

"I knew him, aye."

I was going in strong here. I knew the kid didn't want to be asked, but then again I knew he would answer. So I kept on.

"What did you think of him?" I asked, and he shot back the answer directly: "Liked him."

The wife was pacing about near the fire; she had entered the clearing only a few seconds after me, so she'd been privy to the whole conversation. I began to hear the sound of a river rolling past.

"*Why* did you like him?"

No sound but the rushing river.

Mervyn said:

"He'd give me presents."

"Like what?"

"Like a dormouse," said the kid, this time fast, and he turned his head once again to the side. "There now," he said, and nodded two or three times.

The wife cut in to spare the lad more of my questions:

"What's your dog called, Mervyn?"

"Alfred," he said.

"Is it safe to stroke him?" she asked.

"It'll be safe for *you*," he said, which put the wife in a fix, leaving her no option but to go over to the animal.

The wife was stroking the dog, which seemed more bored than anything else by the attention.

She asked, "What is this place, Mervyn?"

"This?" he said, looking about him. "It's t' set-up."

"The set-up?"

Mervyn coloured up at hearing his name for the place repeated, but Lydia's more amiable questions gradually put him at his ease, and it all came out.

The set-up was his seat of operations against rabbits, or a place he'd come to eat his snap after a morning's toil in the fields or at the inn. He was half pot boy at the inn, half farmer's boy, for he would do turns at all the local farms, helping at harvest and threshing, picking thistles in summer and stones in winter. The Handleys had once farmed land leased from the Hall, but the man later murdered — Sir George Lambert — had turned them out and given them the pub instead. When I asked why, the boy said, "Not rightly sure."

Anyhow, Mervyn did not seem especially down on the late Sir George Lambert. The boy described him to us as a great man for hunting and cricket — a very loud and hearty gent from the sound of it, but "all right".

"Would you like to manage an inn when you're older?" Lydia asked Mervyn, and I could see she was taken with the boy, even though he spoke the broad Yorkshire she was forever trying to lead our Harry away from. Mervyn shrugged.

"Or you might think of the North Eastern Railway," I said. "The present lad porter at Adenwold's not up to much, I'll tell you that."

Mervyn kept silence. Having laid down his shotgun and given the fire a kick, he was moving towards the river.

"Lad at t' station?" Mervyn said as he walked. ". . . I steer clear."

"What's his name?" I called after him.

But he didn't seem to hear.

I indicated by a nod of the head to Lydia that we should follow the boy over to the river.

"Don't press him so," she said, as we followed in his wake. But I knew she was as keen as me to find out more.

"What about the station master?" I asked Mervyn when we were all at the river bank.

"'Im?" he said, "'im wi' t' little men?"

"That's right," I said. "The model soldiers in the booking office."

Mervyn was drawing what looked like a great rubber bag from out of the river. It had been tethered to the bank like a fisherman's keep net. He upended it and . . . well, it was like watching a whale vomiting out dead rabbits, for the rubber bag held half a dozen of them.

"He's a weird one all right," said Mervyn, flinging away the bag. I looked over to the wife; her face was a picture.

"Hold on," I said to Mervyn. "What's all this?"

"Keeps the rabbits cold," he said.

"It's an old mackintosh, I suppose?" put in the wife.

Mervyn shook his head.

"Cover for an invalid mattress," he said. "At least that's what me mam says."

"Where d'you find it?"

"In t' wood. Soon as I saw it, I knew it'd come in."

"It's a clever use of it," said the wife.

"It *does*," said Mervyn in a modest sort of way.

84

He told us that the village carter, a fellow called Hamer, would give him tuppence for each rabbit and then sell them on to the butcher in East Adenwold. There was no butcher in Adenwold itself.

"Why do you have a fire going, Mervyn?" asked the wife.

"In case I pull summat out o' there," he replied, indicating the river.

"You can take a fish by hand?"

"At odd times, aye."

He was stuffing the rabbits into the sacking.

The wife asked, "Have you ever been to Scarborough, Mervyn?"

"I 'ave not."

"It's only an hour's train ride," I said.

"I don't 'old wi' t' railway."

"Why not?"

"It did for all t' farms round 'ere."

Railways were bad for farms. They brought cheap food from abroad.

"There'd be no lemons here without the railway," I said.

"Well then," said Mervyn, "I don't like lemons."

The wife asked him: "Do you never use the railway to get about?"

He shook his head.

"I just walk over t' fields."

"It sounds a very nice way to travel, I'm sure," said the wife.

"Aye," said Mervyn, "it is."

I asked him: "Mervyn, who were the villagers beating on the rabbit shoot? When Sir George was shot, I mean."

"I've no notion," he said, eyeing me.

I nodded, saying, "Where's the Hall from here, Mervyn?"

And he stood pointing.

CHAPTER
TWELVE

"And now?" I asked the wife, as we walked fast through the woods.

The boy's talk of the murder had flicked her imagination. I could tell that by her silence.

"We're not going to *call*, you know," said the wife.

We were not in the habit of leaving cards. We did not have any cards to *leave*. If I became a solicitor then we would do.

"We'll just have a peep at the place," I said.

We were moving now along a wider track. There seemed a whole roadway of tracks in the woods, with great junctions under the branches but never any people.

We came to an edge of the trees, and there was the Hall. There were seas of corn to left and right, and pasture directly before it, across which two telegraph wires were carried towards the house by a line of poles that seemed to originate in the woods. A long drive ran through the pasture and ended bang at the front door. It was dead straight but went up and down a good deal, like a long sheet being shaken out. The drive seemed longer than the house required. It was only a moderate-sized mansion, but made up for that in handsomeness.

"It's not so big that you couldn't imagine living in it," I said, but the wife made no answer. Looking at the house, she was off in her own world.

In the pasture stood a couple of dozen oak trees, set widely apart, Each looked like a green planet, and each had a white wooden railing around its base as if to say: this tree is special, not like that common lot in the woods. The cattle were all lying down and swishing their tails, worn out after their day of great heat, but the house stood proudly. To the left side of it from our point of view stood a group of buildings like something crossed between churches and farm buildings. As we looked on, a man moved from behind one of the great trees. He had on a light white suit and seemed — even from two hundred yards' distance — to be under some great strain. He held a book under his arm.

"What's *he* about?" asked the wife.

"It's *him*," I said, as the white-suited man approached.

As he moved closer, I saw that he wore thin wire spectacles, also that the book he held was a Bradshaw, so that I immediately thought of him as a man important enough to require a timetable always to hand. He might have to go anywhere at any time by train. But he was not important-looking in the normal way.

"Fine evening," he said, in a very sad tone that stopped everything in its tracks.

He was well-spoken, of course, but he didn't look the part of a country squire. He had the same out-of-the-way, almost feminine looks as his brother. He was as pale as Hugh Lambert, but even thinner and more sickly-looking. His close-trimmed beard fitted under the curves of his cheekbones in a way I thought Jesus-like. Unlike his brother, he was inclined to be bald, and such black hair as he did have was rather damp, making him seem feverish; his shirt was disarranged, and his tightly knotted white necker was more like a garrotte, as his brother's had been. But he was the sort that did not need to be smart. He was from brass, in other words.

"You are John Lambert," I said.

He did not deny it, but touched his spectacles, and looked over to the far edge of the grounds, where a man was cutting grass with a scythe.

"That man's been hard at it all day," he said, "and he hasn't had a cup of tea since four o'clock. He told me that himself just now."

We watched the fellow about his work.

"Rather late to be cutting grass," I said.

"It's not a job for the middle of the day in weather like this," said John Lambert. "The temperature touched ninety-five here this afternoon."

"Ninety-six in York," I said.

"Well, York's south of here," said Lambert. "It's practically tropical. Who are you?"

And in the moment of asking that question, he *did* look like the squire of Adenwold. I decided that I would still keep back my occupation.

"Stringer," I said, and he shook my hand, saying nothing.

"I fell into a conversation with your brother at York station," I said. "He was changing trains there, being transferred to Durham gaol. I suppose you *know* he was transferred?"

He looked down at the timetable in his hand, then up at me.

"How did you come to be speaking to him?"

"I work at the station," I said.

He looked at me, as if to say: that's no answer, and you know it.

"Why did he come off the train?" he asked.

"There was a delay. The fireman was taken sick."

"Where?"

"Shortly after Retford."

"At Doncaster?" he asked sharply. "Selby?"

"I don't know exactly," I said.

It was time to give him the hard word.

"He told me there may be people who perhaps . . . mean to kill you."

John Lambert suddenly tipped his head up, as though revolving this notion.

"That may very well be," he said.

It was like finding that a dream of your own matched exactly someone else's. He touched his glasses again, as though a defect in his vision was his main concern of the moment. *Here's a man who's read too much*, I thought. I longed to say the word "Ponder" and see whether he started at it.

90

"They may be here already or they may be arriving by train," I said.

"Mmm . . ." said Lambert, in a comical sort of tone.

He, like his brother, had a taste for grim humour.

"Who are they?" asked the wife from behind me. "And why do they want to harm you?"

I turned about. She looked strange saying that with flowers in her hand, and it was as though the man *did* feel the question impertinent, for he gave answer to me and ignored Lydia.

"I am not at liberty to say."

Lydia asked, "If they're going to kill you anyway, then what do you have to lose by speaking out?" and I was torn between annoyance at her cutting in like this and the thought that it was a good question.

But John Lambert kept silence.

I tried another approach:

"Why do you not make off?"

"Fatalistic disposition," he said with a shrug, and he nearly smiled again, adding: "Let me put the matter less whimsically . . ."

"*Could* you?" said the wife from behind.

"If I made off," said Lambert, "they would find me anyway."

"One 'up' train stopped by request at Adenwold this evening," I said. "We came in by it, and a bicyclist got off as well."

Lambert nodded, and he now seemed distinctly amused.

"Sounds fairly benign so far," he said.

"You've no reason to fear a bicyclist?" I enquired.

"We've all got reason to fear them," said Lambert. "They've no brakes at *all*, half of them."

"Then," I went on, "at 8.41, a scheduled 'down' train arrived. A man from Norwood came in by it."

"Norwood?" said Lambert.

"It's in south London," I said.

"I know."

"He carried papers written in German."

I watched him for a reaction, and he watched me back.

"There are three further trains tomorrow," I said.

"The 8.51, the 12.27 and the 8.35p.m.," Lambert cut in with a faint smile. It was as though the Bradshaw was not so much in his hand as in his very bloodstream.

"And each of those also *leaves*," I said. "You might keep that in mind."

I looked at the Bradshaw in his hand. There were a thousand pages in it. He might go *anywhere*.

"The governor of Wandsworth gaol believes your brother to be innocent," I said.

"I share the gentleman's opinion."

"If he didn't kill your father, then who did? Do you know? And do you plan to let on? Is that why you're in danger?"

John Lambert just eyed me, and he seemed very remote behind those thin glasses of his. He was very likely remote from everyone.

"My brother has sent me here to help you," I said. "And yet . . ."

"And let *me* help *you*, Mr Stringer," he cut in. "As long as you are connected to me your life is in danger."

92

Well now.

I wanted a little time to think in. I must send the wife away for one thing. And I ought to bring in the Chief.

"You mean to save your brother from the gallows," I said at length, "but how?"

"Mr Stringer," he replied, "I am sure that you have better things to do on a fine week-end like this than to fret over the private troubles of a stranger."

"We were on the point of going to Scarborough," said the wife, in a hollow sort of voice. "Just like most of this village."

"*Go* to Scarborough," said Lambert, again address-ing me.

"All the hotels are full," I said flatly, and at that I saw a new and deeper complication in the man's face — a sign of great trouble.

"Mr Lambert . . ." said the wife, and I knew that she had relented somewhat towards him in that moment. He looked directly at her for the first time, and nodded as though to thank her for the step she had taken but she seemed to hesitate on the point of speech. Lambert nodded at us both, turned on his heel and walked away. Ought I to have shown him the papers of his brother? They were in my pocket. I raised my hand to them. But instead I called after him one of the hundreds of questions I might have put:

"What is your profession?"

He stopped, and half-turned towards me, saying, "I fill notebooks, Mr Stringer."

CHAPTER
THIRTEEN

We walked fast through the woods. The darkness was drawing down, but still the heat hung heavy in the wide, tree-made tunnels. In the light of John Lambert's warning, the woods looked different. The trees either side of us were monsters — great spiders with even their highest branches swooping right down to the ground.

"Do you believe it now?" I asked the wife.

"I think there's something in it all," she said.

Whether she believed it or not, she would be leaving Adenwold in the morning, I would make sure of that. One murder had happened and another was coming, or at least an *attempt*, and I would have to put myself in the way of it. It struck me again that I ought to get the Chief over to Adenwold first thing in the morning. I knew he was generally in the office of a Saturday.

We came out of the trees and we were at Mervyn's set-up, which was more than ever like the scene of an explosion in the woods. As far as I could make out, the lad had gone, and taken all the dead rabbits with him. We walked on, and struck the railway track, which we followed a little way, walking under the telegraph wires.

The wife was ahead of me, stumbling now and then on the track ballast.

"Hold on," I said, "we're heading the wrong way."

But she'd come to a stop in any case. The wires from the pole before us were down, and lay by the side of the tracks, all forlorn like a dead octopus. They ran on as normal from the next pole along, but of course one break was all that was needed.

Was this to prepare the way for the killers?

Or were they already in the village?

This doing would cut off the station's telegraph office — very likely the only one in the village — from all points west, and it was odds-on the line would be cut the other way, too. How could I contact the Chief now, short of taking a train out in the morning? But if I did that, I would miss the ones coming in. And would the trains run? It was possible to operate a branch line without telegraphic connections, but special arrangements had to be put in hand.

The wife stood silent, with arms folded as she kicked at one of the stray wires. She said, "They have ordnance maps of the whole countryside, you know — the travelling agents, I mean. They're picked up from time to time, but it's all hushed up."

We walked on in silence through the dark woods. Every so often, there came a crashing as a bird tried to fly through the trees, and I did wish they would *stop* trying, for they put me in a great state of nerves.

When we gained the top of the road that rose from the centre of the village, we saw a greenish light through the windows of The Angel. I opened the front door, and we stepped into the little hallway where we had the options "Saloon" or "Public", or the stairs that led up to our room. There was no question but that Lydia would take the stairs. She didn't drink, and had never set foot inside a public house, but when I asked, "You off up, then?" she said "Not just yet", and stepped into the public bar with me.

Was it fear or curiosity that had made her do it?

We pushed through the door, and half a dozen — no, eight — faces looked back at us.

It turned out that, whichever door you walked through, you got the saloon *and* the public, and that the bar — on which stood six green-shaded oil lamps — was a sort of wooden island in-between the two. The "public" side was wooden walls and wooden benches. The "saloon" side was a little smarter. It had the red rose wallpaper and a fish picture over the fireplace similar to the one in our room. This one showed a pike, but with no instructions and no display of hooks. (If you wanted to catch a pike, you could work out how to do it yourself.) All the windows were open, and a warm breeze occasionally wandered through from the "public" to the "saloon" side. Mr Hardy, the fat station master, stood alone at the bar on the "public" side, and there were a couple of agricultural fellows talking and smoking at a table behind him. The two arrivals-by-train — the bicyclist and the man from Norwood — sat in the saloon side, and each had a small round table to himself. The man from Norwood had a pipe on the go, and was reading documents. The bicyclist was eating a pie — the Yorkshire pie, I guessed. Every now and again, he would lay down his knife and fork and give a loud sigh. After a while, it came to me that this might be connected to the fact that Mr Handley the landlord, sitting on a high stool on the saloon side, was addressing him. He did so again now, in a very deep, drunken voice, an underwater sort of voice like a deaf man's, and I couldn't make it out, but the bicyclist sighed again and said, "It certainly cannot be ridden in its present condition — not with the inner tube holed. The wheel would zig-zag intolerably."

His machine was evidently punctured. Like most who take to biking he was middle class — might have been a university product. As I watched, Mr Handley was served a pint in a pewter by his wife. It must have gone hard with her that he wasn't paying.

Mrs Handley smiled — still cautious, but I had a persuasion that she was warming to us. I ordered a pint of bitter for myself and the lemonade for the wife, and Mrs Handley seemed quite chuffed at this. Her husband being a man for strong waters only, and her boy not liking lemons, I supposed that she was glad to find a taker for her home-made brew. She poured the lemonade and then said to me: "We have John Smith's bitter, and Thompson's ale. The Thompson's is a little stronger."

"Oh, my husband knows all about that," the wife cut in, and I thought with excitement: *Now she's definitely nervous.* Unpredictable things happened when the wife became stirred-up.

Mr Handley made some further remark to the bicyclist. I couldn't understand a word he said, yet the bicyclist seemed to have no trouble in doing so.

"Cycling is certainly beneficial in that way," he said, in reply to Mr Handley. "It is said to promote a general activity in the liver," he added, at which he gave a pitying look to Handley, as if to say, "But *your* liver has enough on as it is."

He then stood up and quit the bar.

I asked for John Smith's, and plunged in haphazard as Mrs Handley passed me the pint.

"Almost everyone hereabouts has . . . well, gone."

She folded her arms and eyed me for a while.

"Moffat's here," she said, "down on the East Green. He's the baker."

"Why hasn't he gone?"

"He doesn't like Scarborough, I suppose."

"Can't credit *that*," said the wife, and she grinned, whereas Mrs Handley did not. Or not *quite*, anyhow.

"Caroline and Augusta are here," said Mrs Handley.

"Who are they?"

"They're the old ladies in the almshouses."

"Oh," I said, "the elderly parties. We saw them. Why haven't they gone?"

"Well, they're too old. They have those houses at a peppercorn rent. They're supposed to be infirm. They can hardly go off . . . enjoying themselves."

And here she did give a quick smile. She was continuing to eye me carefully, however.

"Who runs the Scarborough outing?" asked the wife.

"Christmas Club," said Mrs Handley. "You see, the Christmas Club here has nothing really to do with Christmas. You put in your money, and you have three days in Scarborough."

"Don't you get a turkey at Christmas?" I said.

"You get a chicken," Mrs Handley said after a while. "But people like the Scarborough jaunt. It's a village tradition."

"I suppose nobody from the Hall's gone, have they?" I asked Mrs Handley.

"Most of the servants have, I believe."

"But not the man who cuts the grass?"

"That's Ross's boy," she said, and she nodded to one of the two agriculturals, explaining that they were brothers from West Adenwold, to which they would be returning on foot very shortly, together with the grass-cutter, who was son to one of them. I decided to put them out of consideration, along with the two old maids in the almshouses.

"I believe there's a new squire in place of the murdered man," I said. "But that it's not John Lambert."

Mrs Handley folded her arms, and smiled at me as if to say, "Well now, you're quite the dark horse, aren't you?"

"That's Robert Chandler," she said, slowly, as though feeling her way. "He's Major Lambert's late wife's brother. He's the new tenant."

"Why doesn't John Lambert have the place?"

"Oh, he *owns* it. It's come to him — only he doesn't want to live there."

"Why not?"

"Bad memories, I expect."

"Does he ever come in here?" asked the wife.

"No fear," said Mrs Handley.

99

"What does he do for a living?" I asked.

Mrs Handley shrugged.

"I can't say. I hardly know him. He's in London a good deal of the time, and in York most of the rest. They say he keeps heaps of books in the gardener's cottage, a little way off from the main house."

"Sir George Lambert," I said, "— what was he like?"

Did Mrs Handley colour up at the question?

"He was a sportsman," she said presently, "always bucking about on his horse. He had the hunt, which came through on Wednesdays and Saturdays like a great whirlwind; he had his shoots, and he had his cricket games . . ."

"This inn is his, isn't it?" I said, with the wife eyeing me.

"'Course it is," said Mrs Handley, as if to say, "Don't you know how a village works?"

"What about his wife?" asked Lydia, no doubt thinking this would be a subject more to Mrs Handley's taste.

"Dead long since," said Mrs Handley.

Well, I had read something of the account of her death in Hugh Lambert's papers — the business of the fire seeming always too cold.

"And so there was no-one to come between him and the boys," Mrs Handley was saying. "He was very hard on the two boys — on Hugh especially."

Mrs Handley had fallen to gazing at Mr Hardy the station master, but I was sure there was nothing in this. He was just a convenient object to look at. Mrs Handley's earlier sadness had returned, and I could see that it was not on account of the murdered father, but on account of the son who was about to swing for the crime.

"Would *Hugh* come in here?" asked the wife, who, having finally entered licensed premises herself, had evidently become fascinated by the question of who else might or might not do so.

"Master Hugh?" said Mrs Handley, and she gave a cautious sort of nod. "He'd take a glass, and he'd sit in the public. The *public*, mark you, not the saloon. He was one of the two young masters, and yet he'd sit in the *public* bar." She smiled, saying, "Always wore the same suit — dark blue worsted. Lovely cloth, and yet the trouser bottoms clarted with muck, and all up his black boots. He told me one day: 'I always wear a city suit in the country and a country suit in the city.'"

As she spoke, she was preparing a supper for us — two plates of cold ham and salad. She handed them over the bar, saying, "What do you reckon to that saying of his? Was I supposed to laugh?"

"Well," I said, "I don't know."

"I'll tell you what — he'd look at me until I *did* laugh."

And she was almost laughing *now*.

"He *meant* you to laugh," I said.

"'Course he did. He was always coming out with things like that."

"Contradictory," I said.

"And he was just ever such . . . fun."

"Unlike John."

"John's clever," she said. "Clever people aren't usually much fun, are they?"

And it was clear from this that she didn't include me in that category.

I looked over at the clerk-type from Norwood — I was pretty sure he couldn't hear our conversation, nor was he straining to do so. I somehow didn't feel I ought to ask Mrs Handley about him and the bicyclist, whereas it was all right to ask about the locals. That was the sort of thing an ordinary tripper might do.

The wife said, "Mervyn told us that Master Hugh had given him a dormouse."

Mrs Handley's smile disappeared for an instant, but it came back as she said:

". . . Came up here, parked himself down on the bench outside, just next to where Mervyn was sitting. He turns to little Mervyn and he says, 'I've rather a bad head cold today,' and lifts his handkerchief out of his pocket. Well, the face he pulled when he saw that dormouse curled up in the middle of this most beautiful red silk handkerchief . . ."

"Master Hugh didn't know it was there?" I asked.

"He knew very well it was there. He was play-acting for the boy, don't you see? It was all for Mervyn's benefit. Well, it fairly slayed me, that did. I laughed fit to bust."

"Was the dormouse dead?"

Mrs Handley stopped laughing, and looked at me in amazement.

"Of course it wasn't *dead*. Where would have been the fun if it had been dead? It was a dormouse. It was *asleep*."

Well, this was all apiece with the feeding of the sparrow outside the police office.

"He doesn't sound much like a murderer," said the wife.

"Driven to it by the father, I expect," said Mrs Handley, in a very business-like way. "There'd been aggravation between them for years, and Lambert kept a house full of guns . . . There'll be an end to the business on Monday morning, anyhow."

She gazed at vacancy for a moment, before adding:

"He's to be hung on Monday — eight o'clock."

"I know," I said.

And she eyed me again, perhaps struggling to withhold the question: "And *how* do you know?"

The wife was staring towards the window, picking at her food. Mrs Handley moved off to serve one of the agriculturals, and as she did so the man from Norwood also left the bar. The wife said, "I'm going up."

"Hold on," I said, lifting my pint, "I'll just finish up."

But she just said, "Don't be long", and was gone.

I told myself she'd been emboldened to leave my side by the meek-seeming behaviour of our chief suspects: the man from Norwood and the bicyclist. But that might not have been it at all.

Station master Hardy, I noticed, was looking at me along the bar. The moment I returned his gaze he looked away, but not before I could get in the word "Evenin'".

"The soldiers you have at the station," I said, moving towards him. "What lot are they?"

"Oh," he said, "that's the York and Lancasters."

It was the Chief's regiment.

"Are they set out just anyhow, or is it a model of some particular scrap?"

"Battle of Tamai," he said, for the first time eyeing me directly. "Thirteenth of March, 1884."

Hardy's tunic was askew, but perhaps it had to be arranged peculiarly to fit round his big belly. He was not drunk, but on the way.

"I know a fellow was in that very show," I said, for the Chief had fought at Tamai.

"You do?" said Hardy, and he was different now — sharper. "Who's that, then?"

I couldn't answer directly without giving away that I was a copper, so I said, ". . . Sergeant major, he was."

Hardy was now holding my gaze for once. He was almost smiling as he said, "Tough as bulldogs, the non-commissioned blokes."

"This particular fellow once marched for fifty miles in hundred-degree heat," I said, at which station master Hardy eyed me for a while, perhaps idling the thought of that long march.

"I'd like to shake that man by the hand," he said presently, and he nodded rapidly to himself for a while, each nod signifying a further retreat from the conversation.

Just then there came through the open windows the roaring of a machine. It caused a slight stir in the room, but the drinkers stood the shock, as though the noise came as nothing out of the common to them. Walking over to one of the front windows I saw by the moonlight two men on a motor-bike that ought only to have carried one. The first man — the one on the seat — I did not recognise until I made out the identity of the one riding on the rear mudguard. He was the villainous-looking lad porter, and the one in the seat was the signalman. They both wore their North Eastern company uniforms, but with no shirt collars or caps. They climbed down from the motor-bike, and a moment later came clattering and dust-covered through the door that led into the bar. As the door swung to behind him, the lad porter called across to Hardy, who faced away from him. The pub fell silent as the porter said:

"The auction poster in the booking office, Mr Hardy — out of date it was, you were quite right. I took it down as per your instructions. You won't catch me shirking on the job, Mr Hardy."

He had an older man's grey, pitted face on a boy's body, and without his cap, I saw that his head was shaved; he looked to me like an evil jockey.

He carried on with his stream of shouted sarcasm:

"I've closed the warehouse — padlocked it good and proper as you asked, Mr Hardy. You'll find no cause to complain of slackness there . . ."

But as he spoke, the man addressed turned and made for the door with head down. The porter, eyeballing him all the way, asked, "Where you off to, Mr Hardy? Early night is it?"

Hardy made no answer but pushed on grimly through the door, at which the lad porter said to the signalman, "Well, en't that the frozen limit? It was a perfectly innocent enquiry!"

The signalman grinned and walked over to the bar, where Mrs Handley was nowhere to be seen. Instead, he called for two beers from Mr Handley, and with no "please" or "thank-you" about it. His companion remained standing in front of the door, from where he kept up his speech:

"He's a hard nut to crack, is Mr Hardy. There's just no bloody pleasing him, is there, Eddie old mate? Treat him with consideration, and he throws a paddy." He shook his head, saying, "Well, we'd best reach an accommodation somehow, or the results won't be pretty . . . Are you staring at me, mister," he ran on, addressing me, "or is it just my imagination?"

I kept silence.

"No," said the lad porter, "you must have been staring at me because, now that I come to think of it, I don't have any imagination, do I, Eddie?"

He was appealing to the signalman, who seemed nothing more to him than a sounding board, a mobile audience.

"Not to speak of, Mick," said the signalman, "— not over-imaginative."

I was weighing the kid up. He had a boy's body in size, but was jockey-like in that he looked as though he could take a pounding or give one. It was very noticeable that he stood directly before the door, blocking the exit.

"Bit keen-eyed you are, mate," he said.

106

It was quite beyond believing, but in the silence of the pub, the two of us had fallen to a staring contest.

"I'll give you some fucking rough music," the lad porter said, after an interval.

I said, "I'd think on if I were you. You don't know who you're talking to."

"I saw you at the fucking station," he said. "Come in with your missus. She's a bit of all right, your missus."

"I'll crown you in a minute," I said.

"Try it if you like. But I don't see you have any cause."

"At the station," I said, "you didn't attend to us . . ."

"And *why* d'you suppose I didn't?"

"Because you were sitting at the top of the fucking signal pole, that's why."

"I was changing the lamps, if that's all right with you, mate."

"You looked set for the evening — smoking 'n all. Paraffin and naked flame don't go together too well this weather."

"Well . . . what do *you* know about it?"

I eyed him directly, and the situation cracked.

"Fancy a pint, mate?" asked the porter, and he indicated to the signalman that he should stand me a glass.

The porter put out his little hard hand.

"Mick Woodcock," he said.

He had a lot off, all right — especially for a kid of . . . well, it was hard to say but he might not have been more than eighteen.

"Sorry about that, mate," he said, passing me the pint of Smith's as Mr Handley looked on, and the agriculturals began talking again. "I'm liable to fly off over anything. You here on holiday, are you? I mean . . . don't suppose you're here on account of our murder, are you? You en't a copper or a journalist or owt like that?"

"On holiday," I said.

He was sharp, this kid.

"The bloke that did it goes up Monday morning," he said.

There was a long interval of silence as we drank on.

Woodcock said, "That business at the station earlier on — I didn't mean owt by it, you know. Fact is I like a high seat. Very viewsome it is, up at the top with the signals and you can take a pot at the odd rabbit. We have to keep 'em down, you know. I mean, they *will* get at the perishables in the warehouse. Of course, I'll come down to give a hand with bags occasionally . . ."

"Very good of you, I'm sure."

"But only if a good tip seems to be in prospect."

"He'll only come down for the gentry," put in the signalman, "and not all of *them*."

I was meant to be riled by this, so I gave it the go-by.

"Very likely," I said. "Thanks for the pint, anyhow."

And as I made towards the door, I heard the lad porter say, "Aye, on your way."

I ought not to have let that *go*, I thought, as I walked upstairs.

What would the Chief have done in my place? He'd have laid the bloke out, and then he'd have gone all out

108

to get him lagged — three months hard for assault whether the bloke had fought back or not. I reached our room, but when I tried the door it was locked.

CHAPTER
FOURTEEN

I rapped on the door, and there came a noise from along the narrow corridor. I turned. The man from Norwood was there, holding a candle and eyeing me in his dressing gown.

"Everything quite all right, old man?" he said.

"Ought to be," I said, thinking of the German papers that had spilled from his bag.

He looked more impressive somehow in his dressing gown, although it was shabby enough. I knocked again, and Lydia answered the door in a flurry, wearing her night-dress. I walked into the room, and saw that the window had been thrown wide open. The wife strode across to the bed and sat down upon it cross-legged like a Hindoo, which she would often do at night — something about being in her night-dress seemed to bring it on. She looked from me to the open window as the curtains stirred.

"Why d'you lock the door?" I said.

"Now . . . what do you suppose about the bicyclist?" she said.

"Eh?"

"I left the bar when I saw him through the window messing about at the back of the pub. I've been watching him from *our* window while you were hammering on the door doing your level best to give me away."

"Where is he?"

"He *was* just down below."

"And what was he about?"

"He was at his bike."

"It's punctured," I said. "I overheard him say so in the bar."

"He held a pocket knife," said the wife. "He took it, and stabbed it twice into the front tyre."

"That *would* give him a puncture."

"It might just," said the wife.

"But he already had one."

"No, he did not. He stabbed the wheel to make what he said true. He *wanted* a puncture."

"It's rum. How will he account for it, I wonder?"

"Sharp stones," the wife immediately replied, as though she'd spent a good while thinking about it. "That man has done everything to convince us that he's a cyclist, short of riding his flipping bike. Why does he *have* a bike if he doesn't go anywhere? And why does the man Lambert have a railway timetable if *he* doesn't go anywhere? It's just as though everyone in this place is *checked*."

She was now looking over at the dresser.

"The second thing," she said. ". . . Your warrant card — you put it in the left-hand drawer, didn't you?"

I nodded.

"When I came in, both drawers were a little way out and your card had jumped to the right-hand one."

I heard the roar of the motor-bike as it left the front of the pub — it couldn't have been those two that had come into the room. They'd entered the bar directly after arriving. Mrs Handley and young Mervyn had seen me put the warrant card in the drawer, but my money was on the Norwood clerk. The noise of the motorbike faded away, leaving nothing but the sound of massed grasshoppers. No breeze stirred the window curtain.

The wife said, "Who do you think's been in, then?"

I sat down next to her on the counterpane, and we went over everything. I undressed by degrees as we spoke, and was down to my undershirt when I looked at the wife, and said:

"You're leaving by the first train in the morning, anyhow."

"No," she said, "I am not. Apart from anything else, I'm set on seeing inside that house."

She meant the Hall. She had a liking for grand houses. The Archbishop of York had his palace at Thorpe-on-Ouse, and the wife would find any excuse to go inside. She aspired to own a grand house herself, although she'd never admit the fact. It was terrible in a way to think that she had all these ambitions kept down.

"Tomorrow, I'm going to fetch the Chief," I said.

In my five years on the force, the wife had never set eyes on the Chief but I knew she was strong against him. He was the fellow who kept me out all hours, who put dangerous work my way.

Talk of the Chief brought me back to the subject of station master Hardy, and how it was the Chief's regiment that he had in miniature in the booking office. I told her a little of what I knew about the Chief's time fighting in Africa:

"All they had to hand", I said, "against the spears of a thousand charging dervishes was —"

"A large quantity of guns."

As the wife said this, she was stretching out on the bed.

She was always down on the army. In the first place, it was all men, and secondly it would be the army who'd put a stop for good-and-all to the women's movement if it took matters that bit too far.

I was beside her now, and my hand was under her night-dress, making its regular explorations.

"Do you suppose the blank papers in that man's bag were written in invisible ink?" she said.

"But then why wouldn't he put the German stuff in invisible ink as well? This is not the time to be seen carrying German papers about."

The wife said, "I've often thought — if you can have invisible ink, then why can't you have invisible anything else? Invisible *bicycles*."

And, not waiting for an answer, she quickly stood up and took her night-dress off; then she walked over to the wardrobe, and fished my darbies out of my suit-coat pocket. She sometimes liked me to lock her hands into them for a while before our love-making. She liked to pretend to be in desperate straits, with no knickers on and her hands fast. I thought it a strange look-out for a

113

reader of *The Freewoman*, but that was the wife all over. She was an unpredictable sort.

We fucked once, and then we did it again, differently arranged, in very short order. It might have been the danger of Adenwold that had stirred her up, and the danger of Morocco, the raging fires and the strikes and all the rest; or just the fact that somebody had been in our room without our say-so. As we turned in, I thought: *Well, she's off in the morning, no question. The Chief will come in and she will go.*

I put the oil lamp to its lowest setting and closed my eyes. But sleep wouldn't come, and I fell to listening to the country sounds — the many desperate rustlings, scufflings and screechings. The chimes of midnight floated up from the village, and I walked over to the chair on which I'd left my suit-coat. I took out the papers and read again from the memories of Hugh Lambert:

And so we began to avoid each other more than ever. If father was in the country, then I made it my business to be in London, and vice versa. According to Ponder we were like the opposing carriages of a funicular railway. "I will run up to London," I would say, but I could never say it lightly. Father told me often enough that this was one of my troubles: "Too much London," and it's true that upon returning from a spell there, I would lie awake at night, still somehow hearing the heavy roll of the traffic, as though the city

were an infection not lightly to be shaken off.
Indeed, the . . .

I could not read the next few lines.
I shuffled the pages, and read:

She is a treasure, but he . . . His speech I find a
kind of chloroform. When he addresses me, I
drift off, and every other sound supersedes him:
the babbling of a nightingale, the wind rattling at
the window panes of the inn. He is often in
drink, of course, but the defect in his speech has
some deeper cause. On the farm, I was never
required to speak to him. He was always on the
other side of a field, working happily. And no
wonder . . . how beautiful that place was! A farm
under sycamores, and with a rookery in each
corner. Does Mr Handley drink to bury the pain
of its loss? I do not know. The man is
incomprehensible to me, but it is all I can do
when in his presence not to apologise continually
for father's conduct.

I put aside the papers.
Sir George had removed the Handleys from one of
the estate farms, and given them The Angel instead. I
had already had this from the boy Mervyn. Was the inn
fair compensation for the farm? Would the loss of the
farm make a motive for murder?
What did John Lambert know about it all? And what
did he aim to do about it?

I walked towards the window with a fast-beating heart, and pushed aside the curtain. But there was only the violet night, and the building heat.

PART TWO

Saturday, 22 July, 1911

CHAPTER
FIFTEEN

In my dream, Mr Handley's blurred voice spoke over Adenwold scenes, giving out country-side facts:

"Here is the hawthorn, the roots are polished black."

"Here is our station — the porter has turned on the danger lamp." "Here are the rabbits running. We kill them at harvest time when they have nowhere to hide."

"Here is a field put to grass."

"This is not like your place — we are all under the great house."

Mr Handley seemed to give a cough, and I woke suddenly to a blare of light and heat beyond the open window, and the distant beat of the 8.51 "up" approaching through the woods. It might be over a mile off yet. The wife was lying on her front and looking as though she'd been dropped from a great height. She was asleep, and yet the day was half done. I stood up and looked down at her. Any person asleep always seems better off that way, and there was nothing for it . . . I had meant to put her on the first train, but I could not wake her.

The counterpane was twisted to one side, her night-dress was up and her brown arse was on full view. What ought a gentleman to do? I pulled the night-dress down; I put on my suit and cap, threw cold water on my face and stowed the warrant card (which was evidently not safe left in the room) and the papers of Hugh Lambert in my inside pocket. The engine gave another long shriek, as if to say, "I have given you fair warning! The station is now approached!" I clattered down the stairs of The Angel. No coffee, no breakfast — fine holiday this was! The long table stood empty before the dusty road, and no breeze moved the wisteria.

Rounding the bend that led towards the station, I ran into a confusion of geese, all flapping to take off, and none succeeding any better than any quantity of madly dashing white-skirted women. Nobody seemed to be attending them, and the green was silent and deserted as before.

I crossed the white dazzle of the station yard, and arrived at the "up" platform just a second after the train. It was a Saturday train — short: two carriages and a guard's van.

Who had it brought?

I walked along the "up", watching the doors, and as I did so, the vicar, who had departed Adenwold the previous evening, climbed down and moved quickly along the platform before cutting across the station yard and disappearing from view. He had *left*, and now he had come *back*, carrying the same bag and wearing the same white suit and flower-like hat. He had perhaps been at a dinner. He was another to be taken into account. Or was he? John Lambert had told Hugh that "they" would be coming for him, and the vicar was not a "they". The same objection could be raised in the

120

case of the bicyclist or the man from Norwood. But either might be an agent of some larger group. Or they might all be in league.

I walked further along the platform, still watching the train. The carriage windows were once again sun-dazzled, but I made out an old man sleeping in Third, and he looked as though he might have been inside that dusty red rattler since it was built, or then again he might have lived and *died* in it, for he made no stir as I looked on.

Coming up to the station house, I noticed for the first time a public telephone attached to the side of it. Pasted above the instrument were the instructions: "How to Use the Telephone", but these were half-obscured by a notice freshly pasted over: "Out of Order". I looked up and saw the west-leading wires reaching away into the woods. They would meet their doom within half a mile, and I could not believe the ones that led in the other direction remained intact either.

I turned again to the train.

All the doors of the carriages remained closed. The engine simmered and waited for its signal; the clock on the "up" moved to 8.55.

In the gloomy doorway of the booking office, I spied the bulk of station master Hardy. What were those soldiers of his in aid of? Some station masters would spell out the name of the station in white stones on a bank of grass, or they'd have a super-fancy flower display — pansies in an ornamental barrow. But the model soldiers were not laid on for the benefit of the passengers — they were entirely for the benefit of Hardy.

The fellow turned towards me from within his hole, and his mouth made the shape of his habitual "Oh", but he kept silence.

There then came the sound of rough Yorkshire voices from the head of the train — from the locomotive itself. As I looked on, a small figure climbed down from the footplate. It was the porter, Woodcock. He was now saying something to the unseen driver or fireman; he carried a cloth bag that no doubt contained the snap and bottle of tea for his turn.

"Your lad comes in on the engine, does he?" I asked Hardy.

He turned in the shadows.

"He likes a ride up," he said.

"He lives along the line, I suppose?"

"The lad? He lives at East Adenwold. First train of a Saturday brings him in just nicely for the start of his duty. Well, a *little* late, but near as makes no odds."

The idle little bugger ought to have biked in like any country station junior, as I had done myself when I'd had my railway start in the village of Goathland up on the Yorkshire Moors. I looked at Hardy, and my gaze seemed to shame him into further speech.

"The boy has a crib in the signal box," he added, "and he sometimes kips up there."

Hardy then looked down at his boots.

I said, "Telephone's bust."

"It is, aye," he said, looking up.

I eyed the communicator and receiver dials of the ABC machine behind him, saying, "Telegraph's out too, I suppose?"

Hardy nodded. "There's been a general collapse out in the woods," he said. "It's not the first time . . . It's all out while they fix it."

"When did you hear of this?"

"Last night."

"By company runner?"

He nodded again, and I thought of the silver-haired man I'd seen the night before, hurrying through the station yard. He'd been *running*, but he hadn't looked like a railway messenger. He'd looked more important than that.

"How's the line being worked then?"

"Oh," said Hardy, "by ticket."

In emergencies, a driver would be given a ticket or token authorising him to proceed even against signals set at danger . . . But I had no clear understanding of the system.

"I've had a look," I said, "and I'd say the line's been cut."

"Oh," said Hardy, "well now . . ."

Woodcock was now eyeing me from a distance of ten feet — it was always a face-down with him. His head was too compressed for my liking — like an old apple. He pursed his thin lips and gave a tremendous fart, staring at me all the while, so that it was very hard to keep in countenance.

"Been burning some bad powder," he said, just as a carriage door opened behind him, and a man stepped down.

He was a dapper dog, this one: blue lounge jacket, white flannel trousers, stiff collar and stripy tie; and the trousers were tucked into highly polished army field boots. I imagined that he'd been arranging his clothes to a look of perfection in his compartment, and that this accounted for his delay in getting down.

The fellow carried a document case and a biggish carpet bag. He was trim, well set-up — uncommonly blue eyes, sunburnt face and sandy hair. He put me in mind of a prosperous sort of colonial farmer, and he had evidently passed a test that I and the wife had failed, for Woodcock put down his own bag and hurried up to the man. Here was a chance to put the bleed on — carry the two bags at a shilling apiece to some waiting vehicle, for this was certainly the sort of fellow who'd be met, except that I could see clear through to the station yard, and it was empty as before.

The man sent Woodcock packing with a word. He then struck out along the platform and out towards the triangular green where he stood getting his bearings. I watched him from the platform as Woodcock moved alongside me again.

"Bad luck," I said.

No reply from the porter.

"Do you know him?" I asked.

"I know his *type*," said Woodcock.

"That chap falls into the class of a mean toff," I said. "Looks a good bet for a tip, but en't. I was a lad porter myself once, and I always reckoned to be able to spot that sort the minute they climbed down."

"Cut the blarney," said Woodcock.

124

I said, "You have a ride in on the engine come Saturday, I see," and I nodded towards the locomotive.

Woodcock muttered something I couldn't catch, before asking in a louder voice, "You okay today, pal?"

He was moving, as he spoke, towards the end of the train, and the guard's van. I looked on as he took down from the unseen guard a quantity of newspapers, a wooden box and a hamper tied about with a leather strap. The newspapers were loosely covered in brown paper, but I could make out one of the headings: "The Moroccan Sensation: Reports of a Further Grave Incident".

"Reckon you were half seas over last night," Woodcock said, standing over the packages, "spoiling for a scrap, you were."

The train was at last pulling away.

The wooden box, I now saw, was a crate of wine.

"Who's this lot for?" I asked, indicating the goods, and shouting over the roar of the departing engine.

"Nosey bloke, en't you?"

I fished in my pocket for a tanner and passed it to him.

"You'd have had that earlier if you'd carried our bags," I said.

"Well then," said Woodcock, looking down at the coin, "I'm glad I didn't bother. This is all for the bloody Hall, of course. Why do you want to know?"

And it came to me that I might put him off with a lie.

"You asked me last night if I was a journalist," I said. "As a matter of fact I am. I'm hunting up a bit of background for an article on the hanging of Hugh Lambert."

"What paper?"

"Various," I said. "I'm with a news agency."

He eyed me.

"Is there anything you'd like to tell me about Hugh Lambert?" I ran on. "Or John, come to that?"

"There is not," he said.

A consignment note was tucked into the leather belt that held the lid of the hamper down. I caught it up before Woodcock could stop me. The delivery came from York, and was marked: "Lambert, The Gardener's Cottage, The Hall, Adenwold, Yorks."

I looked across the station yard towards the triangular green. The dapper man in field boots was still gazing about. He was a stranger to Adenwold, that much was obvious.

"Lift the lid," I asked the porter, pointing at the hamper.

He made no move.

"Irregular, that would be," he said. "Mr Hardy might not like it."

He nodded towards the urinal, where station master Hardy was making water, the top of his head just visible over the wooden screen.

"You don't care a fuck for what *he* thinks," I said.

"That's true enough," the porter said. "Give me a bob and I'll do it."

He was a mercenary little bugger. I handed him the coin; he unbuckled the strap and pushed the lid open. "Aye," he said, looking down, ". . . seems about right."

126

Inside the hamper were perhaps fifty railway timetables, all in a jumble. At the top was one of the Great Eastern's, with a drawing of one of that company's pretty 2-4-2 engines running along by the sea-side. But in the main, the basket held the highly detailed working timetables that came without decorated covers and were meant for use by railwaymen only.

Woodcock kicked the lid of the basket shut.

"Timetables," he said. "Bloke's mad on 'em."

As he spoke, I watched the dapper man in field boots striding across the green. He moved with purpose, and I knew I'd better get after him.

"When'll they be carried to the Hall?" I asked Woodcock, indicating the timetables.

"Carter'll take 'em up presently."

"When?"

"When it suits him — don't bloody ask *me*."

"Who's that bloke just got down?" I asked Woodcock, pointing towards the man in field boots.

"Search me."

"Well, don't worry, mate," I said, keeping one eye on the bloke. "Everything considered, you've been surprisingly helpful."

"That's me all over," said Woodcock.

"I'm obliged to you," I said.

"I'm more surprising than I am helpful," he said as he made off, "so look out."

The man in field boots was walking amid the cawing of rooks towards the two lanes on the opposite side of the green from the one leading to The Angel. Of this pair, he was aiming towards the lane furthest away from the station, which was bounded by two towering hedges. I made after him, but lagging back a little way.

The hedges made two high walls of green with brambles and flowers entangled within. A ladder stood propped against one of the hedges, and it looked tiny — only went half-way up. But it was a good-sized ladder in fact. The only sounds in the hedge-tunnel were our footfalls and the birdsong, and I thought: *It must be very obvious to this bloke that he's being followed.* But he did not appear to have noticed by the time we came into the open again.

Here was a clearing, and another triangular green, this one better kept than the first and with — for all the heat — greener grass. A market cross stood in the centre of it. A terrace of cottages ran along one edge of the green. They looked pretty in the sunshine, and quite deserted. Their owners were having a holiday from them, and they were having a holiday from their owners. A row of three shops ran along another side: a baker's, a saddle-maker's and a tobacconist and confectioner's, this last with the sun kept off by window posters for Rowntrees Cocoa and Player's Navy Cut that looked as though they belonged in York and not out here in the wilds. Only the baker's looked to be open, and there was a good smell coming out of it: hot and sweet, to go with the dizzying smell of the hundreds of flowers blooming all around.

The shops stood opposite to me, the terrace to the left. On the right was Adenwold parish church, which was contained within the half-ruined skeleton of a much larger church, and covered over with ivy. In the graveyard were little enclosures made of thick hedges, like natural rooms, and inside these were clusters of graves — whole families of the dead. Alongside the graveyard was a grand pink house. This must be the vicarage, and I was sure it had claimed the vicar who'd just left the station.

The lately-arrived man in field boots was now examining a finger-post that pointed towards a narrow road running away to the left of the baker's. I came up behind him and read: "TO THE HALL".

"You're for the Hall?" I asked the man.

He wheeled about, but he hardly looked at me. Rather, he seemed to be looking into the *far distance*, and I had the idea that he might have learnt that gaze in Africa. But he also had London written all over him — expensive education and five hundred pounds a year. He gave the shortest of nods. He *was* for the Hall. At this, I gave him my name but again kept back my profession. The man put down his bags and shook my hand, but didn't introduce himself. His eyes were exactly the same colour as the sky.

He was a tough-looking bloke, and if one of those bags of his held a gun — which seemed to me more than likely — and if he *was* on his way to shoot John Lambert, I would not be able to stop him by force. All I could do was try to put him off by saying what I knew.

"There's a man staying at the gardener's cottage which is connected to the Hall," I said. "His name's John Lambert and I believe him to be in danger of . . ."

"Of what?" asked the man, and it was not sharp, but in the manner of a polite enquiry.

"In *mortal* danger," I said.

There was a silence. Or rather the air was filled with the sound of bees.

"How do you know?" the man eventually asked.

"He said as much. I spoke to him yesterday."

The man put down his bags.

"Did you seek him out, or just come upon him?"

"I'm here on holiday," I said. "I was out strolling with my wife, and I just came upon him."

The man put his hands behind his back, and placed his legs wider apart.

"Did you not recommend that he summon the police?"

He'd forced my hand.

"I *am* the police," I said, and I showed him my warrant card, saying, "Do you mind my asking your business at the Hall?"

But, still with his hands behind his back, he put a question of his own:

"You're here on holiday, you say?"

"I am."

"Who's your officer commanding?"

And that *was* sharp.

"That don't signify," I said, feeling like a lout. "I've asked about your business at the Hall."

"I have an association with John Lambert," said the man. "I am . . . a confidant of his. The poor fellow is considerably agitated at present."

It struck me as I spoke that John Lambert might be a mental case, and that this might be his doctor. He picked up his bags, and said, "You can be assured that my visit is in Mr Lambert's own best interests."

"Then you're not here to do him in?"

By way of answer to this stab, the blue-eyed man merely changed the angle of his head.

"I'm going to have to ask for your name," I said.

"That's confidential," he said, and he looked at me levelly. "Do you mean to arrest me?"

I had never yet arrested a man of a markedly superior class. Anyhow, I had no reasonable cause to suspect him of any crime.

"Arrest?" I said. "Not a bit of it" — and I added, by way of a touch of humour, "I'm for easy going."

"Good day to you, Detective Stringer," he said, and I watched him walk off, my head seething with the word "ass" directed at my low-class self.

CHAPTER
SIXTEEN

I needed more authority. I would summon the Chief from York.

But how?

A girl in a very white pinafore with black-stockinged legs that looked too thin, making her seem somehow spider-like, came out of one of the houses. And I'd thought they all stood empty. She skirted the green and walked over to the baker's.

I pictured Hugh Lambert in Durham gaol. He had forty-seven hours left to live. Did he wish it was more, or less? A condemned cell was bigger than the common run of cells, and was a kind of open house. There was always a warder looking on; the governor would come and go; the priest, too. Lambert was about to die, but was not yet *dying*, and this was an odd notion: as though time itself had been meddled with.

I followed the girl into the baker's. The interior was dark and unbearably hot. There were twelve loaves on the shelves behind the baker, I counted them as I waited for the girl to buy her loaf — only she didn't buy it but was given it gratis. I bought the smallest one remaining, and said to the baker: "You're about the only person left in this village?"

He grinned. He looked a decent sort, gave his name as Moffat.

"Only two of us here on the East Green," he said. "My daughter and myself."

"Was she the one in just now?"

"She was."

"Hardly any point baking today, I'd have thought."

"I've just done a few," he said. "We generally have a couple of trippers by."

"There was a murder here, I believe?"

"I believe so," he said, and that rather threw me. "Before my time," he ran on. "We've only been here three months."

I decided to rule him out of account. He could have no interest in stopping John Lambert from speaking out about the murder of Sir George.

I asked him: "Do you know if the village carter's about?"

"That's Will Hamer. He should be coming by here in just a minute."

I came out of the baker's, tore off a bite of bread and waited. Moffat was now leaning in his shop doorway whistling, and the tune wove its way steadily through the birdsong: "My Grandfather's Clock". The sun was raying down, everybody was waiting for everything and I ate my bread with half an ear cocked for the sound of gunshots from the Hall.

I heard instead a rattling of cartwheels, and looked up to see a load of hay creaking along the narrow hedge-tunnel with not an inch to spare on either side. The load was like a barn on the move, and yet only one horse did the dragging, and only one man led the horse.

At the same time, a rulley drawn by the lop-sided combination of a horse and a donkey was coming from the opposite direction — the way that led to the Hall — and I decided that the man driving this must be the carter, Will Hamer. He had two beasts to the farmer's one, and yet he carried no load. He looked far wiser than a carter needed to be, with a white halo of hair and beard.

Will Hamer and the man leading the load of hay stopped and had a good laugh at how they'd come to be on the same bit of road at the same time. Presently the farmer sauntered on, his great haystack rolling behind. There was a placard on the side of the cart reading "Sidebottom: West Adenwold". I would rule him out of account as well, provided I did not see him around again.

I walked across to Hamer before he could get going again. Standing next to the donkey, I held up my warrant card. He gazed down at me with a bright smile on his face, which by degrees became a frown.

I said, "Can you make it out, Mr Hamer?"

"Bits," he said. "I can read bits. I can't read *all* words, like."

"Well," I said, pocketing the card, "who can? Now I'm on police business, and I'd like a message sent. Could you do that?"

He nodded.

"I can take you a message anywhere," he said. "East Adenwold, West Adenwold . . ."

"The lines are down here," I said, "and I need a telegram sent. Can you carry a message to West Adenwold for me? West Adenwold is the nearest of the two, isn't it?"

"The nearest to *where*?" asked the carter.

"To here."

He frowned again.

"And there is a good-sized railway station there?"

No reply, but I pressed on: "And there is a telegraphic instrument in that station?"

"Aye to both of those," Hamer said presently, and with a smile returned. The fellow was as slow as a wet week; there again, it suited me that he couldn't read. I took out my indelible pencil, and began scrawling in my pocket book as follows:

To Chief Inspector Weatherill, York Station Police Office.
Come to Adenwold by first train. Matter of the gravest . . .

I broke off. The gravest what? The gravest *gravity*? I scratched out the sentence and wrote: "Life or death matter at hand."

I passed it up to Hamer, saying, "What's the cost?"

"Well now," he said, "what d'you reckon?"

"They ought to send it for nowt," I said, "since it *is* police business — and how about two bob on top for yourself?"

The carter had such a big grin on him when I passed up the money that I thought a bob might have been

135

nearer the mark. Thanking me, he moved off, which was a matter of waking up the donkey and horse with a shout of "Come on, men!"

He went off a little way, and then stopped. He turned about and said, "Line might be down at *West* Adenwold "n" all."

"Let's leave it that you are only to send the message if you can," I said.

"Oh, all right," he replied, as if this was a very interesting new idea. "Only if I *can*."

A thought struck me, and I said, "Mr Hamer, you wouldn't have brought anybody into this village today, would you?"

"Me?" he said, and he looked at me for a while. "I should say not!"

And then he winked very slowly, which I wished he hadn't done.

He re-started his beasts, and I took out my silver watch. It showed 9.45. Hamer ought to be at West Adenwold station by ten thirty, and the wire ought to reach York within five minutes of that. I guessed that the 12.27 arrival at Adenwold would leave Pilmoor at about midday, which meant that, if the Chief received the wire as soon as it arrived at York station (which was odds-on), he'd have an hour and half to *get* to Pilmoor. That would be simplicity itself. Being on the main line, Pilmoor was served by a good many fast trains from York, and it was only sixteen miles to the north. The only weak link in the chain was Hamer, who had now disappeared from sight in the hedge-tunnel.

I pocketed my watch and looked up.

Lydia was dawdling along the hedge-tunnel, moving slowly, which was out of the common for her. I called out to her and she quite ignored me. I wondered at this until I saw that the clerk from Norwood, the one who'd spilled the German documents, was coming along behind her. He walked briskly, and carried once again the Gladstone bag. I called again to Lydia, and once more she ignored me, but cut across the green making straight for the shut-up confectioner's shop. The Norwood clerk had stopped and was looking about. I had a persuasion that it wouldn't do to be seen by him, so I pulled down my cap, and turned a little aside as I watched him walk through the churchyard wicket. Lydia was watching the man from the shop doorway.

"What's the game?" I asked, walking up to her.

"I'm following him," she said, pointing to the clerk as he tramped across the graveyard in his cheap suit and high-crowned brown bowler.

"But you were in front of him," I said.

"I was following him *from* the front," said the wife.

The Norwood man had now cleared the graveyard and was leaving it by the opposite wicket.

"He's off to the parsonage," said the wife, as the man opened the gate of the big house behind the church, and walked up to the door.

"Come on," said the wife. "I want to know what he's about."

So we too entered the graveyard, moving in the great, delaying heat between the compartments of the dead bounded by the thick dark hedges. As we walked, I told Lydia about how I'd sent for the Chief and how I

137

expected him by the 12.27 train. I told her about how I'd met the earlier train in and collared the man in the field boots, and she in turn said that she'd had breakfast at the long table outside the inn, where entertainment had been provided by the sight of the bicyclist making a show of mending his puncture.

"He was making such a palaver that I challenged him directly about it," she said.

"Oh Christ," I said. "What did you say?"

"I just said, 'Surely this hole is of your own making. I saw you attack the tyre last night.'"

"Pitch right in, I would . . . And what did he say to that?"

"He said, 'I had a fancy that it was punctured, but I thought I'd make quite sure.'"

"He never did," I said.

"That's what he said."

"Did he seem put-out?"

"Yes."

"I'll bet. I'll bet he was creaking in his shoes."

"I couldn't imagine how anybody could behave more suspiciously," the wife ran on, "until about two minutes later when *that* man came down to breakfast, and started looking over his German papers while drinking coffee."

And she pointed towards the vicarage, where we glimpsed through low graveyard trees the Norwood clerk, still waiting to be admitted. We'd come to a stop before one of the newer graves, which stood outside the green enclosures and lay exposed to the bright sun. "In Memoriam," I read, "Sir George Arthur Horton Lambert,

Baronet. 1855–1909. Deus Fortitudo Mea." That meant something like "God give me strength". No, couldn't be. It was a very simple inscription anyhow, but then I supposed there were many things you couldn't very well put on a murdered man's gravestone. "Died peacefully" was out for starters; so was "Loved by all". There were no flowers on the grave but just a single bush growing up from the grass mound.

"He was reading his German papers over coffee at the front table," the wife repeated, looking across at the Norwood man, "and when I walked behind him, pretending to be interested in the wisteria, he folded them up. A moment later, he turned to me and said, 'I say, you're quite sure your husband ain't Franklin? It makes no odds either way to me. Only, I know Franklin's expected.'"

I looked surprise at the wife. She had made a very fair imitation of the man's cockney accent.

"I've already told him I'm not Franklin," I said.

"Well then, he doesn't believe you."

"Wait a bit," I said. "What if the man in the field boots is Franklin?"

The door of the vicarage remained unopened, but as we looked on, the red-faced parson appeared from around the side of the house, and shook the clerk's hand. He then took him back around the side with him.

"Come on," said the wife, and we closed on the house.

From the front gate, we could hear the vicar talking to the man from Norwood, but could not make out the words. The two were in the back garden.

"We'll walk round the side of the house, only we'll do it slowly, listening out all the while," said the wife, pushing open the front gate.

"What'll we say if they see us?"

"Hello," she said, "we thought it was part of the common."

"That won't wash," I said.

"Then we'll ask about service times in the church."

"Push on, then," I said.

The wife opened the gate, and we both stepped into the garden. She let go of the gate, and it clanged shut. It was on a spring. The wife turned to me and gave a look of alarm with eyes extra-wide, which she did half in jest. I thought: *She was worried for a while last night, but now she's back to larking about.* The fact that we'd been told we were in danger seemed to have faded completely from her thoughts.

The vicar's garden was well-kept and well-watered. The grass was bright green. The flowerbeds were as bright and various in colour as Turkey carpets, but what stood out was the red: red apples hanging from the trees, red roses — and the red ribbon in the hat of the red-faced vicar as he led the man from Norwood through the rear garden. He was escorting him towards the opened doors of a round wooden summerhouse, and the surprising thing was the tone of his speech. He had that glorious house and garden — his own little Yorkshire Eden — and yet he sounded glum; sounded like a right misery, in fact.

"Servants, curate and verger gone away to Scarborough," he was saying, as the birds in his beautiful garden sang like mad. ". . . I had to see to my own breakfast, and not an egg to be found . . ."

The two entered the summerhouse, and were lost from earshot.

It was little more than a circle of French windows — mostly propped open — with a wooden roof on top. It stood at the very end of the garden, and just behind it were iron railings separating the back of the vicarage garden from the woods that were everywhere around Adenwold. To the left side of the summerhouse (as we looked) stood a row of sweet peas supported on canes, making a kind of wall. Lydia eyed me, and we had the same thought in the same instant. We dashed past the sweet peas and so, screened from the summerhouse, gained the rear railing. We climbed over, and were in the edge of the woods.

Here, we could loiter and watch through the glass without being on trespass, and without having to account for ourselves.

And that's what we did.

CHAPTER
SEVENTEEN

The summerhouse was bare except for a couple of occasional tables, and deckchairs pointing in various directions to catch the sun at different times — it was a sort of temple for sun worship. As we looked on, a fox terrier walked into it from the vicarage garden, wagging its tail and happy as you like. The Norwood man made to stroke it, but the vicar roared "Out!" and it bolted in terror. The parson then turned to his visitor: "Now, Gifford," he said (so that at last the man's name was disclosed), "shall we get down to business?"

They moved over to one of the small tables, and Gifford removed from his case the objects in the cloth bags that he had spilled onto the road the night before. There were four, as when he'd had his spillage, and he placed them on the table before the parson, saying:

"These are hot from the factory in Germany as you might say, sir. Direct from the boys in Nuremberg. They come with all the usual etceteras."

The fixed agent meets the travelling agent — was that what I was seeing?

Gifford was now taking papers out of his case — no doubt the ones written in German, although I couldn't see them in detail.

"I've looked them over, but it's all Hebrew to me," he said, passing them to the vicar.

I kept glancing across to look at the wife's face. She'd removed her straw boater, and was so intent on the summerhouse that it was like being at the music hall with her, looking at her as she strained forward to see what would happen next, quite ignoring the man at her side. The parson looked over the papers, and he could obviously read German. Nothing so surprising in that: he was an educated man. Meanwhile, he held the object that was inside one of the cloth bags. Why wouldn't he remove the bloody thing?

"You haven't had a letter from Franklin, have you, sir?" Gifford asked him. "The bloke that lives in Islington?"

"I've had no letters at all," said the vicar, pulling the object from the cloth bag in his hand.

It was a red miniature locomotive that he held, and the sight came as a let-down to me. I'd pictured some species of weaponry, something devilish and German.

"That's jolly," said the vicar, contemplating the little engine. But he didn't sound over-enthusiastic.

Gifford said, "It supersedes the . . ."

(I couldn't catch the final word.)

The vicar put the engine into its cloth bag and took out another, from a second bag.

Gifford leant over and said, "Valve and valve gear that work properly, you'll see, sir."

He was an ordinary salesman, and the vicar nothing more to him than a likely — though not, as it appeared, a *very* likely — customer. Gifford had had an appointment to see the vicar, and had been anxious that a fellow called Franklin, apparently a business rival of his, had an appointment for about the same time, and he had thought that I was Franklin. He had not believed my denial and had then (finding the door unlocked) walked into my room and hunted through the drawers in the bureau in hopes of discovering my true identity. He'd have had a shock when he saw the warrant card and found out I was a copper. He'd have left that room at a lick.

We were wasting our time. It was the man in field boots that really mattered. Was the murder already done? Had he put John Lambert's lights out immediately on discovering him? I did not think it would work like that. There would be some parley or negotiation to begin with, and I was thrown back on hoping this would somehow carry on until the Chief pitched up.

In the summerhouse, Gifford was recommending another of the engines to the vicar, who now seemed thoroughly bored.

"Looks well, doesn't it?" Gifford said. "I've seen nothing to match it in the 'O' gauge."

It was not his part, as the seller, to be saying that. The vicar ought to be saying it. Instead he gave a glance towards the woods, and I met his eye for an instant. But he saw only a couple spooning under the trees — rather too close to his property perhaps, but harmless anyhow. He was a burly man with a rough-skinned red face. He had a summery look: neatly pressed white suit, and the shirt under his white collar was sky blue. The sun was not good for him: it burned his skin, but he took it full in the face all the same. He would drink a good deal of wine, and it would be fine wine. He had what I believe they call in the church "a good living" and he did himself well. Or other people did well for him.

Lydia had already given up on the scene within the summer-house, and turned her back on it; she was resting against the railing and eyeing me, as if to say, "Have you cottoned on yet? This is a false trail."

The vicar was saying, "Taken all in all, I think I'll let these go."

Gifford's long journey north had been for naught, and I admired the way he gulped down his disappointment.

"Will you not take just the little one, sir? The red single-driver? Have it on approval for a month, sir. Return it by post if not completely delighted."

But under the heavy gaze of the vicar, he was already packing his bag.

"Want to go back round the front?" the wife said. "Catch him coming out?"

"Why?"

And she shrugged while picking at a dandelion.

We did it anyway, avoiding the garden this time, but cutting along towards the graveyard by means of a narrow snicket that led between two of the cottages.

"Lovely country," Gifford was observing at the front of the vicarage, as he said goodbye to his host. His words were almost drowned out by birdsong, but he hadn't given up on the niceties, for all his disappointment. His behaviour towards the vicar reminded me of mine towards the man in the field boots.

"Lovely garden too, sir," said Gifford.

"It might be moderately agreeable, I suppose," said the vicar, "if the head gardener gave it half a chance. He will insist on planting out far too high a percentage of late-flowering . . . But you don't want to hear my troubles, Gifford!"

And he clasped the salesman's hand, saying, "Pleasant journey back, now!"

Gifford stepped into the lane that stood between the vicarage and the graveyard, and gave a start of surprise when he saw the two of us lounging there, no doubt recalling in that instant his secret visit to our room.

"You're the pair from The Angel, ain't you?"

I could see the sweat leaking out from over his stand collar.

"We've just taken a stroll around the back," I said. ". . . Saw you chatting to the parson, and couldn't help over-hearing a bit."

"Not a lot *to* bloody well hear," said Gifford in a glum tone.

"Came out badly, did it?"

"Don't it always?" replied Gifford, and he removed his brown bowler to mop his brow. He had not made his sale, and he was stifled besides. His centre parting looked like a guide-line for a saw. His moustache was also arranged in two halves. The man was a martyr to his fine-toothed comb.

"I travel in model locomotives," he said. "You might think that's a pretty good joke?"

146

And he looked at us expectantly.

"But I ain't seen the funny side in years — not in years."

We had entered the graveyard, and come to a stop by Sir George's grave.

Gifford was saying, "Steam-powered, electrical and spring-motor mechanism — well, that's clockwork, if you must know. But it's all a bloody mug's game, pardon my French, lady. He's one of the biggest collectors in the whole country," Gifford continued, indicating the vicarage. "'Well worth a visit to Reverend Ridley,' I was told. 'Makes a purchase every time. Never misses.'" He shook his head. "Calls himself a vicar . . . Christian thing would've been to buy the little red loco. Brass boiler, steel frames. Double action piston valve cylinders with reversing motion worked from cab. All wheels to scale throughout."

Gifford stepped back from the grave, and his boot-heel went into some fresh sheep dung.

"Who let a bloody cow in here?" he said, and I hadn't the heart to put him right. "Bloody cattle!" he said, looking down. "They do make a litter. I'll be bloody glad to be leaving this 'ole, I can tell you."

I looked towards the vicarage, where the Reverend Ridley was standing at one of the ground-floor windows, watching us with folded arms.

"Have you two heard of his layout, by the way?" Gifford continued in a lower voice, as though he felt the vicar might be able to hear him. "Famous, it is — been photographed in all the railway papers. It's in his dining room I believe, though the pill wasn't about to show me

147

it, and I hadn't the nerve to ask. King's Cross and environs in one and a quarter inch to the foot. Shown in the rush hour, the Cross is. Hundreds of little lead people charging about all over the shop — well, they're not *charging*; they're completely fixed, but that's the effect. Thing is, being a parson, he's rotten with money and ain't got anything else to do."

"Except save the souls of the villagers," said the wife, who was one of the religious sort of feminists, and set a lot of store by the behaviour of vicars.

"Do leave off, lady," said Gifford.

"You have a line in German models?" I said.

Gifford pulled at his collar.

"The best models today are German," he said. "You'll generally find with your German models the smoke-box door will be made open-able. Little touches like that. It's in the finishing too, of course. The enamelling and lining is always of the first order. But try telling him that!"

It struck me that the vicar might be looking on because he'd seen us stop by Sir George's grave. Did he think we were discussing the murder?

"That's the fellow was murdered," I said to Gifford, indicating the grave.

"I know," he said, which surprised me. "It's a queer spot this is, just the place for a murder. Gives me the jim-jams, I don't mind telling you."

"Do you not find it peaceful and quiet?" asked the wife.

"The quieter a place is," he said, "the *noisier* it is. You hear every little thing. Here now, I meant to have a word with you," he continued, addressing me particularly. "You're a copper, aren't you? Railway police."

"Hold on," I said. "How do you know?"

He stopped dead; all the life went out of him. But he rallied after a few seconds, saying, "I don't rightly know. Just something about you, I suppose. Something about your looks."

"And a railway policeman looks different from the ordinary sort, I suppose?" the wife cut in.

He'd been in our room all right.

"What did you want a word about, anyway?" I asked. "Something touching on the murder?"

"I believe so," he said, thoughtfully, but before he could answer, there came a cry from the vicarage.

The Reverend Ridley was standing in the doorway and hailing Gifford.

"God help us, he's changed his mind!" said Gifford. "He's seen the sense of going for the single-driver."

The vicar called again.

"I've half a mind not to go to him," said Gifford.

"I *wouldn't* if I were you," I said.

"Are you nuts?" said Gifford, and he was off, bag in hand, calling "Just coming, sir!" to the Reverend Ridley.

"What did you want to tell me?" I shouted after him.

"Speak to you at the inn," he called back. "One o'clock suit?"

"Well, that's that as regards him," said the wife, looking on as he was taken into the vicarage.

"How do you mean exactly?" I asked her.

"He's not a spy."

"No," I said, "I don't believe he is."

"We ought to see John Lambert again," she said. "Really have it out with him once and for all."

I reminded her that there was the complication of the man in field boots.

"Oh, I don't care about *him*," she said.

CHAPTER
EIGHTEEN

We'd followed the finger-posts to the Hall, which had taken us, by a new route, to the gates at which we'd earlier discovered John Lambert. We'd walked through these and were now passing between the great globe-like trees, approaching the house with its dozen windows staring down at us.

I'd meant to wait for the arrival of the Chief before braving the Hall again. I'd been warned off the place both by Lambert and (in a roundabout way) by the man in field boots, and with every step I expected some alarm, shout, objection to be raised. Most particularly, I expected some gun to be fired. Over against that, I was a police officer about my duty.

As for the wife, she just seemed entranced by the house.

"It's middle Georgian," she said. "Very simple."

Many green plants stood in tall urns across the white gravel of the carriage drive. These and the green door, the brown bricks and the great heat bearing down somehow put me in mind of the Roman Empire.

I said to the wife, "What's the programme?" and I thought: *Now hold on, Jim, you can't be asking* her.

A man came walking fast round the side of the house, and he wore knee-length boots, but not field boots. He was a footman or groom or some such — had a horsy look about him.

"Where's the gardener's cottage?" I asked him, and he said, "Follow me round."

We crunched over the dazzling white gravel to the left side of the house, and there stood a lot of stables and out-buildings of one sort or another, the lot of them looking Roman to me, like temples or villas. We walked through the maze of these for a while, passing dark farm machinery standing in open doorways, until the horsy bloke pointed to a very plain cottage standing amid burnt brown grass fifty yards off.

"That's you," he said.

"I'm obliged to you," I said, and we set off in that direction.

The groom called out:

"You're with Captain Usher, are you?"

"Don't answer him," said the wife, in a low tone as we walked on. "He's a servant, so you don't have to."

She wouldn't as a rule have said that, but in her mind she was established as mistress of the house. The notion made her headstrong — not that she wasn't already, and for the first time the notion composed in my mind: *I wish I hadn't brought her along.*

The man in field boots was Captain Usher. That was no surprise. He had a martial air, he had the boots, and he had the firearm somewhere about him, I was sure. But he was nowhere to be seen as we closed on the gardener's cottage, which was a small, plain building, newer than the rest and with its own territory — a garden within a garden — bounded by low hedges.

152

Beyond the cottage, on a yellow hillside a quarter-mile off, I saw a harvester pulled by four bullocks, the whole arrangement tilted so far to one side that it threatened to topple over.

But the gardener's cottage now came between us and that vision. The curtains were closed but the door was on the jar. As we crossed the garden, I cut in front of the wife — which was by way of reminding her that I was the certificated detective.

I tapped on the door, and John Lambert was just inside it.

He stood smoking a cigarette, in a living room that had been put to use as a study in the place that he preferred to the Hall. There were two desks, one either side of the dead, dusty fireplace, and these two desks seemed to signify great effort, like a double-headed train. Lines of bright light leaked through the closed curtains, and they showed up twirling clouds of dust. There were papers everywhere, covering all the means of ordinary living: papers on top of the sofa, on the carpet, all about the hearth and the hearth rug. They were scrawled with both letters and numbers, and some of them were maps, and some were maps of the *sea*; and where there weren't papers there were railway timetables.

John Lambert looked disappointed to see us, but only moderately so.

"You're still living, then?" I blurted, all my rehearsed speech going by the board.

"I can't deny it," he said, breathing smoke, ". . . in the face of all the evidence."

He looked over-strained, as he had the day before —
but no worse. His beard, growing in the shadow of his
hollow cheeks, still looked as though it had not been
intended. Instead, it was a mark of decline. His white
suit was of a good cloth, but did not stand close
scrutiny.

"A man has arrived to see you," I said, "A Captain
Usher."

He nodded once, touched his spectacles and looked
at me shrewdly.

He said, "How do you know?" But he seemed only
moderately curious on that point, and as to the reason
for my interest in the matter.

"He came by train," I said. "Not many people do, so
it's easy to keep cases on the arrivals."

John Lambert nodded again.

"Usher has been here once today already," he said.
"And is about to return. I wouldn't be here when he
does if I were you."

"Is he the one you're in fear of?" the wife put in.

(I would allow her that one question.)

"I'm not in fear of anyone," Lambert replied. And he
kept silence for a moment, before adding: "That said, I
do not much expect to see out the day."

"And you won't say why?" I enquired, in horror.

"I will not. It is all a secret — a profound secret."

"And do you know the identity of your father's
murderer?"

He kept silence.

Why would a man about to die have any interest in
keeping a secret?

"You make . . . timetables," said the wife, from over near the sofa.

"My wife will step outside now," I said.

Lydia — giving me not so much as a glance — was leaning over the sofa, fanning her brown face with her straw boater, which I knew was meant as a deliberate provocation.

"Would you please move away from there?" Lambert rather coolly requested.

Lydia stood back, saying, "You needn't worry. I do not understand railway timetables."

A beat of silence.

"Actually you will find that many perfectly intelligent people do not," said the wife. "They are very badly designed. Your brother was not married, I believe," she ran on, "but is there a fiancee perhaps, or some special woman who will be thinking of him this week-end?"

I looked white at her. Here was a man who did not expect to outlive the day, and she was making tittle-tattle.

"My wife will leave the room now," I repeated.

Lydia eyed me for a full five seconds before turning on her heel, and walking out, which left a strange silence between me and Lambert, during which he smoked out his cigarette.

"Well, congratulations," he said, "you worked your will in the end."

So saying, he turned and pitched the cigarette stub into the fireplace, where it joined dozens — if not hundreds — of its fellows.

"Is it difficult to be married?" he asked, turning back to face me.

"She's rather strong-minded," I replied.

Lambert looked as though he might have said a hundred things in answer to that, but settled on none. He glanced at his watch.

"Will you join me in a friendly glass?" he enquired. "Just before the return of friend Usher?"

He caught up a tumbler from the mantel-piece, and poured into it from a whisky bottle that stood by the sofa. But this glass was evidently his own, so another was needed, and as Lambert hunted about for it I let my eye run over his papers.

There seemed an eastern bias to it all. Two timetables of the Great Eastern; a town plan of the port of Harwich; sea charts for the Channel and the North Sea; a book on the railways of East Anglia. The written documents gave little away, but were just dense masses of handwriting. I made out a few phrases — "Principal entraining stations", "provision of hospital trains" — and one sentence I read in its entirety. It stood out almost luminous: "There must be kept, throughout the emergency, open lines for out-going, so that trains can be kept running, as it were in a circle."

And that was when the picture composed.

As Lambert handed me the whisky, I was in a flat spin of excitement, and I drank it in a draught to steady myself. John Lambert did the same — and it wasn't his first of the day, either. It was agony to understand something of the matter at hand, and yet to be checkmated by his silence.

156

He was now peering through the gap in the curtains at the window that overlooked the fields. He turned to me, and said, "Drink up, Usher's coming. You can go out by the way you came in."

"Now hold on," I said. "We can face him down together."

Lambert smiled and shook his head.

"A small chance remains that he and I might reach an accommodation, but there'll be no chance of it if we have company."

And there was somehow nothing else for it. I would leave, and I would return directly with the Chief. If I was too late, then it was too bad.

Lambert walked towards the far door. He unbolted it, stepped into the back garden and, as I quit the room by the *front* door, I heard him say "Hello again" in a fascinating, dead tone. There was some smooth answering murmur from Usher, and then Lambert said, "Look — let's talk out here in the garden. It's pleasant here, don't you think?"

I stepped through the front door, and there stood the wife, kicking her heels.

"This way," I said, indicating the most direct route towards the woods, and she stood still for a moment, just to show that she would not take any more orders from me.

I waited for her at the railing that bordered the woods. I had managed the angle so that we could not be seen from the rear of the gardener's cottage, and the wife had followed my footsteps very precisely along the scorched grass, although keeping at twenty yards' distance.

"And are you any the wiser?" she said, looking at the sporting cap, which I had fixed back on my head.

The railing stood between us.

"Yes," I said. "Come out of the grounds."

"You left in a tearing hurry," she said.

"Usher came up to the cottage by the back way. The two of them are talking in the garden now."

"I think you should have stood your ground. If you're dead set on filling up our week-end with this business you should go about it properly."

I made no reply.

"You're scared of that man Usher, why don't you admit it?" she said, climbing over the railing.

I put out my hand to help her.

"Don't you dare," she said, and struck out for the main woodland track.

Now it was my turn to follow *her* at a distance.

"Do you want to know what all those papers of Lambert's are about?" I called after her.

No answer. She walked on with swishing skirts.

"It's the mobilisation of the British Army," I said.

The wife said nothing to that, but I knew by the change that had overcome her walk that she was impressed.

CHAPTER
NINETEEN

We tramped on through the woods.

We'd missed the best route back to the village, but I knew the general direction. Sometimes I walked ahead, sometimes the wife. Sometimes we walked parallel on separate narrow tracks through the trees. Every so often the wife would shoot a look of fury at me, and at my green sporting cap in particular.

As we walked on, I thought of the timetable clerks at the Company offices in York, who worked amid heaps of graphs and diagrams and maps and were considered the brightest sparks of the place, while the men in charge of them were the leading intellects of all. John Lambert was evidently one of the men in *charge* of the men in charge. He would have the brains to overturn a conviction for murder. If he spoke out against a hanging, people would listen. But who did he plan to speak out *to*?

Was Usher the man? Or was he out to *silence* Lambert?

I'd read in the railway papers of the mobilisation schemes, but the subject was always very cagily approached: "It is likely that plans are in hand . . ."; "It would be expected that at such a critical time . . ."

I glanced again towards the wife.

It was crazy to be rowing, for we'd struck a business of the very gravest sort. Everything, from the Moroccan crisis to the women's question to the strikes and riots flaring all across the country — it was all wrapped up in the War Question. France had been the enemy for a while (there always had to be *one*), but the French had given way to the Germans, who fitted the part much better. You didn't hear much about Anglo-German friendship any more.

Instead, it was all war talk — and war talk and railway talk overlapped more and more. I'd heard of a scheme to connect the barracks at Aldershot with East Anglia without going through London. Get the regular army out fast — push 'em out through the Essex ports. But there was more to the planning than that. The whole question had to be looked at contrariwise as well: you'd need a programme for getting the troops into defensive positions in the event of invasion, and another for bringing back the dead or injured — a scheme for hospital trains. You knew the planning went on, and all you could do was trust that it was being done well.

But for all that, the row with the wife was just as strong in my thoughts. It was hardly our first one. We had small ones regularly about the late hours I was called on to work. It all boiled down to the demands the Chief placed upon me, which the wife did not understand. The Chief's wife seemed to stand anything; he lived his whole life in a man's world.

"I'm sorry I packed you off," I called to her through the trees, after twenty minutes or so.

"You did not pack me off," she called back, crashing through some ferns. "I chose to leave."

"Well, I'm sorry that I made you choose to leave then," I said. "I just think it was a bit of a distraction to start telling him that you couldn't use a railway timetable."

"Credit me with some intelligence, please. I wanted to keep him talking," said the wife.

"Funny way of going about it," I said, ". . . by talking *yourself*."

"I had the idea that I was on the verge of a discovery."

"What?"

"Oh, get back in your box," she said. "And take that flipping cap off."

"I will not," I said. Indicating a path, I stopped and said to the wife, "After you."

"Stow it," she snapped back, but she led off in the direction I'd shown her.

The woods gave out and a cricket ground came into view. The pavilion put me in mind of a white wooden railway station. At one end of the ground stood three tall poplars, and they might have been giant wickets, only they stood some way beyond the boundary. The wicket was a strip of especially bright green light.

I followed the wife along the lane that bounded the pitch, which turned out to connect with the second village green of Adenwold. We walked past the silent churchyard, the shops and cottages, and began drifting along the hedge-tunnel, where the bees whirred as they worked the great green walls. The neglected ladder remained in place, looking very forlorn, for the hedge could grow and it could not.

I heard what might have been a motor-car in the far distance, and stopped to try and make out the sound, but the wife kept walking, drawing her straw hat against the left-hand hedge, and taking down her hair, which you would have thought a complicated business but which she accomplished with two impatient strokes of her right hand. When she took her hair down, that always meant she was going off into her own world.

As we trudged on past the station yard, the hour chimes from the church floated up, the bell tolling with great effort, as though climbing a steep hill to the maximum number: twelve o'clock. Hugh Lambert had forty-four hours left; his brother possibly fewer still. The train that might bring the Chief was due in twenty-seven minutes' time. I called up to the wife: "I'm off to meet the train in. I'll come up, presently."

But she just walked on towards The Angel.

I crossed the station yard, and walked up onto the "up", where a smell of white-wash, combined with the great heat of the day, made me feel faint. The whole of the platform seemed to tilt for a moment and the signal box lurched.

The signalman was up there, leaning on his balcony. Eddie by name. He appeared to be grinning down at the porter, Woodcock, who sat on the fancy bench smoking, and looking at a pot of white-wash set down by the platform edge. He'd started renewing the white edging, but had got only about a third of the way along.

162

I took my top-coat off, and draped it over the fence that separated the "up" platform from the station yard.

"You had enough of this place, mate?" said Woodcock. "Are you making off?"

I made no reply to that, but removed the Lambert papers from my coat pocket, and sat down by the fence to read them:

The dog is everything to the boy, and accompanies him at all times. He uses it a good deal for rabbiting, of which he knew I disapproved, but Mervyn Handley has an innate diplomacy, which always prevented him from speaking about his pursuit of rabbits in my presence. I would often think that he would have been the perfect son for father to have. Aged eight, I fell off the cob, and had concussion of the brain; later, I perfected the art of going backwards on a pony. I doubt that Mervyn would have required a leading rein for year after year, as I did. The boy has taught himself shooting, but I'm sure that he "shoulders" a gun (if that be the correct expression) in the right manner, and I'm sure that, given the chance, he would be the "hard man to hounds" that Ponder and I were always supposed to become. He could never be categorised as a booby or a mollycoddle, even by a man so keen to employ those epithets as father.

I do not mean to be patronising about the boy. There is more to him than pluck and a keen eye. He is intelligent, and who is to say that he does not have the brains to take a first at Cambridge as Ponder did? This, of course, will remain undetermined.

Approaching the bottom of the page, the writing became scrawl and I shuffled the pages once more, but I found that I couldn't break in again: every new page seemed equally crabbed. I sat back, and closed my eyes.

When I opened them, the clock on the platform said 12.27 dead on, and I felt my face stiff with sunburn. I didn't like the idea of having slept in Woodcock's presence. He remained smoking on the bench just as before, but as I lifted my coat off the wicket fence, I checked through its pockets for warrant card, pocket book and watch, and found them all present.

"Any news of the 12.27, mate?" I called over to Woodcock. "It's not running late, is it?"

"Don't know," he said, "and I'm not your mate."

It had been a daft question. How *could* he know? The telegraph line was down.

"You leaving without your missus?" he said.

"Meeting a pal," I said.

"Another journalist?" he said.

"Yes, since you ask."

He didn't believe me.

Did John Lambert's timetable work somehow connect him with these blokes at the station? I looked from Woodcock to the paint pot.

"It's almost too hot to work today," said Woodcock, "and I never thought I'd hear myself say that. Anyone who knows me would be amazed to hear me coming out with those words."

I watched him blow smoke.

"In a state of shock they would be," he said.

"Where's your governor?" I enquired, and it seemed to me possible in that instant that Woodcock and the signalman had killed and eaten station master Hardy. But Woodcock looked along the platform towards the small sidings and the goods yard. As he did so, I heard the bark of a small engine from that direction.

The station master was on the warehouse platform, swivelling in the driving seat of a steam crane, the steam and smoke rising up from his rear — from the little motor that was located behind him like a bustle. He fitted so snugly into the seat of the crane that he looked like a steam-powered man. A good-sized crate was attached by canvas belts to the jib of the crane, and station master Hardy was loading it onto a flat-bedded wagon that had been drawn up by the warehouse. The wagon would be taken away on the next pick-up goods to come through Adenwold. That would be on Monday.

How many Lamberts would be dead by then?

I wondered again about station master Hardy's miniature soldiers. Did he move them about at intervals like chess pieces, the movement on one side requiring movement on the other? How did a miniature soldier die? How was that event signified? If you were a boy, you just knocked the soldier over — and you usually didn't stop at one.

The man Gifford . . . Perhaps I ought to have directed him towards Hardy, who might have an interest in scale models in general. Then again, did model soldiers come in the same scale as model trains? This was the connection that John Lambert was required to make: the connection between soldiers and railways. And who had charged him with the task? Surely the government: the War Office. In which case, who employed his seeming opponent Captain Usher? They couldn't both be in the service of the state; couldn't both be on the side of right.

The sound of the crane was by degrees drowned out by the beat of a louder engine, and I saw the 12.27 coming around the track-bend in the woods, two minutes late. As I crossed the barrow boards to the smaller platform, I watched the bundles of black smoke enter the woods by different gaps in the trees, like so many parcels being sorted.

The train stopped on the "up", and a carriage door opened.

Well, the first man down was the Chief, and I felt a great sense of relief and duty-done at the sight of him. He was holding a kit-bag, and looking at his watch. He hadn't seen me yet, for I stood by the guard's van, and he'd been riding in the carriage behind the engine.

He held his trilby hat, and I looked with enjoyment at his battered face, and thin strands of hair lashed by sweat to his great dinty head. At first he might charge me with having dragged him away from his Saturday dinner-time bottle of wine in the Station Hotel for no good reason. But I was sure he'd see the sense of the wire I sent once I'd explained all.

The Chief gave a glance along the platform, and would have spotted me at that moment had not a younger man stepped down from the train, blocking his line of vision. I'd barely had time to take in this new arrival when another man came, and then everything went wrong, for a dozen carriage doors opened and a dozen or more young blokes climbed down. They were all in the twenties or early thirties. Some wore hooped caps, and all carried long canvas bags, some with bat handles protruding. They were all bloody *cricketers* and they were all bloody suspects. I cursed the North Eastern Railway for bringing them.

To turn up in this way at a village with the shadow of an execution hanging over it did not seem right. They all stood on the platform, joshing and larking about, and the Chief was fighting his way through, coming towards me and looking none too pleased. Cricket wasn't one of his games. As he closed on me, I pulled off my cap by way of a salute, and started in straightaway by asking whether he'd had the story of Hugh Lambert's lay-over at York station, at which the Chief shook his head briskly, and spat.

The train was noisily taking its leave (nobody had boarded), and the platform was clearing as the cricketers streamed over the barrow boards towards the station yard and I began telling my tale to the Chief. He listened with head bent forward and eyes closed as though making a great effort to understand.

Or was he drunk?

That was not out of the question. Saturday was the Chief's principal boozing day, and his breath came over a little sour.

The Chief was nodding occasionally, and looking over towards the station yard, where a charabanc had drawn up. It had many seats — looked like a sort of omnibus with the top deck sliced off. At the wheel sat that bad shilling of Adenwold, the fucking vicar, the Reverend Martin Ridley, who was climbing down now as the cricketers straggled across the yard towards him. He moved towards the first of the blokes and greeted him by miming the bowling of a very fast ball, which caused a good deal of dust to fly up in the station yard and the vicar's hat to fall off.

As I carried on with my explanations, the Chief was agitatedly moving his hand over his head, shifting the strands of sweaty hair, so that they were one minute like so many tangled S's, the next drawn straight as railway lines. Station master Hardy had abandoned his seat on the steam crane, and was watching us across the tracks from the booking office doorway; porter Woodcock also looked on from the "up" platform, where he'd advanced a little way towards his pot of white-wash, but had still not laid a hand on the brush. I did not believe that either could hear my talk with the Chief.

The porter had made no move to cross the tracks to help the Chief with his bags, so my governor had evidently failed the test. Any one of the cricketers might have passed it, but none had looked in the least need of assistance.

168

The charabanc was now driving away from the station yard amid the sound of more explosions. The scale of it seemed out, for it did look a normal-sized car at first glance — and yet there were more than a dozen men in it.

The little station was left silent except for the high birdsong, and the ceaseless rattling of my own voice as I went on with my story.

The clock on the "up" said 12.35. Station master Hardy remained at the doorway of the booking office looking, as he ever did, in fear of some catastrophe coming around the corner. Porter Woodcock had disappeared.

"It's a good job you were in the office when the message came," I said to the Chief.

He gave a grunt. "Now where's the Hall?" he enquired.

"We'll go there directly," I said.

"Don't get past yourself," said the Chief.

I turned about and eyed him.

He said, "It'll only take one of us to see whether there's anything in this."

Well, it came to this: he hadn't believed my story.

. . . Or did he want to keep the business for himself? In the past, when I'd struck something big, he'd given me a pretty free hand. But this was very big: one death certain, and another threatened. And the gentry were involved.

I'd had visions of walking up to the Hall with the Chief. We'd take the place over. He'd be my authority, but I'd be in the lead. We'd get John Lambert out of the clutches of Usher, force him to say what he knew — the thing that Usher wanted him to keep back — and then we'd lay hands on the true killer, which for preference would be Usher himself.

I was in a stew of sweat; I dragged my handkerchief over my brow, and could think of nothing better to say than, "It's too hot."

"You want to get your coat on," said the Chief.

"Well, it's not as if I'm on duty, is it?"

The Chief made no reply but lit another cigar.

"Have you come armed?" I asked.

He eyed me over the flaring Vesta. "Are you trying to scare me, sonny?"

Our pint of the day before had been amiable enough, but I had perhaps bested the Chief over the matter of the bank's man on the platform. I'd pointed out his error, and that might have rankled.

"The Hall is that way," I said, indicating the direction of the second village green. "It's signposted."

I was buggered if I was going to tell him about The Angel, or offer to take his bag up there.

After the Chief had quit the platform, the station master called across the tracks to me:

"Was he the one?"

"Eh?" I called back. "How do you mean?"

"The one that was at Tamai?"

It was unlike Hardy to be coming forward. He seemed galvanised for the first time since my arrival. He ignored Woodcock, who sat on the bench, smoking.

"How did you know?" I asked Hardy, as I cut across the barrow boards.

"Well," he said, as I gained the "up", "he looked the part . . . about the right age . . ."

"What do you mean by that?" I said, challenging him — although to say *anything* to Hardy was to challenge him.

"Oh," he said, and he took a step back into the booking office.

Somehow emboldened by the Chief's rejection, I stepped into the booking office after him.

Trapped heat and dust made the place suffocating. The tall desk was still covered with a jumble of papers, but some of the books had now been stacked on the counter where stood the ABC telegraph machine. But that must be dead since the line was down. As before, the arrangement of soldiers had pride of place on the strong table, and it seemed that Hardy was minded to talk about it.

"The push for Khartoum," Hardy said, indicating the soldiers on the table. "Thirteenth of March, 1884, east coast of the Sudan. I show the British square," he ran on, as he knelt down beside the table, quite heedless of his uniform. His head appeared over the brown-coloured board like a desert moon. As he spoke, he touched the tops of soldiers' pith helmets with his fingertips, moving from one to another like a kind of blessing.

"The square was formed against a massing of the Mahdi's forces . . ."

"The dervishes, as they were known?" I said. "The fuzzie-wuzzies? They wanted to kick Egypt — and us — out of the Sudan?"

171

"Correct," he said, "quite correct. In the square there were all sorts: York and Lancasters, Marines and other regiments besides, but I show the York and Lancasters only. You might have brought your friend in for a look," he said.

This was a turn-up: a bit of steeliness in his voice, as if I'd let him down.

"He was in a hurry," I said, "— business up at the Hall."

Hardy appeared to show no interest whatsoever in what might or might not be happening at the Hall, but carried on moving his fingers across the ranks of little soldiers. They wore khaki uniforms with white bands on the tunics and pith helmets and white puttees. Some wore moustaches, and these did not come standard but were various in shape and size.

I asked Hardy: "Did you paint them yourself?"

"Sable brush," he said briskly.

"It's well done."

This compliment seemed to check him for a second, but he made no acknowledgement of it.

"We have three poses. First, standing," he said, indicating upright soldiers; ". . . then kneeling to repel," he went on, indicating others; "and finally kneeling to fire. It's the Winchester rifle, of course," he added, standing back, as if for a better view of his own creation.

"You haven't modelled the Mahdi's men," I said.

He blew out his cheeks.

"Leave those chaps to the imagination," he said, "and they don't bear thinking about too much. They

172

slashed hands and arms first — then go for the head and body. Wouldn't take prisoners, mind you, but then nor would we — not at Tamai. It was life or death."

He advanced on the table again, and shifted a couple of the kneeling figures a few eighths of an inch.

"The square was broken, you know," he said, looking up. "I don't show it broken, but it was, and you saw the character of the British soldier: officers and men risking their lives for each other."

All I could think to say was "Yes," for I'd been quite knocked by Hardy's speech. He lived for this miniature display.

"I should imagine that if you'd been in that lot," he said, indicating the display, "then everything that happened next in your life would be of quite minor importance."

I thought of the Chief. Certainly he was not over-anxious.

". . . quite minor importance," repeated Hardy, who then took a deep breath and looked at me. "All my paints and all my brushes," he said, ". . . all stolen last week."

"Well, don't look at me," came a voice from the doorway, and it was Woodcock the porter.

He leant against the door frame, smoking.

"This is Mr Hardy's little war," he said, addressing me. "*Nice*, en't it?"

I kept silence.

"His big war's summat different," said Woodcock. "That's against me. No — joking aside — he wants me stood down, don't you, Mr Hardy? He's got his monkey up with me, has Mr Hardy."

"Clear off, you," said Hardy.

"You wouldn't believe it," Woodcock said, "what with him always acting so friendly like, but he's plotting against me. You want to be careful that board don't get kicked over, Mr Hardy."

"And why might it?" asked Hardy, looking down at the floorboards.

"Somebody might just come in and give it a bit of a fucking *boot*," said Woodcock as he moved away from the doorway.

CHAPTER
TWENTY

Mrs Handley was peeling apples in the middle of the trestle table that stood before The Angel. There were a couple of documents in front of her. Mervyn sat at his end with his terrier but without his ferret. His gun was propped against the end of the table.

My silver watch said five to one. Perhaps Hugh Lambert would be taking his second-to-last dinner. It would be brought to him in the condemned cell, and he would eat observed by guards, who would then watch him walk it off in the exercise yard. Later they might watch him smoke a cigarette or even, since he was condemned, a cigar.

As I walked up, the wife came out of the inn, and sat down opposite to Mrs Handley. It seemed that they'd become fast friends in my absence. I didn't much fancy telling the wife I'd been put off by the Chief.

"What are these, Mrs Handley?" the wife asked, indicating the papers, and looking sidelong at me as I stepped up to the table.

"Oh, pictures of Master Hugh," she said, and I saw that she was once again a little teary. She passed two photographs across to the wife, and I stood at Lydia's shoulder and looked at them. In the first, Master Hugh wore a harlequin outfit and held a frying pan as if it was a banjo. He was in a beautiful garden and he was smiling, but it was a quiet, secret sort of smile, not the jollity you might have expected given his rig-out.

In the next photograph he was more himself, or so I imagined. You'd still say he was smiling but if you looked carefully his mouth was turned down. He wore a dusty black suit. He was in the country-side somewhere — some wild-looking spot — and indicating an object on the ground amid a mass of ferns.

Mervyn had risen from his place at the end of the table, and joined us.

"That's him up at the ridge," he said.

"It's up above the old quarry," said Mrs Handley. "He'd take Mervyn and me up there."

"See brock," Mervyn put in.

"To look at the badgers," said Mrs Handley, by way of explaining.

"He knew just when they'd come out of their holes. He would say it was the last train — the last train of a day that did it. The badgers would listen for it going away, and then they knew it was safe to come out."

"Was that another of his jokes?" I asked, and Mrs Handley frowned at me.

"Certainly not," she said.

In that case, I wondered what the badgers did for an alarm clock on Sundays, when there was no evening train.

"Just look at that suit," Mrs Handley said, gazing fondly at the photograph. "You'd never believe he'd been at Eton, would you?"

"You might not," I said, "but then again, he doesn't look like a murderer either."

Mrs Handley kept silence. The matter was not to be spoken of.

She rose to her feet, asking, "Would you two like some food?"

The wife asked, "Oh, what do you have, Mrs Handley?"

"Cheese, pickled walnuts and salad. That do you?"

"It sounds just lovely," said the wife.

I knew that Lydia could not abide pickled anything, but when she was "out" with me she was always extra-friendly to whoever else was around, so as to let me see what I was missing.

Mrs Handley collected up the two photographs and put them on top of the pile of papers; then she went inside The Angel.

Looking directly ahead, the wife asked me, "Did your Chief turn up, then?"

"He did."

"And where is he?"

"He's gone to the Hall."

"So you've given the whole matter over to him?"

"Isn't that what you want?" I said, "So that we can get on with our holiday?"

The wife made no answer, but just looked at me for a while before nodding towards the front of the pub, and saying, "The bicycle's gone, you might care to notice."

"Isn't it round the back?"

"It is not," she said.

She'd been onto that bicyclist from the very beginning. But his behaviour — and that of every other train-arrival — was no longer any concern of mine. Let the Chief figure it all out.

Mervyn was saying from his end of the table: "Mam writes letters to him, you know."

"What's that?" I said.

"Master Hugh," he said. "Mam's been writing to him."

"Oh," I said. "And what does she put?"

"She'll generally just ask him: 'Are you going on all right?' "

"And what does he *reply*, Mervyn?" asked the wife.

"He'll generally put: 'All right just now. Thanks for asking.' "

"But he's about to be executed," I said.

"That's why he puts 'all right *just now*'," said Mervyn. "All right *for the present*."

That doubtful look came over him again, as if he wondered whether he ought to have spoken out at all. Mrs Handley came out with the food, a jug of aerated water and two glasses on a tin tray.

"Do you suppose they'll pray over Master Hugh in the church tomorrow?" Lydia asked.

"Well, that's not our church, so I wouldn't know. We're Catholic, and the nearest church for us is St Joseph's, out at East Adenwold, which is a bit of a way."

I had the idea that this was a highly convenient state of affairs as far as Mrs Handley was concerned.

". . . But I shouldn't think so," she ran on. "Not if the vicar has anything to do with it."

178

"Did he not like Master Hugh?" the wife asked.

"He liked the *Major*," said Mrs Handley. "The two of them got on thoroughly, and he would always take his part in Sir George's arguments with the boy. Ridley would ride out with Sir George every morning, hunt with him as well."

"What's become of the hunt?" I asked.

"Stopped," said Mrs Handley. "It was the vicar himself led all the hounds down to the station, where they were packed into a van and taken to some chap in Lincolnshire."

"What did you think of him?" I couldn't resist asking. "The vicar, I mean?"

She folded her arms and eyed me.

"He wouldn't last long in a Catholic church, I'll tell you that much."

"Why not?" the wife cut in.

"He's hardly ever at home. He's always running about the place."

"Doing what?" asked the wife.

There was a beat of silence.

"He has a lady at Barton-le-Street."

"A lady?" said the wife.

"Well," said Mrs Handley, "a *woman*. And she's thought to be one of a few. 'Live and enjoy' — that's his motto."

You'd take a "down" train to get to Barton, and the vicar had done just that the night before. He'd returned this morning by an "up". Was this fancy woman the explanation for his journey? It did not seem possible to pursue this subject with two women present, and so I fell silent.

"The new tenant at the Hall . . ." the wife began.

". . . Robert Chandler," Mrs Handley supplied.

"Yes," said the wife. "Is he there at the moment?"

Mrs Handley nodded. "He's been here all summer."

"Do you think *he* shot Sir George really?" the wife asked, and she laughed after she'd said it, just as though it was a joke, which I didn't think it had been.

"I'm quite sure he didn't," said Mrs Handley. "I believe he was out in India at the time of the shooting. He certainly wasn't here, anyhow. And how would he know that John would want him to take it over? Besides, it's not as if he wants it. He's only come in as a favour to John."

It seemed that *nobody* wanted the Hall, or the running of the estate. "Master Hugh was found in the woods," Mrs Handley ran on. "He had the gun in his hand which was later shown to be the murder weapon, and his father was dead at his feet."

"He pleaded not guilty, though," I said.

"Well, wouldn't you?" said Mrs Handley.

Her line, then, was that she liked Master Hugh, but was in no doubt that he had done the killing. She might perhaps have *approved* of his having done it.

"Happen the new man will give you the farm back?" I said, and Mrs Handley gave me a very choice look at that, eyes fairly burning into me. At the end of the table, Mervyn had started scuffling with his dog Alfred. He didn't want to hear any more about Master Hugh.

Mrs Handley shook her head once, saying, "That's gone."

"The fellow that came upon him," I said, "Anderson, Constable for the Adenwolds. Where does he live?"

"Retired to the city," she said.

"Which city?"

"York," said Mrs Handley. "Where do you think?"

It struck me again that she thought me an idiot.

"Who's the new copper?"

"Don't recall his name," she said. "We hardly ever set eyes on him. He lives out at East Adenwold."

The fellow might as well have lived on the moon.

Mrs Handley had gone back to apple-peeling, and Mervyn was walking away up the dusty road with his dog and his gun. *Watch out, rabbits*, I thought. The wife rose from her seat to call out after him: "Bye, Mervyn!"

She missed our lad Harry, and she'd taken to Mervyn in his place.

She said, "I'm off up for a bath," and she went inside the inn.

She was in a strange mood — torn: half-friendly, half not; half wanting me to be investigating the Adenwold mysteries, half not.

Above all, she was annoyed at the arrival of the Chief, for it reminded her that I was not the top man even in the York railway police.

Had the heat got to her? Not a bit of it. She was always agitated — feverish, so to say, even at the best of times. It was just womanliness and you couldn't cure that with a cold bath.

A single breath of breeze shifted the wisteria growing on the inn front, like a summer sigh. The shadow of a branch waved over the table and became strange when it struck the aerated water. Mr Handley, standing in the pub doorway, boomed out something that might have been "You've had a long chat out here," followed by the question: "Don't appeal?" or "No appeal?" and I somehow had the idea he was talking about the water. I was never a great one for water, aerated or otherwise, and I took this to be an invitation to take a pint, at which I said, "I'd quite fancy a glass of Smith's, thanks," but no sooner had I said it than it occurred to me that he had meant Master Hugh had not appealed against the verdict of guilty and sentence of death.

I stepped through into the public bar after Mr Handley, and the place was empty except for the bloody bicyclist, reading a book. I nodded to him, and said, "I see your bike's gone. Still jiggered, is it?"

"Took it up to the blacksmith," he said, only half looking up from his book. "Chap called Ainsty, but he wasn't about. He's off fixing some motor, apparently."

Well, here was more data for the wife, fascinated as she was by the movements of the bicyclist.

The bar smelt of wood and wisteria. All the windows were propped open. On one side they gave onto the golden cornfields and The Angel garden; to the other, they looked onto the trestle table, the dusty lane and the woods.

Mr Handley was at the barrel of Smith's pouring me a pint, and one for himself. He boomed out a remark in his habitual blurred manner, and I could not understand. I asked him, as politely as I could, to repeat it, and it was hard to keep in countenance as he made the same baffling noise again. I looked over to the bicyclist for help, and sure enough he looked up from his book and reported with a sigh:

"He says, 'There are as many crimes committed high as low.'"

I nodded at Mr Handley, and said, "You're right over that," although I was thinking of the constant succession of working men I'd given evidence against in the York police court. You hardly ever saw a toff before the magistrates.

"Mr Handley," I said, "did Sir George Lambert have any military connection?"

Mr Handley shook his head as he raised his glass to his lips. He then *touched* the glass to his lips, and half the beer went down in an instant. I raised my own glass and tried the same, but I didn't have the trick of it, and my glass went down by just two inches and I nearly choked. To cover up the embarrassment, I said, "Does the pub pay?"

Well, I had to listen very carefully, and say "Pardon" a lot, but I got the gist. The pub did not pay. The village was in decline. The limestone quarry had been worked out, and farming had been in a bad way for years. His talk became a constant low moan on a theme of everything going to pot: the timber in the woods round about was not of the sort wanted by the modern house-builders, and the holiday trade was nothing to what it had been at the height of the cycling craze.

Whole fleets of cyclists, it appeared, had once passed through the Adenwolds every week-end.

At this news, I looked across towards our own bicyclist, but he'd quit the room. Mr Handley talked on, and I pictured Lydia in the tin bath upstairs. I always liked to hang about when she took a bath, and if she didn't tell me to clear off, that meant we would have a ride. Mr Handley was running on about how he was thinking of removing with his family to York. I asked him, "Where in York?" and — not being very interested in the reply — revolved my own thoughts as he gave it.

What was the Chief up to at the Hall? Had John Lambert killed the Major, and did he mean to make a confession to it in order to save his brother? No. Couldn't have, because he'd been in London at the time, and the court must have heard evidence to that effect.

What — if any — was the connection between the timetables for the military and the murder?

And the man Usher . . . If he meant to murder Lambert, why hadn't he just gone ahead and done it directly? How did things stand between Usher and the new owner of the Hall?

Who had been the man in the dust-coat running away from the station?

And what was the bloody bicyclist up to?

I thought of Gifford, the man from Norwood. I took out my silver watch. It was ten after one; I was supposed to have seen him at the inn at one.

184

"Gifford," I said, interrupting Mr Handley, "the commercial traveller . . . Have you seen him about?"

Mr Handley shrugged, muttered something like, "Not lately."

I drained off my glass and — telling Handley that I was off to take a turn in the woods — I quit The Angel.

I didn't mean to go into the woods, though. I meant to bang on the vicar's door to ask questions as follows. One: why had he been staring at us in the graveyard? Two: why had he called Gifford back? Three: where did he suppose the man might be just at present? Bugger the Chief. He was an old man, shortly to be superannuated. I would pursue that matter independently of him.

But I wasn't long out of the front door of The Angel when, looking to my left as I walked towards the first green of Adenwold, I saw something wrong-coloured lodged in the greenery of the woods. I went in after it.

The road was lost to my sight within ten seconds as the barriers of green fell between it and me. I might just as well have jumped into a green sea. I twisted my way between the trees and holly bushes, brambles and ferns, all connected by spider webs of ivy and bindweed, and after half a minute of battling I came to the hat: a brown, high-crowned bowler. It hung on a brier bush in company with thousands of red berries glowing in the green darkness. No name was written in the crown, but it was Gifford's, I was sure. I caught it up, and fought my way through to the wide clearing that lay beyond the brier bush.

This I took at first to be an expanse of flat moss, but a slip of my boot proved it to be a green and black pond over which a hundred insects swooped, the lot of them looking like man-made flying machines going through their paces. Why had Gifford, the man from the London suburbs who hated nature, entered this abandoned world?

I skirted the pond as he must have done after losing, or abandoning, his bowler, and pressed on, picking my way. Low, sharp branches kept whisking off my own hat as if to say, "*Keep* it off: show us some respect, won't you?" At every turn, my boots broke the twigs beneath my feet, and I began to feel unsure about what lay beneath, like a man walking over the rotten rafters of an ancient attic.

I called out "Gifford!" a few times, but there came no answer.

Of course, he might have gone the other way around the pond. My route led in the direction of a golden light coming through the trees, and as I came to the limit of the woods — and re-entered the heat of the day — I saw that the golden-ness was made by the sun and a cornfield combined. The edge of the woods was marked by clouds of cow parsley, just as the border of a fancy handkerchief is marked by lace.

I walked along a little way, and then I saw another wrong colour, this time on the ground. I picked up the red model engine: the single-driver. It was made of stout soldered tinplate, and beautifully finished. The maker's name was stamped in German underneath. It might have been something like "Gastin", with two little dots over the "a", but the letters were too tiny to be made out.

Turning the model over in my hands, I thought of the German railways. It was said that you had to show your ticket to the guard on all trains with no exceptions, and that the guard saluted you like a military man when you did so. The station masters saluted passing trains all along the line, whether those trains stopped at their stations or not. As a people, they were lacking in humour, and they carried method too far.

But Gifford, surely, was neither German nor a travelling agent of that country. As he had said himself, he was a traveller in small locomotives. Yet he had possessed some secret, some knowledge touching on the Adenwold mysteries, and he had meant to tell me it.

Had he been observed in the course of observing someone? Had the vicar brought him into the woods to put his lights out, only to drop in on the railway station and collect the cricket team?

The locomotive had spilled from its bag, which was hard by in the grass. I looked up and there, lying under cow parsley, was Gifford's Gladstone bag . . . not six feet from the man himself.

He was half in a ditch, his head pointing down into its depths, his boots higher than his head. Directly above was the stout branch of a giant oak. Had he come down from it?

Or had he been pursued through the woods, only to come a cropper as soon as he escaped the trees?

He seemed to have attained a kind of peacefulness in his position. His eyes were closed, and he looked to be having a pleasant sort of dream, but his head was cut by brambles, his face was bluish and a quantity of dark-coloured blood had flowed from the corner of his mouth.

I held my hand over his mouth, and felt nothing. I knelt down and put my face directly in front of his, at which I detected faint breaths. If he had come down from a height, and suffered a smash, I ought not to touch him.

Had he tried to make away with himself by leaping from the tree? Perhaps he was in low water financially. He'd sounded desperate enough, and the vicar had evidently not purchased the red engine.

It seemed wrong that I should be able to view his head so closely. I touched my hand to his hair, and my fingers came up rust-coloured. Blood (and a good deal of it) was working with the Brilliantine to keep Gifford's hair fixed in place, and shining. I touched again, and there was a groove under the hair. I pulled my hand away fast. Had he taken a bullet?

I sat up on the edge of the ditch; ten yards to my left, a wooden bridge ran across it, half-hidden by brambles. Two white butterflies danced in the air before my face, as if to say, "Isn't this all a lark? You may have your troubles, but we're on holiday just at present."

I set the little engine down next to the Gladstone bag, and looked at my silver watch: one thirty-five.

CHAPTER
TWENTY-ONE

Flying along the margins of the cornfield, I kept a look-out for the telegraph poles that ought to be somewhere ahead. They would indicate the territory of the railway line.

I rounded a bend and came upon the silent poles, and their confederates, the silent tracks. I slowed somewhat as I went past the downed stretch of cable. It struck me that railway policemen ought to be issued with portable telegraph instruments. With these, and a length of cable looped over the right wire, it was possible to send your own messages.

Running now along the railway sleepers, I looked up. The poles carried six wires: telegraph and telephone either way — that accounted for four. The other two would be the wires linking the signal boxes of the branch, for the sending of the signalmen's bell codes. To send a message, you'd have to know which was which; you'd need the portable doings, and you'd need to go beyond the point of the cut. Then you'd be within reach of the normal world, and sanity.

I kicked up my boot-heels and I flew on. The station, waiting on the far side of a tree-made arch, seemed to swing and shake as I pounded down the track.

I found it quite deserted, like a ship becalmed. But Will Hamer and his horse and donkey stood dreaming in the station yard, with the rulley hitched up behind.

I ran at the fellow, gulping at air and unable at first to speak.

Instead, Hamer spoke.

"It's you again," he said, smiling.

"There's a man badly injured in the woods," I said. "I've just come from him. He's near the bridge over the ditch."

"I know that spot," said Hamer, who was now not quite smiling but still looking amiable, "On the edge of Clover Wood."

So there were separately named woods within the woods.

"He may have fallen out of a tree," I said.

"Aye," Will Hamer said, "I expect so."

"Will you fetch a doctor?"

"Aye," Hamer said again, making no move, "I will do."

"Where *is* a doctor?"

"Well now, East Adenwold," Hamer said. "Doctor Lawson — deliver to him regular like. Very good man for an emergency if you can catch him in."

"You'd better look sharp," I said. "I reckon the fellow's dying. Might you un-harness the donkey? I mean, wouldn't the horse be quicker on its own?"

Hamer looked at his horse for a while. Presently, he said, "Wouldn't move at all on his own, wouldn't that bloke. Pair of 'em might go a *bit* faster, though, and don't think I en't tried a few tricks. I've had 'em this

190

way and that: him to the left, *him* to the left. You name it, I've tried it."

I stood silent. Was there any other way of getting help to Gifford apart from employing this blockhead?

". . . Mangel wurzels I've tried," he was saying. "Short rein, long rein . . ."

He turned and fixed on me a sort of questioning smile.

"You look down-hearted, mister," he said.

"There's blood coming out of the bloke's mouth," I said, "and that's always a bad look-out."

"Might be his . . . tooth fallen out?"

"Will you go off just now?" I said. "I'll go back to guard the bloke, and I'll see you at the place."

I indicated the rulley.

"You'll get that along the edge of the field — there's a track of sorts."

"Oh, no bother," he said, and he fell to smiling at me.

I felt in want of a whistle to blow and a green flag to wave.

"Come on, men!" Hamer shouted at last, and the horse and donkey first awoke, and then moved.

I took off my jacket, and watched them cross the station yard, but as before they rolled to a stop after twenty yards.

"While I think on . . ." Hamer called out, and I thought: *Christ, he wants to be paid.* But that wasn't it, He was passing a paper to me.

"Your wire was delivered," he said, "earlier on, like."

It was an acknowledgement of sending, written on a chit stamped: "The Booking Office, West Adenwold Station."

"Obliged to you," I said, "but I knew it had gone off, because the fellow I sent for arrived."

"What fellow?" said Hamer, and instead of answering, I gave his horse's arse a good slap, which set the three on their way again. I watched them out of sight, then raced back through the station and around the woods.

I came to the bridge just as two rabbits went flying across it. I looked about. Birdsong twisted through the drowsy air. I walked a little way along the margin of the wood. I looked about once again. The sun beat down on the brambles and the cow parsley.

Neither Gifford, nor his bag, nor the little red locomotive, were anywhere to be seen.

I stood still for a space, thinking of everything and nothing. Finally I sat down by the bridge, exhausted.

This place Adenwold, I thought . . . It'll be the bloody finish of me. I made no further attempt to scout about. There was no sound but the steady, heavy drone of insects. I looked at my silver watch: five to two. I felt honour-bound to wait for the doctor. It was important that *somebody* kept up sensible behaviour. When the chimes of two o'clock floated over from the village, I moved under the big oak for shade, and took the papers of Hugh Lambert from my pocket.

"Mr Richardson, the station master at Adenwold during our childhood," I read . . . and that pulled me up short, for starters. It was hard to imagine the station without Hardy: he seemed such a fixture of Adenwold, his own strangeness matching that of the village. I read on:

. . . Mr Richardson would bring Ponder on in his railway interests, and father would undoubtedly have written to the Company demanding his removal had the man been anything less than a model official. His top hat was lustrous, and the staff were most punctilious under his eye, as even father admitted. Richardson personally sent telegrams by the dozen for father, using the station machine, and always with a smile and always without charging. But he would talk trains with the boy!

And how could father state that the railways were neither sporting nor aristocratic? That they had paid grandfather too little for right of way over his land, a fact serving to remind father that the estate was small, the family not as well-off as commonly imagined, and he only a Baronet? Father expressed himself delighted at Richardson's retirement, but the new man wore a bowler instead of a topper and did not keep the place so well.

How many times did father cancel Ponder's subscription to the *Railway Magazine*? And how often did he wearily reinstate it during a fit of guilt? It wasn't so much my brother's reading and collection of the *Railway Magazines* that antagonised father, as the sending-off for the special binders with the railway crests. (I should say that Ponder, an incredibly untidy person for all his orderly mind, liked the idea of binders more than the act of binding.)

The writing-in of letters by Ponder was still more to be deprecated, and the publication of articles under his own name doubly so. I remember Ponder showing the first of his letters to appear in cold print. It appeared under the heading: "A correspondent asks for information concerning the vacuum brake now installed". He pointed to the word "correspondent" and then to himself, and he grinned. He then promptly won a carriage clock for one of his railway essays. I asked him whether it had been an essay on carriages but nothing so modest: "How to Improve the Summer Services" was his theme. Not some of them, but all.

And Ponder ought to know, for he'd spent almost the whole summer lying on the croquet lawn and reading timetables, relayed to him in batches free of charge, I believe, by Mr Richardson. Ponder would seek out the innovations; a new restaurant car between St Pancras and Leeds; a train from York to Hull booked one minute later than the previous month. It was the drag of interrelatedness that fascinated him, the way that one train couldn't be moved until another had been. He was quite lost to it all; and he was lost to father, too. Ponder did not retreat so much as fade from the battleground, with the result that father and I concentrated our fire on each other, and in this connection too the railway figured, for it was the railway that took me to London, and my other life.

Trying to make out the words had brought on a headache. I put down the paper. What was this other life? I had half an idea.

I looked up to see Will Hamer's wagon rumbling over the sun-hardened mud. Another man was sitting up with him: Lawson, the doctor from East Adenwold.

He turned out to be a very crabby little man in a salt and pepper suit, who wouldn't take no for an answer. I felt like offering to lie down myself on the canvas stretcher he was waving about, just to save him a wasted journey. Hamer smiled through the whole palaver. It took more than an unexplained disappearance to jolt him out of his groove.

"Do you think the man had been drinking?" Lawson demanded.

"More likely shot," I said. "There was something very like a bullet wound on the side of his head."

"Have *you* been drinking?" asked Lawson.

He seemed to have a very limited imagination: everything started and finished with alcohol. I stood shaking my head as Will Hamer turned the rulley about and drove the doctor back down the track. I ought to have given him a couple of bob for his trouble, I decided, as I set off back to The Angel. He'd proved himself not such a dope after all, for he'd delivered my wire without any hitch, *and* he'd fetched the doctor.

At The Angel, the bar was quite deserted. I climbed the stairs and the wife was sitting cross-legged reading her paper, *The Freewoman*, which she immediately tossed to one side. I knew right away that I was properly forgiven, and that there was some important business at hand; or business she thought important, at any rate. It didn't matter what it was, though. Gifford had very likely been shot at because of what he knew, and I would not put the wife in the way of a bullet. I had to get her out of Adenwold.

There was a pleasant scent of soap in the room, and I saw that the wife had placed cut lavender inside a glass on the dresser. She was looking at me bright-eyed. She started saying, "You'll never guess . . ."

But I cut in on her, telling her that I'd found Gifford in the woods; that I'd fetched a doctor; that Gifford had disappeared meantime. I did not mention the possibility of a shooting. She kept silence for a moment when I'd finished, before saying:

"Well, whatever he was about, it's connected to the man at the Hall, and to his brother. The centre of everything is the Hall, and we're invited there this evening."

She would not be going; she would be on the "down" train at 8.35p.m. But I asked, "Invited? Who by?"

"Why, the tenant of course. Who else would presume to do it? Mr Robert Chandler — he came by the front of the inn just now."

"How? On foot?"

"In a very smart little trap."

196

"We can't be invited to a place like the Hall. We're not their type."

"It *is* a little irregular," said the wife. "But it's not a dinner invitation. It's for rather late on — nineish — and Mr Chandler said we were not to dress."

"Just as well," I said, "since we've nothing to dress *in*." And, seeing my way to a grievance, I added: "He fancied you, I suppose?"

The wife went quite blank at that. She never admitted that any man fancied her. It was as though her womanly spell might be broken if she once did so.

"He was with his wife," she said at length, "and she seemed just as keen. They were very friendly. You see, I was sitting outside at the long table and Mr Chandler drove up and said something about it being a lovely day. Then he asked me, 'What brings you to Adenwold?'"

"The train," I put in. "The *train* brought you to Adenwold."

The wife ignored this, saying:

"I told him that you'd brought me here but that I'd been hoping to go to Scarborough, not that this wasn't a very pretty spot, and he said, 'I know, but Scarborough's my favourite summer place.'"

"Why didn't he go on the outing, then?"

"I don't see him in one of your horrible rattling excursion trains," said the wife.

Everything bad about the railways was my personal responsibility.

"I then said that I'd been particularly looking forward to the Chinese lanterns strung all along the

197

garden walks, and he said, 'Well, we've Chinese lanterns at the Hall, why don't you come up and see?'"

"Did you tell him I was a policeman?"

"I did not."

"Did he mention the Chief?"

"No."

"And will Usher be there?" I asked. "And John Lambert, who's under threat of death because of what he knows about his father's murder? Where do they come in? Are they invited to this little jolly?"

"I don't know," replied the wife, "but that's what makes it all so exciting."

It was *one* of the things that made it exciting to the wife.

Presently, she went back to *The Freewoman*, and I looked at Hugh Lambert's papers again, but I kept striking bits of bad handwriting, or bits I'd already read.

The wife said she'd like a look, so I passed the bundle over. "I never went well on a horse," she read out loud. "Ponder did, but he simply refused . . ."

"Who's Ponder?" asked the wife.

"The brother, John," I said, "on account of his studious ways, I suppose."

". . . Ponder did, but he simply refused," she repeated. "However, he would ride out with father and I if father had been especially bold with the brandy, which would make him liable to violence. He saved me from countless thrashings, just by riding in-between us, playing the part of a mounted policeman . . ."

And she read on from there in silence.

198

"What we have here," she said, when she eventually put the bundle aside, "is *impressions*."

"That's it," I said. "It's literature, worst luck, written only for his own satisfaction."

"But then why do you suppose he gave it you?"

"Well, it's all in there, I suppose, in a roundabout way."

"What do you make of him?"

"I don't know. I don't understand him at all."

"Do you know why, Jim Stringer?" she said, and after giving me a strange look for a while, she went back to looking over the sheets of paper.

"Who'd want the verdict to stand?" I asked her a little while later (my silver watch gave ten to four). ". . . Or, to put it another way, who'd have wanted Sir George dead in the first place?"

"The pheasants of Adenwold, I should think," said the wife, still reading Hugh Lambert's papers.

CHAPTER
TWENTY-TWO

Come eight twenty-five by my silver watch, Lydia was standing by the door of our room in her best blue cotton dress. It was set off to a T by the high black belt, and the white fancy blouse that showed through at her neck and shoulders. She carried her little leathern bag that was half-bag, half-purse.

"Look alive," she said, as I did up my bootlaces. "And remember that it is not fashionable to be intoxicated."

"We'll see about that," I muttered, following her through the door.

I had her railway ticket in my inside pocket, but I knew I'd have a job to get her on the train, especially since I meant to go to the party myself. This would strike her as unfair. No self-respecting woman Co-Operator would stand for it.

We'd both slept a little in the early evening; then I'd lain on the bed making notes in my pocket book of the week-end's events so far. Later, I'd kept station outside the pub with a pint in my hand watching for any sign of the Chief, but he'd not pitched up. Did he mean to stay at the Hall? And would he be at the beano? *Would* Usher be there?

I could have done with more than just one pint to set me up, but I supposed that a glass of wine would be put in my hand directly I stepped under the Chinese lanterns. You got wine directly on arrival at the Christmas party given by the Archbishop of York for the whole village of Thorpe-on-Ouse. There was no messing about there — the Archbishop was certainly going to be drinking, and he didn't want to stand out.

Along the lane leading down from The Angel, a doorway in the low, bent houses stood open and one of the old ladies stood by it, as though presenting the place for inspection. Lydia, walking ahead, gave her good evening but received no response. I tried the same, with the same results. She might be near-blind. She looked as though she could see, but only very far-off things. I then overtook the wife, and stood with arms folded in the station yard. She walked towards me shaking her head.

I indicated the station.

"You're off in there," I said. "The 8.35 is an 'up'. It'll take you to Pilmoor, and you'll change there for York."

"That's what you think," she said, standing before me on the dusty stones.

It was a good thing the village was empty, because we were all set for a scrap.

"Here's the return half of your ticket to York," I said.

"What do you think I am? A consignment of goods?"

I could hear the beat of the approaching train.

"There's been a bad business here. A man is waiting to hang for it, but I don't think he's the guilty party. Gifford was nearly done in because of what he knew.

There's a man at the Hall threatened with death if he spills the beans. It's no . . ."

"Well, *you're* not about to spill the beans," the wife cut in. "You don't know anything."

"It's not me I'm worried about."

"I'd have thought you might want a bit of moral support when you see that man Usher again."

The beat of the train was loud now. It was approaching at a lick.

"Harry will want to see you anyway," I said.

"You know perfectly well that he'll be having a lovely time with Lillian Backhouse and all her kids. She'll have given them lemonade today, and they'll all have gone swimming in the river."

"But you told her not to take them swimming in the river."

"But I know perfectly well that she will do, and that Harry loves going."

"Why did you tell her not to take him, then?"

"Because it's *dangerous*."

The 8.35 was bustling through the woods, dragging its banner of smoke.

"For once in my life I've been invited to a party at a grand house," said the wife, "and if you think I'm going to climb up into a filthy third-class carriage and ride to Pilborough with some lecherous old man eyeing me from the corner seat . . ."

"It's Pil*moor*, and there won't be any lecherous old man."

"There will be. There always is. Ask any woman."

"It's coming too fast," I said, turning.

The two of us looked up at the station, and the train was there, rattling and thundering; each coach was itself for a small second, and then . . . a shocking silence. It had run right through.

I ran across the yard, and onto the "up" platform.

Woodcock the porter was on his high perch, turning and laughing. The signalman, Eddie, laughed back at him from his balcony. They hadn't bargained on the train not stopping. Station master Hardy was in his doorway; he retreated into it, back towards the little soldiers, as I approached, asking, "Did you have a traffic notice about that?"

He shook his head like a little boy.

"The lines are down," he said, "and no-one's come by."

"Then the driver's had orders from . . ."

"Oh, from Pilmoor, most likely," Hardy said.

"It was to stop anyone leaving," I said.

"But no-one *wanted* to leave," he said, and he indicated the empty platform.

The 8.35 had left a smoky tang in the air. I looked up at the signals. Woodcock and Eddie were both smoking, looking down with the remains of smiles on their faces. Were they on the inside or the outside of events? Where had they been in the afternoon? Slacking in the village ? The urge was suddenly strong on me to see whether John Lambert was still living, and to try my luck again with the Chief.

I walked through the wicket and back into the station yard where the wife stood waiting.

"More mysteries?" she said, as I approached, and she didn't wait for an answer, but just said, "Come on, we'll be late."

It was getting dusk as we struck out along the lane indicated by the sign reading "TO THE HALL". The wife was walking a little way ahead, and it seemed to me that she turned into the woods early.

"Hold on," I called out.

She'd taken a woodland track we'd not seen before.

"It's this way," she said. "We're going to the back of the house."

"That's a bit out of it," I said. "We might as well be servants."

After three minutes in the wood, we came to a tall gate, propped open.

"Cap off," said the wife, as the Hall came into view.

The back of the house looked the same as the front but even handsomer, as I might have guessed, for the aristocracy would beat you all ends up. There was a stone pond immediately behind the house, and a very mathematical-looking garden had been made around this. Two stone staircases curled down from either side of this garden to reach the terrace, which was dramatic like a stage, except that it was sunken rather than high. Two wires were strung high across the terrace, and the paper lanterns hung from these. They held my attention, each like a little paper concertina: orange, red, green, and giving a beautiful soft glow, but one had got scorched and smoke was racing away from the top of it as the paper burned.

204

The lanterns were like toys, childish things, and yet the Chief stood underneath them. He was to the rear of the terrace and the sight of his clothes hit me like a station buffer.

The Chief wore an evening suit: trousers with braided seams, varnished shoes, white bow tie — and the hairs on his head were mustered into parallel lines and held down by Brilliantine. The perfection of the suit pointed up his natural imperfections, and I knew that I was for once seeing the Chief out of his element. The fellow he was speaking to, on the other hand, looked practically born to wear an evening suit, and he had one foot raised on a white iron garden chair which gave him a confident look. He was smoking a very white cigarette, and this made him seem to be pointing all the time, saying, "Now look here, it's like this," while the Chief listened and looked as though he *wanted* to smoke but daren't.

This second man was Captain Usher.

A couple also stood waiting on the terrace and these I knew must be the Chandlers: the brother-in-law of the murdered man and his wife. Robert Chandler was a bald man whose head went in slightly at the middle like a peanut shell; his wife was a round and pretty woman in a lilac dress with a train. They were both somewhere in the middle forties, which made them about of an age with Usher.

Of John Lambert there was no sign.

"But they told us not to dress," the wife was saying, in a tone of voice I'd not heard from her before, for it seemed to hold real fear. We were approaching two avenues made by dark firs that had been cut into cones like witches" hats. Which one to choose? Would there be a right one and a wrong one? You could bloody well bet there would be. "

But before we reached the trees, an advance party approached us: a chambermaid and a manservant of some sort — two servants kept back from Scarborough. Both carried trays holding bottles and glasses. They closed on us and then divided, the parlourmaid making towards the wife, the manservant heading my way.

I realised that he was the servant I'd seen that morning, the amiable one who'd directed me to the gardener's cottage. He no longer looked horsy, but like an expert on wines.

"Hock or claret, sir?" he said.

I took a claret because it was nearest. But I felt I moved too fast, because the man said, "Or there's champagne at the table, sir?"

Looking over, I saw a small table covered by a white cloth, and over-crowded with bottles and ice buckets. I had the notion that the four people standing around it and waiting for us were all adults, and that the wife and I were children. Evidently the four had all eaten supper, and we had received an invitation of an inferior sort after all, and I knew this would go hard with the wife. I knew also that her nervousness and embarrassment on this account would far exceed in her any anxiety about any murderous doings.

We were not approaching the terrace by the two proper walkways, but had somehow ended up going haphazard over the grass. Having drunk off my claret, I found that I was now making towards the hosts with an already empty glass, which also didn't seem quite etiquette. The wife, of course, carried no glass, since she was tee-total.

It was Chandler's wife who was waiting to greet me at the margin of the terrace. *Do not on any account say, "I see that you do yourselves pretty well here,"* I told myself. *Do not say, "This is laying on luxury."*

She shook my hand, she might even have curtsied; she said something I didn't quite catch and then, after a long beat of silence, I heard myself saying, "Lovely place you have here."

Meanwhile Lydia was being greeted by the host, who said, "It is lovely to see you again," and the two "lovelys" seemed to clash.

From the rear of the terrace, I heard a laugh from the Chief as he spoke to Usher, and it was not quite natural, not quite *him*. Had Usher got him under the gun? Had he bested him as he had bested me?

And where had the Chief got his bloody dinner suit from?

The hostess, who stood before me, was looking down at the ground. Beneath the folds of her dress, she moved one of her feet, as though testing the bricks beneath. She looked up again, and a ruby necklace rose on the slopes of her white bosom as she took a deep breath. I had the idea that she was at once very distant and very near, and that she was a little squiffed. She then spoke all in a flurry:

"We had such a friendly talk earlier on at the village with your wife, Mr Stringer. She said she was absolutely

just dying to see some Chinese lanterns, and —
anything to oblige!"

She turned and smiled with arm outstretched,
presenting the lanterns of which there was now one
fewer, the scorched one having burnt right out. I looked
from it towards the Chief, who had certainly noticed
me, but had not yet given me any acknowledgement.
Mrs Chandler, spotting the direction of my glance,
said.

"You won't believe it but those two are talking about
camels."

As the manservant poured more claret for both of us,
Mrs Chandler said something about how the two men
had been in Africa, so what could you expect? There
was practically nothing in Africa *but* camels. Then the
host, Robert Chandler, came over with his arm in
Lydia's.

I looked at Lydia's white-gloved hand, and there was
a glass of champagne there, and the sight was so
all-of-a-piece and so elegant that for a moment the
shock did not register. As I looked on, she drained off
the rest of the glass and shot me a look that clearly said,
"You put away gallons of alcohol every week, so why
shouldn't I take a glass now and again?" I understood
straightaway that it was the shame of not being invited
to the meal that had made her do it, but the sight of the
glass so knocked me that I said to the host:

"By the way, Mr Chandler, where is John Lambert?"

"John?" he said. "Well, we hope to see him here. But
I think he is a little over-strained just at present."

"That's what everyone says," I said.

"Do they?" said Mr Chandler, and he looked put out. "I was rather congratulating myself on my — y'know — insight, He's not a very forward party exactly, and he's been conferring with Captain Usher all day, so I expect he's pretty worn out. Now that sounds as though I'm being rude about Usher when in fact he seems a perfectly pleasant chap who knows a very great deal about camels and horses and dogs and things like that. Tell me, do you know that fellow that runs The Angel? What's wrong with him?"

It hardly mattered what I said in reply. I was becoming confident that Chandler — who at some stage after the arrival of my fourth glass of claret told me to call him Bobby and his wife Milly — did not really know Usher, and that he was out of the picture as far as any bad business was concerned. As he burbled on in his amiable way, he kept glancing over to Lydia, who was talking to Milly, while I heard the Chief say to Usher, "Strange that is, sir . . . I always took the General for a base wallah," at which they both laughed, but especially the Chief.

Of course, that *would* be how things stood between them. Chief inspector was a higher rank than captain, but Usher was an *army* captain, and it was the army that signified. The Chief had only been a sergeant major in his service days, so the Chief "sirred" Usher just as I "sirred" the Chief. Only that word sounded wrong on the lips of a man who'd seen as much as my governor.

Another glass of claret was presented to me by the footman, who seemed to have become a special ally of mine. I looked across to the Chief again, and Usher was watching me. Had he been forewarned that I'd been invited? His gaze was not over-friendly, and I was quite sure that if he'd had his way I would be nowhere near the Hall at this moment, but it seemed that he was a species of guest just as I was, and so caught between good manners and whatever business he had in hand.

I drained off my glass at a draught, and said to Bobby Chandler:

"There was a murder here, of course."

"Ah!" he said. "Good subject for a party conversation!"

I gave a sudden nervous laugh, quite unintended, and Bobby Chandler made to give me a nudge with the back of his hand, saying, "Could it be that we share the same sense of humour, Mr Stranger?"

And then he fell to looking at Lydia again.

"It's *Stringer*," I said.

"Yes, my brother-in-law . . ." he said. "Perfectly blameless existence walking about this place blasting animals to kingdom come, and then made away with by his own son — what do you think of that?"

"It's a bad look-out," I said.

"*Damned* bad," said Bobby Chandler. "And with his own thirty-inch barrel, one-hundred-and-fifty-guinea twelve-bore."

"It's a bad look-out," I said again, and I thought: *I'm canned already*.

"When I got the news," said Bobby Chandler, "I was absolutely devastated for about — well, not that long if we're quite honest. I didn't know my brother-in-law all that well, and he wasn't really my sort."

He was looking at Lydia again.

"It's a shame about young Hugh of course, in a way, but I hardly knew him either . . ."

So it was not really *such* a great shame.

"Good-looking boy, Hugh," he said vaguely. "Had a governess absolutely devoted to him. Absolutely *devoted*. Now governesses are always either terribly pretty or absolutely grim-looking, don't you think?"

I wondered at the question, since it must be obvious to him that I was not acquainted with many governesses. Was this generosity in him or plain ignorance? Had he expected us not to notice that we hadn't been invited to the supper, but only the afters? He'd very likely not thought about it either way. His chief goal was avoidance of boredom, and proper form and "the done thing" could go by the board as far as he was concerned.

Well, it was all right by me.

". . . And if you knew anything about my brother-in-law," Bobby Chandler was saying, "you'll know which sort young Hugh's governess was. Can you guess?"

"Pretty," I said.

"Decidedly," said Chandler. "I only saw her twice, and even though she was a servant of sorts . . . Now I'm not quite drunk enough to say what I'm going to say next, so change the subject please, Mr Stranger."

"What was her name?" I said, and the sharpness made Bobby Chandler take a step back.

"That is not changing the subject of course," he said, "but I believe her name was Emma. The vicar here," he said, leaning forward, "was distinctly keen on her."

"Did either man conduct a . . ."

And the world stopped, and the sliver of moon winked down at me encouragingly, as I found the word "liaison".

"I think that possibly they both did," he said with a sigh, as though suddenly extremely bored.

"Both at the same time?" I said.

But he didn't seem to hear. He had turned a little way away from me and, keeping half an eye on Lydia, began instructing the waiter about opening some more of the right kind of bottles.

The vicar, who was supposed to be such a great pal of the murdered man, would not be dismissed, would not be stood down from the ranks of suspects.

Bobby Chandler was still speaking to the manservant, having quite forgotten about the governess. Lydia was still speaking to Mrs Chandler, who was drinking hock, but Lydia had not re-filled her own glass; the first one seemed to have done the trick, and it had emboldened her to bring out her hobby horse, for she was speaking about one of her great heroines, Emmeline Pankhurst, until Mrs Chandler interrupted, saying:

"I know Emmeline Pankhurst slightly."

The wife was shocked at this, but tried not to show it.

"Oh," the wife said, "and what does she say about the progress of the cause?"

"Well, I don't really speak to her about that."

212

"Really?" said the wife. "That's rather like knowing William Shakespeare and never mentioning his plays."

"But William Shakespeare is *dead*," said Milly Chandler, and the force of the last word made her stumble slightly.

"I admire her daughter Sylvia very much," the wife was saying. "She works tirelessly for the poor in the East End."

"Yes, she's *very* tedious," said Milly Chandler, and she eyed Lydia for a moment, looking to see her response to this. But she burst out laughing after a second in any case.

The small table seemed to have been replenished with red wine; there were also now walnuts, almonds, crystallised fruits in silver bowls, cigarettes and cigars in silver boxes. The manservant was at my elbow, and it seemed that he intended to take my glass away. Perhaps he'd noticed that I'd had enough. But as it turned out he only meant to give me a new one. "This is the '98, sir," he said. "It's a better vintage."

"Reckon so?" I said.

Bobby Chandler was facing me again, and to test my theory about him, I said, "Where were you when you heard the news of the murder?"

"India," he said, very simply. "We were visiting people we know out there."

"Where do you actually *live*?" I asked him.

"Well, *here* now," he said, "most of the time."

"But where were you before, exactly?"

"Oh, London, you know. We're not really country people."

"Ten to one your place in London is not as big as this," I said, gesturing up towards the Hall.

Chandler glanced thoughtfully up at the great house.

"Perhaps not quite," he said. "But there's a lot I don't care for about this place. It has no cellar, for instance — well, it won't do after tonight. John doesn't drink, and my brother-in-law left very, very few decent bottles, so I thought we might as well drink them off so that we know where we stand, do you see?"

"How do you mean?"

"Well, if there's nothing left, there's nothing left. It's an extremely straightforward position."

The Chief was at my elbow.

"Will you step over here, lad?"

He took me by the arm, and moved me a little way to the side of the terrace. He held one of his small cigars. He was friendlier than before.

"Lydia's looking well," he said.

"Good," I said, and then, after a pause, "Is it all in hand, sir?"

"It is and it isn't, lad."

The Chief was normally as straight as they came, but now he looked and sounded shifty.

"I came upon a fellow lying in the woods," I said. "I thought he must be . . ."

"We can't speak of it here," said the Chief — and he was eyeing Usher.

"You had supper earlier on?" I enquired, after an interval of silence.

214

"Aye," said the Chief, and he almost smiled. "Roast quails . . . and it went from there."

On the terrace, Usher was pacing and smoking.

"Where's John Lambert?" I asked the Chief.

"He'll be joining us presently."

"Usher means to kill him," I said. "I'm certain of it."

The Chief took a pull on his cigar, and made a movement of his head that was both a nod and a shake.

"Do you know who Usher is?" he asked, putting one eye on me.

"No," I said. "Do you?"

He put his cigar out just then, stamping on it with his patent shoe. He did not mean to answer the question. He meant to keep whatever he knew on important points muffled up.

I was looking the Chief's tail-coat up and down.

"Where did you get the suit, sir?"

"This clobber?" he said. "It belongs to the boy."

"Hugh Lambert? The one that's about to swing?"

"Twenty years of PT," said the Chief, looking over towards the terrace. "That's the only reason I can get into it. Not bad going for a bloke of my age. Trousers are pinching a bit, mind you."

The Chief must think it only fair that a man convicted of murder should have to forfeit his clothes as well as everything else.

"You know Usher from the colours?" I said. "He must be a decent fellow if he fought with you?"

I couldn't let up with the questions.

"Some of the biggest cunts I've ever known have been soldiers in the British Army, lad."

Here was a flash of the Chief I knew, but his heart wasn't in it.

"He was in the same regiment, was he, sir?"

"Same brigade, lad, same brigade. Usher was in the Royal Marines."

"Did his lot fight alongside your lot at Tamai?"

"Tamai was a bit of a mess," said the Chief, "but that was the general idea, yes."

He looked all-in, and I noticed that he wasn't drinking, which was out of the usual.

I said, "The station master at Adenwold — chap called Hardy — he's made a model of that battle."

"A model of it?" said the Chief, still watching the terrace. "There were ten thousand fucking dervishes . . ."

"Oh, he hasn't included *them*," I said.

The Chief shook his head.

"The fact that you and Usher were both at Tamai, sir — can't you use it to get a leg in with him? Find out what's going off as regards John Lambert? Have you seen Lambert at all yet? Seen all his timetables?"

The Chief dropped his cigar stub, and put his boot-heel on it.

"You're not to speak of any of it, lad," he said. "It's a pretty delicate situation."

It was not like the Chief to find anything delicate.

I said, "What *can* I speak of?"

"Don't talk," said the Chief. "Just drink."

"I'm half seas over as it is," I said.

"I'll put you straight about everything before long," he said, and the Chief was eyeing the right-hand stair to the rear of the terrace, which John Lambert was

216

descending. Looking at him, my first thought was: *Well, here's another condemned man*. In his dinner suit, he might have been dressed for his coffin. He was operating on habit alone as he came down those stone steps, to be greeted by the host and hostess, with Usher waiting behind them.

Looking on, I said, "Well, Usher can't very well do for him at a *party*, can he, sir?"

"'Course not, lad," said the Chief. "It'd be considered very poor form."

And he walked slowly back towards the terrace.

CHAPTER
TWENTY-THREE

I followed the Chief back onto the terrace, where I crossed the wife, who was making towards Milly Chandler.

She said, "Can you smell the lovely musks and damasks?"

"Is that what they are?"

There was a beat of silence.

"John Lambert's here," I said, indicating him with a nod.

"I see him," she replied.

"He looks rather seedy."

"Yes."

"What's going off, do you suppose?"

"Don't ask me," said the wife. "I thought your Chief might be putting you in the picture just now."

I could only shake my head.

I sat down on one of the stone steps to the rear of the terrace — and when I sat down, I *really* sat down. I found a glass of claret near my perch, and drank it off. Someone had placed an oil lamp on the steps to supplement the Chinese lanterns, and it had drawn any number of drab-coloured moths. This terrace was really a room without walls; it was very hard to credit that a man who'd had the run of it, and the house too, was now in a cell in Durham nick.

Usher was speaking in low tones to John Lambert, who would meet his gaze by some great effort, and then turn away. It was rather cheering to know that two members of the upper classes did not always see eye to eye. The Chief, not being upper class, was not privy to this exchange, and he stood on the edge of the terrace looking spare. After a few minutes, Usher broke off, sighing, from the conversation and drifted towards the white-covered table, while John Lambert went over and sat on the far steps, so that he and I balanced each other as the two gloomy onlookers at the party.

It seemed to me that of all the people around the table, Lydia was in the greatest request. She had recovered from her early shock, and I saw that this was a world to which she was very well-suited, and from which she was being unfairly kept by her low-class husband.

Milly Chandler was saying to her: "I don't agree with you about religion. I think it's all lies."

"Is that why the vicar's not here?" asked the wife.

"I notice you make a connection between God and vicars," Milly Chandler said. "I find that interesting. In fact, the Reverend Ridley's not here for the simple reason that he's a perfectly horrible man who once put his hand on my — well, let us say my *derrière*. It was after matins," she added, and at this she started doing a little dance with her glass held high in the air. As I watched her — and watched especially her white, rolling bosom (that ruby necklace was a very brave adventurer) — the manservant and three other servants new to me came down the stone steps carrying a sofa and a divan.

I thought: *Christ, is this for me?*

But Usher indicated the sofa to the ladies, and they sat down in it. He then invited the Chief and Bobby Chandler to the divan, while he remained standing, letting everyone see his perfectly pressed trousers, and the golden watch chain stretched across the silk ribbon that ran around his middle.

During all this, the wife was talking once again about the women's movement, and Usher flashed me a couple of glances as she did so. What had the Chief told him of me?

As the wife spoke, the Chief looked down at the glass of champagne in his hand. He was not in favour of the women's cause: the suffragettes were too pushing. And yet he sat silent. He knew something of what was happening, and was silent on that account. The Chief had once described himself to me as "self-educated" and I wondered whether I fell into that bracket. I had been taught how to fire engines, but did that really count as an education? I knew a dart from a pricker or a paddle, and that "little and often" was the best way with coal and water. But my work had never impressed Lydia, and she'd thought it a blessing when I'd been stood down from the Lancashire and Yorkshire Railway. Well, I'd known what I was taking on when I married her. She was always trying to climb, both for her sex and for herself. She wanted everything a woman could have, and everything a man could have, too.

220

The manservant came over again, and poured more claret. The stuff was too warm. They would have an ice chest somewhere for the champagne.

"Might you stick the claret in the ice for a while?" I said, but the man had already gone, and I was glad about that. *You had a narrow squeak there, Jim!* I thought. Cold claret! The stuff had to be warmish, like blood.

I walked after the manservant, and asked him where the water closet was — I had never called a jakes a water closet before. He directed me through a dark arch cut out of a yew bush, and I was in the territory of the kitchen garden. On low black trees that looked like old men, lemons grew. They glowed in the deep darkness, but *lemons?* Could that be right, even in the heat of this summer? I walked a little way of the gravel path towards them and saw that they were lemon-shaped yellow apples. Anything seemed possible as (having given up my search for the water closet) I pissed by the sweet-smelling compost pens.

When I returned to my former post on the terrace, Usher was speaking to the wife, and I did not like this connection between them. If it continued, I would have to put aside my claret, top-class vintage though it might be, and lay the bastard out.

"Are you quite opposed to violence on behalf of your cause?" he was asking Lydia.

"Not absolutely," replied the wife. "Are you in the case of yours, Captain Usher?"

He gave a half-smile that made his handsomeness double. Lydia never called a man handsome, but you

221

could tell when she thought it. I put my hand into my inside pocket, and there was a single paper there. Lydia said something else about the women's movement, and Usher, lighting a cigarette, said, "Hear, hear!" He seemed to be making out that he agreed with her, but how could he? A man like that was sure to be an Ultra.

I heard the faint sound of the Adenwold clock striking midnight as Milly Chandler stepped onto the lawn with a glass in her hand, calling out that she was looking for glow-worms. A bottle of whisky and a siphon were now on the go, and a cigar box started doing the rounds. As long as both of these stayed away from me, I would not be sick.

Instead, Bobby Chandler came over.

"Lydia and the Captain are hitting it off rather well," he said, but I would not rise to the bait. Instead I asked him in a rather slurring voice about Hardy, the station master.

"I've seen him once or twice," said Chandler. "My brother-in-law told me to look out for him as one of the leading curiosities of the village. To George, the man was a buffoon, plain and simple, but I wonder. He's an amateur historian, you know — hides from the world. His only refuge is with those toy soldiers of his. Seen them, have you?"

"A lot of people around here like midget objects," I said, for some reason.

More claret came.

"Could you manage some more?" asked the manservant, and I replied "Yes" but I knew it would be a struggle. I was crippling myself with this stuff — it

222

was beyond all reason. Was I alcoholic? If not, it was probably because of Lydia. That was the great thing about having a wife. She checked your drinking.

Chandler was moving away from me; John Lambert remained sitting on the far step. My hand still rested on the paper in my pocket. I took it out, and saw the docket that Will Hamer the carter had given me — the proof of the wire having been sent.

Usher was still speaking to Lydia, and still his speech was well-greased.

"The ladies might break a few windows in Oxford Street," he was saying, "but is that so serious a matter? It seems to me they are driven to it not by a deep malice, but simply by the excitement of the moment."

"No," the wife cut in.

"I'm sorry?" said Usher.

"They are not driven to it by the excitement of the moment, but by the injustices of the centuries."

"The excitement of the moment or the injustice of the centuries," said Usher. "I am not going to split hairs over that. The point I wish to make is that they are handled too roughly by the ordinary constables."

I watched the wife's face. I knew when she was likely to give trouble, and all the warning signs were there, but Usher of course could not see them. He was lighting another cigarette. He drew a line of fire in the dark-blue air as he waved out the Vesta, saying:

"The ladies have a will of iron. Unfortunately, their bodies are not made of iron, and all concerned should act accordingly. The watchword of the constables ought to be: 'Remember these are ladies — handle with care.'"

The wife stood up from the sofa and folded her arms. Poor old Usher had jarred, for if there was one thing the wife disliked more than unkind remarks about the women's cause, it was *kind* remarks about it.

I addressed myself again to the data on the docket or receipt in my hand, which seemed to be perpetually being replaced by another version of itself dropped from above, like raindrops repeatedly falling on the same spot. I would make out one or two words, and then it would drop again. As I finally made sense of the receipt and lowered it slowly onto my knees, I noticed that the Chief was looking across the terrace towards me.

He had arrived before the telegram had been sent.

PART THREE

Sunday, 23 July, and
Monday, 24 July, 1911

CHAPTER
TWENTY-FOUR

The butler or manservant gave us a storm lantern, and we used it to light the way back to The Angel. It made the trees swing and rear up as we pushed on, the wife talking about Usher, and how he'd said the women's cause could "bring the women up", and other wrong things.

"I don't think John Lambert's in any danger," she said. "Usher's an ass. But still, you can see that Lambert needs to be taken in hand. He has a condition of some kind, a mental . . . a sort of hysteria, I'm sure brought on by what's going to happen to his brother."

Her success at the party had made her over-confident, it seemed.

"We women have wills of iron but very frail bodies, you know," she ran on. "I suppose Captain Usher's body is made of iron. I'd say his brain probably is."

She broke off in her speech when our light showed a fox on the track before us.

I was drunk but not, as it turned out, in the worst way, for it had been good wine. I felt outside of myself somehow, and revolved my new discovery just as though it had no power to harm me. The paper in my pocket showed that the wire asking the Chief to come to Adenwold had not been transmitted until 12.30, whereas he had arrived by the 12.27 train. I had no idea what had gone wrong with Will Hamer, his rulley or his beasts, but there were any number of possibilities. The Chief had not come to the village on my account; he had arrived quite independently.

I began trying to explain this to the wife, but she was hardly listening, and did not take the point.

". . . It was only a coincidence that we coincided at the station," I said, and she asked, cheerfully enough:

"How drunk are you, Jim?"

In our room, we kissed in a friendly way, for she knew she'd been the star of the evening, even if wrongly dressed and not invited to the meal. Then I turned out the lantern, and the slice of moon moved right up to the open window. I watched it from the pillow thinking: *I am investigating my own Chief.* Nothing could be worse for my prospects or more generally shocking, but I went directly to sleep nonetheless.

I awoke at the chime of three, however, and knew that I could not put off finding an answer.

I stood up, dressed and caught up the lantern we'd been given at the Hall. The wife changed position twice as I did so, but she slept on. Outside the front door of the inn, I lit the lantern, and set off back for the Hall.

The lantern showed swinging, grey-coloured pictures of Adenwold: closed doors, shuttered windows, high blank hedges. I took the early track through the woods, and followed it to the rear gate of the Hall, which now stood unattended. I moved fast across the grass, approaching the lines of cone-shaped trees.

228

The Chinese lanterns on the terrace were now only so much dangling litter, objects of no significance, long since burnt out. The table had been removed, but a line of empty bottles remained on the bottom step of one of the two staircases.

Light glowed from two of the house windows. I turned the lamp off and went up the steps into the mathematical garden. I was not sticking to the complicated paths: I went as the crow flies, and I could feel ornamental plants falling under my boots.

The light in the sky was ash-coloured, a sort of emergency light. There was just enough to see what was important. I had now reached the low windows of the rear of the house, and a voice in my head put the question: *Where are you going?* A sash window standing open gave the answer. I ducked down and I was in, coming bang-up against a piano. I took out my matches, and relit the lantern. The room grew as the light flared — a long yellow room with multiple sofas, as if the contents of many ordinary drawing rooms had been taken into it.

It held no fewer than three wide, peaceful billiard tables. The lantern showed me a dark painting of a boy and a greyhound over the fireplace, and I pictured Sir George Lambert and his sons in this room, each playing his own game on his own table.

I moved now into the hallway, which offered the front door and the main stairs as ways of escape. But I could not have said whether I was aiming to find or avoid the occupants of the house. I began a circuit of the hall, and the first room that I came to contained a harpsichord and many photographs, both on the walls and on the mantel-pieces. They were all of men shooting or hunting, and one showed a cricket game. It ought to have been possible to work out which man was Sir George — his would be the face that cropped up the most often — but I had no time to examine the pictures.

My lantern was like a *magic* lantern, showing me dream-like pictures. The next room along was done out in a Chinese style with tall vases and delicate black cabinets holding pottery that was Oriental in looks but otherwise mysterious to me. The main object in the room was not in the least Chinese, however. It was an old soap crate, and it held more photographs — some framed, some not — and a stack of handwritten papers.

I picked up the first framed photograph. The young man pictured was Master Hugh. He was standing before a tree, and looking as though taken by surprise, but quite happy about it. He was grinning, perhaps on account of his hat, which was completely shapeless in a countrified way. I picked up the first of the papers that was to hand. It was a short note, and the address was Park Place, London S., which I took to be a *good* address.

"My dear Hugh," it began. "This is up to the mark. It has the music of the place. You pretend not to know it, but if you heard a note wrong in the happy speech of the public bar in that pretty village of yours . . . this you would instantly detect. Have you tried Heinemann's? If they bite, you would perhaps be five pounds to the

230

richer, for one book of poetry equals one very good dinner in Mayfair, or one good lunch and a *haircut*."

It was signed "Paul".

I picked up another paper, which carried the heading "Station Hotel, York" and was evidently from John Lambert:

Greetings and thank you for the verses, which I find beautiful, although whether that means anything coming from a railway drudge, I doubt. You asked how my work is going here and you can damn well endure the answer. Many of my supposed talents go to waste in this business, but it might be regarded as useful. Are you bored by railway timetables? You might not be if you knew how they were put together. (How's that, by the way, for the beginning of a chapter in *The Wonder Book of Railways for Boys and Girls*?) . . .

A voice came . . . a woman's voice from the top of the stairs. She was calling out a name I couldn't catch. Bundling some of the letters into my pocket, I reviewed my options. I could retreat into one of the rooms I had so far visited or sprint for the front door. I sprinted, as the voice called again from lower on the staircase. I was quickly at the door, where I set about trying to work the latch.

"You there!" called the voice just at the moment I got the trick of it.

I slid through the door, turned right and dashed across the front of the house, reaching the territory of the dark out-buildings. Some of their doors were open, disclosing a deeper darkness. The dung on the stone walkways combined with the stagnant black air and the smell of engine oil to make a drugged and drowsy atmosphere. I leant against the wall of a workshop, getting my breath and looking towards the gardener's cottage, which stood fifty yards off.

A voice was at my ear.

"Have they brought you in, sir?"

It was the footman or manservant, the one who'd been forcing the claret on me. He wore no tie; his clothes looked hastily put on.

"Into what?" I said, shocked.

"Well," he said, "the search."

"I know that a . . . difficulty has arisen," I said, with fast-beating heart.

"I mean to pray for him, sir," said the manservant. "I believe his soul's in danger."

I eyed the man. It was strange to hear somebody say they meant to pray when they were not in a church.

"He's not well in himself," the man ran on, "and Captain Usher wanted to keep an eye on him. But he burst out of his room about half after one in the morning and he hasn't been seen since."

"Was he not under lock and key?" I asked.

"He is the owner of the house, sir," said the manservant.

"It was Usher who gave chase?"

"Captain Usher and Chief Inspector Weatherill."

232

"Were any shots heard?" I asked, and I saw by the lantern light that the man had closed his eyes. Was this the prayer in the process of being delivered up? He opened his eyes after a few seconds, and carried on briskly, as though he had just sent a telegram.

"How do *you* know that, sir?" said the manservant. "I heard two shots at two o'clock, but I'd gone back to bed by then, and was half-asleep. I just looked at the clock, and I suppose I thought: *Well, it's two for two, like church bells striking.* A few minutes later, I went over to the window again and light was coming across the lawn. It was Captain Usher and Chief Inspector Weatherill. I dashed down to see them, and they said they were looking for Mr Lambert, and I believe they've been about it ever since."

"Did they carry guns?" I asked.

"They both held shotguns."

"*Why*, do you suppose?"

"Well," said the manservant, "suicide is feared."

I supposed he meant that Lambert, bent on suicide, might have been assumed to be armed and generally inclined to shoot.

I shook my head.

"That won't answer," I said.

"I must go to the housemaid, sir," said the servant, "She's very upset."

And this man — a very dutiful fellow indeed — headed off in the direction of the house.

The Chief and Usher were giving out that John Lambert was missing. But I believed they'd done for him.

I held up my lantern and contemplated the gardener's cottage.

As before, the door was on the jar. I pushed it, and entered, setting the lantern in the middle of the floor. Aside from a jumble of what looked like belts and webbing bags on one of the two desks, the room had been cleared and tidied: all the timetables and papers had been piled against the left-hand wall. A blanket was partly draped over the stack of documents. I moved towards it, and saw a last year's Bradshaw. There were thin folded papers inside, acting as bookmarks. One marked a page for "London, Barking, Tilbury" and certain railway stations and times on the "down" line had been circled in ink pen. Here was the easterly drift again. I imagined that John Lambert read timetables in the same way that an art expert looks at a painting, forever spotting curious little details here and there.

I unfolded the paper that had marked the page. It was pale blue, and headed "Sartori's Park View Hotel, Hyde Park Corner, London, S.W." The date was 9 October, 1908, and I recognised Hugh Lambert's writing:

My dear John
  Well, the Squire's chucked me out again, so I'm lodged just around the corner in the above mentioned pensione — very modern with all hygienic desideratas. You entrained for York last week, I think. How do you find the place? I have

spent more time there than you, and feel I ought to be able to supply a few pointers.

I strongly recommend the peacocks of the Museum Gardens who look very proud but are not above taking rolled pellets of bread from your fingers. They can "fly" to the top of the tree, but it looks to me suspiciously like a jump accompanied by flapping of wings. I dragged the Squire to the Museum Gardens once, and could only persuade him to show interest in the peacocks by telling him they were a species of pheasant, which gave him the opportunity to imagine killing them. Peacocks' tails are beautiful: blue and green and iridescent, but the poor peahens come in drab browns. The case is the opposite with the peacocks and peahens here at Sartori's . . .

I heard an approaching voice outdoors, at which my eyes flicked to the bottom of the letter, and the words: *Your disgraceful brother, Hugh*. I dropped the letter back into the Bradshaw, and moved to the front door, ignoring the lantern. I'd made the garden gate by the time I heard the clatter of boots on the flagstones that lay between the out-buildings and the cottage. Usher loomed into view a second later, a blue-eyed shadow. He carried a shotgun by a strap over his shoulder, and it looked about right — this was the fulfilment of the man.

He tilted the gun slightly, and pumped it once. A cartridge was ejected, twirled in air and clattered somewhere in the darkness about his boots. I knew that by this action he had also chambered a new cartridge, ready for firing. He said nothing, but levelled the barrel at me as the Chief appeared from around the same corner. He looked glad to be back in his tweeds and his dinty old trilby hat. He also carried a shotgun — the two of them had perhaps plundered the armoury of the Hall — and he too levelled it and took aim at me.

"Thought you'd have a bit of a poke about, did you?" he said.

With a jerk of his head, he indicated the cottage to Usher. It was permissible, I supposed, for a sergeant major to make a suggestion to a captain in the heat of an engagement.

I walked, under their guns, back into the cottage, and was directed to the main room where the timetables were stacked and my lantern glowed. I was driven by the gun muzzles towards the back of the room, where the two desks stood, and in so directing me I perceived that the gunmen had made rather a bloomer.

A beautiful bone-handled revolver lay in the tangle of martial-looking goods on the desk, and it looked very questing and forward-pointing and eager to be up and at. I watched the shadows of the two shotguns as I contemplated it, and I made my goodbyes to the world and the mysteries of Adenwold, as I picked it up and turned about.

CHAPTER
TWENTY-FIVE

There were now three pointing guns in the room. My own was aimed at the Chief. Two days ago, I might have asked the man's permission before going to the jakes and now I proposed putting a bullet in him.

"You'll put that fucking gun down at once," he said, but he seemed to be only trying the words out for size, hardly believing they'd be heeded.

"I'll fucking not."

"I'll fucking not, *sir!*" roared the Chief.

He took a step forward.

He might threaten to lag me for decades now, or offer me a glass of beer by way of alternative. I stood in exactly the same relation to him as the bank's man had on Platform Five of York station, only not *quite*, for as I met the Chief's gaze I drew back the hammer of the revolver.

"Now you're *threatening* to put me into a baddish temper," said the Chief.

"Between the two of you," I said, "you put a bullet in John Lambert."

Usher flashed a sidelong look at the Chief.

". . . And I can't think of any reason why that might have been a lawful and right thing to do," I said.

A long beat of silence.

"I've told Captain Usher a good deal about you this past day or two," said the Chief. "Your ears must have been buzzing."

"It's more than his ears that'll be buzzing in a minute," said Usher, whose pale-blue right eye looked along the level of his gun barrel.

"*What* did you tell him about me?" I asked the Chief, indicating Usher.

"That you were determined," said the Chief, "hard to put off."

". . . Hard to put off, *with an intact cranium*," said Usher.

"You were seen by the manservant coming back to the house with guns in your hands," I said. "Ten minutes before, two shots had been fired."

Another beat of silence.

The Chief said, "You'll only fire that thing once, you know — and there are two of us."

I said to the Chief: "I don't think I've been properly introduced to your confederate, sir."

The Chief flashed a glance at Usher, who made a movement of his head that I could not interpret. Anyhow, Usher spoke next.

"Why have you taken such a liking to the brothers Lambert?" he asked, looking along the length of his gun. "Can you not see that one is a traitor to his country, and that the other is a member of the cult of —"

"Of what, for Christ's sake?"

"Of Uranus," said Usher, at which the Chief gave a great roar of something like fury and something like amusement, and walked three fast paces towards me with his gun still raised and ready to fire. I dashed down the revolver and he swung at me with his right fist; I swung back with my right *and* my left, and then he was bouncing strangely — hard bald head kept low. He was by repute a heavyweight of the rushing type, but before he could live up to that billing, I rushed at *him* and crowned him again, and his nose was changed by this. He came at me with his left fist raised, but it was the right that struck home, and the Chief had a very good right. A strongman might have picked me up by my boot-heels and swung my head through a full circle into an iron pole.

After an unknown interval of time, I came up to a sitting position with a feeling of having been swimming in heavy seas, a headache and blood in my mouth. The chief was on a level with me and grinning. His nose was like a sign indicating "left" to all his features and his grin seemed to be directed that way, too. His knees were raised and his arms were around his knees. He sat like a happy boy at a camp fire. The Chief liked automatic machine guns and drinking beer under a very hot sun — awkward things — and he had enjoyed our scrap.

I looked at him, and he was all ablaze.

"Go again?" he said, like a man forty years younger. How could I have thought that he was ripe for superannuation? Behind him stood Usher, who was beyond speech, but who still had his shotgun trained on my chest. I did not fear him now, though.

The Chief held his hand over his nose. He seemed to be trying to push it back towards the right.

The revolver still lay on the floor, close to the lantern.

"Why'd you give it up?" the Chief said, indicating the revolver with his boot.

"Because I knew the two of you were right," I said.

"About what?"

"About Hugh Lambert. It was something the wife said."

She had asked me why I did not understand the man, hinting at missing knowledge.

"I knew that if you weren't lying about his . . ."

But I broke off, for the Chief was still adjusting his nose. It was somewhere about middle now but at the cost of a faster flow of blood. Usher walked forward with a silk handkerchief.

"If you weren't lying about *that*," I said, "then I knew you weren't lying about not having killed John Lambert."

"I'm not sure we ever did deny it, did we, sir?" the Chief asked Usher, who was lighting a cigarette.

"I personally never deny anything," Usher said, shaking out the match.

"But you didn't do it," I said.

"The limit," said the Chief, with the handkerchief still held at his nose, "the absolute fucking *limit* was when you said we'd taken two shots over it."

240

The Chief was shaking his head, still with the handkerchief pressed to his nose.

"Why were the shots fired?" I asked.

"Two warnings," said the Chief. ". . . Try and stop him as he raced into the woods."

"And how is he a traitor?"

The Chief flashed a look to Usher, who sighed and said, "It's highly inconvenient that he was invited here tonight. I suppose he can sign the paper, but it's up to you — he's your man, and you know his qualities. By the way, do you think a whisky and soda might help that difficulty of yours, Chief Inspector?"

The Chief rose to his feet, gathering up the revolver; he looked at me, then down at it. He raised the revolver, grinning and levelling it at me, and then with the flourish of a conjuror he made the cylinder swing out and I saw the bullet chambers — saw clean through them, in fact.

It was not loaded.

CHAPTER
TWENTY-SIX

We were in the very long yellow room. After an interval in one of the sculleries involving the ruin of many clean towels and the emptying of most of a bottle of carbolic (both supplied by a parlourmaid), the Chief and I had stanched our wounds, and were kitted out with new, pressed white shirts, which we wore without collars, so that they looked like military tunics. I somehow hoped that they belonged to the manservant rather than any of the Lamberts. Beyond the windows, dawn was breaking, and the heat rising.

The Chief paced with a whisky glass in his hand, but otherwise looked like a barrister in a courtroom as he indicated Usher, his chief witness or exhibit, and the hero and leader of all men not of the Hugh Lambert kind.

His full name, not very surprisingly, was Captain Joscelin Usher — a girl's name, in fact. And while he was known as "Captain" in memory of his glorious exploits in the Royal Marines in Africa and elsewhere, he was currently employed as a detective inspector of the Special Police on commission from the Secret Service Bureau, of which accreditations he was evidently happy to carry no proofs whatever. He operated always in secrecy, but I wondered — as the Chief spoke on — whether it wouldn't have been better for him to have carried some form of identification, instead of just looking put out whenever anyone asked who he was and what he was about. It seemed that the Chief had some connection with the intelligence division of the Army, and in turn with the Secret Service Bureau, and it had been arranged in advance that he, a trusted man, would come to Adenwold to assist Usher in his mission, which amounted to this: put the frighteners on John Lambert.

That was not quite how the Chief put it, of course, but not far off. The two of them had certainly been willing to go as far as threatening to put John Lambert's lights out and the matter might very well have (and might *still*) come to a killing, for the highest interests of the state were involved.

John Lambert had been a very clever student indeed at Cambridge University. He had then joined the North Eastern Railway, which was a surprise move, for men of the graduate sort were only just beginning to enter railway careers in numbers. He'd quickly brought himself under notice for quickness of understanding, and by age thirty he was District Superintendent of the Traffic Department of the Eastern Area, whereas the last man in that post had been in the fifties or older.

"He was then", said the Chief, "taken into a special body of men selected from all the railway companies, and charged with —"

He stopped at this and looked over at Usher, and then the Chief seemed to begin all over again, saying:

"Men and arms can be carried anywhere on rail —"

"And they *will* be, Stringer," Usher put in from the sofa. "Troops, provisions and *matériel*."

At which — as Usher leant forward and put out his cigarette — I wondered whether this "*matériel*" was the same thing as "material".

"I make no predictions as to the nature of any European war," Usher went on, "but the continental railways were laid out with an eye to military considerations and German railways, for example, are owned by the state."

The thought seemed to agitate him to the point where he had to stand up.

"They can hurl their army to any given point at a moment's notice," he said, rising, "and we must be able to do the same. It is not necessary for you to have the full details, Stringer, but since you've thrust yourself forward so far, and on condition of absolute confidentiality . . ."

He walked over to the nearest mantel-piece and collected his own glass of whisky which stood next to my empty one. I had downed it in a single draught, and it had been fuelling my headache ever since.

"A committee was formed," Usher continued, "and provided with imperial funds to formulate working notices — schemes of transportation — to be employed in the event of an emergency."

"Meaning a war with Germany?" I put in.

"There are other, equally dangerous possibilities, Stringer."

"Such as what, sir?"

244

There was a beat of silence, and then the fellow coloured up and grinned, looking almost girlish; I liked him for it, and I grinned back at him.

"Imagine the complexities, Stringer," he went on, replacing his glass. "Offensive and defensive railway schemes to be created, supply depots to be nominated. The coaling of the home fleet to be accomplished — now how do you suppose *that* is to be managed in time of war?"

"That's to be done under heavy guard from Hull," said the Chief, lighting up a new cigar.

Usher was checked for a moment by this intervention of the Chief's, whose nose looked different again with a cigar beneath it.

"The schemes are constantly tested with practice mobilisations," Usher continued, "during which ordinary services are to be carried on as far as possible. The committee men work in the offices of their own companies and at a central co-ordinating office in London, They are few in number — kept to a minimum by the requirement of absolute secrecy — and the weight of work is very great. I am told they are all very brilliant, and with intellectual brilliance comes a degree of waywardness, as I'm sure you appreciate, detective sergeant."

"Try to picture yourself as intellectually brilliant, lad," the Chief cut in. "Imagine yourself into that situation."

Usher caught up his whisky glass again, and sipped at it.

"That said," he ran on, "John Lambert had appeared until lately to be a man of impeccable character. But his defect has been disclosed, and it takes the form of an excessive loyalty to his murdering brother."

"I don't believe he is a murderer," I said.

"Hugh Lambert had a liking for the country-side," said Usher, ignoring me, "but he would also spend a good deal of time in London making — well, making free." Usher replaced the glass once again, adding: ". . . Making free in *Mayfair*."

He was looking at me, but I had never been to Mayfair.

"The long and the short of it, Stringer," he said, "is that John Lambert has tried to black-mail us — *Britain*, I mean. He has proposed to disclose a digest of the mobilisation notices to our enemies unless his brother is reprieved and the sentence commuted."

"He means to disclose the information *to the Germans*?" I said.

"If you want to put it like that, yes," said Usher.

He saw off the remainder of his whisky, and sank back down into the sofa.

"Has he told you who he thinks did the murder?" I enquired.

"He has not been good enough to do that," said Usher. "The limit of his contention is that his brother did not have the character to do it."

I nodded.

"What happened to the man Gifford? Why did the train not stop? Why were the wires cut?"

The two exchanged glances. They would ration their answers.

"The wires are cut", said the Chief, "because we cut 'em. Had to be done. They were newly connected to the telephone — this place and the station both."

"You see, the possibilities are three," said Usher. "One: John Lambert was merely making an idle threat. Two: he genuinely intends to pass on the scheme of mobilisation but hasn't yet. Three: he has already done it. We have kept an eye on him here, and removed the danger of a telegram being sent that might direct the recipient to where the data is located. But Lambert has hinted that a message might be conveyed to some intermediary through no action on his part. It might be transmitted by *default*, do you understand?"

I did not.

"Some bugger down in London might be primed," put in the Chief. "If you don't hear from me by such and such a time on so and so date, give the package held in locker number one at Euston station to Mr X."

"Or the middleman might have been here in the village," said Usher.

"If that happens, then three years of concentrated brainwork is lost," said Usher. "On top of that, our enemies may prefer to act quickly, directing an invasion force to those parts appearing from the plans to be less well protected."

"You'll see now", said the Chief, "why I was a little offhand with you at the do last night."

I looked towards the French windows, which stood open. The heat of day was present, but the light of summer was quite missing.

"We mean to lay hands on Lambert," said Usher. "A detachment of ordinary constables is coming here by motor from Malton."

"How were they summoned?"

"Never you mind."

"John Lambert believed you meant to kill him," I said.

Usher nodded once.

"It was my own favoured solution," he said. "It seemed to have the benefit of elegance."

"Only trouble being," said the Chief, "that if we'd put his lights out, then we wouldn't know whether the documents had been passed on or not."

"And my instructions were to employ diplomacy in the first instance," said Usher.

I said, "Wouldn't it have been worth reprieving Hugh Lambert to avoid all this bother?"

"You're the first person involved in this case to make such a suggestion, Detective Stringer," said Usher; and he evidently considered this answer enough, for he sat down again, saying, "That's all, Stringer. In due course you will be required to sign a contract pursuant to a new Act of Parliament. It binds you to secrecy on pain of prosecution."

"Do you not want me to give a hand with the search?" I asked, standing.

Usher shook his head, and I knew why. The constables would be kept in ignorance of the reason for the search, and he thought I might give it away. He wanted me kept well clear of all developments. He'd told me as much as he had in order to satisfy my curiosity, and so remove my need to solve the puzzle of John Lambert.

"Right then," I said, "I'll be off."

I took the sporting cap out of my pocket, put it on my head and walked under the steady blue gaze of Usher towards the opened French windows.

"Remember, Detective Sergeant Stringer," Usher called out as I left, "*absolute* secrecy."

I stepped through the French windows, and a noise made me look to the right, where the wife crouched just beyond the last of the windows. As I approached her, she stood up and joined me just as though she'd been marketing in Coney Street, York.

"You heard every word of that, I take it?" I said.

"All except the last words Usher spoke," she said. "But I think he was telling you again that the matter must not go beyond the four walls of that room."

She turned and gave me a grin. But it didn't last, for the silver-haired man in the white dust-coat now stepped between us.

"Back inside with you two," he said, in a strong Yorkshire accent that I would never have expected.

CHAPTER
TWENTY-SEVEN

The room was in the eaves of the house. There was next to nothing in it besides a truckle bed, a locked cupboard, a table and a hairbrush that could have been a man's or a woman's. A photograph of a young woman stood on the tiny window-sill, and she must either have been the occupant of the room — when not in Scarborough — or the sweetheart of the occupant.

Coming upon us late, the dust-coated special policeman — name of Cooper — had got the false idea that we'd both been eavesdropping on the Chief and Usher. But he hardly relented when the true situation was explained. He had found us to be making light of a grave national danger, and there was more than a hint in his arguments that we would try to come to the traitor's aid. The Chief had put a word in for me, but it counted for nothing. Cooper was junior to Usher, but Usher agreed with his man, and so we were stowed at the top of the house, and the door locked behind us.

The wife hadn't seemed to mind too much.

"At least they're not trying to be gentlemanly," she said.

She sat on the bed, and asked for another look at Hugh Lambert's papers.

250

"Now we're in a cell just like him," she muttered, after leafing through them for a while.

A few minutes later, she passed me one of the sheets, saying, "This is interesting."

I read:

Father and the Reverend Ridley hit it off splendidly. The Reverend never mentioned that father did nothing besides romp around the estate blasting animals, and father returned the favour. Father was unsettled to discover that Ridley kept a model railway in his house but the only other point of antagonism between the two of them was Emma, my former governess, who continued to appear at the Hall long after her efforts had secured my admission into Eton. Her new role, according to father, was to give him "French lessons". He often accused me of being too familiar with gutter slang, but some acquaintanceship with it on his own part might not have come amiss.

I am sure that the Reverend, however, saw nothing amusing in the situation, for he liked Emma. She could stop him in his tracks, even with a cricket game in prospect.

I handed the papers back to the wife, telling her I'd heard something similar from Chandler at the party.

"Didn't Mrs Handley tell us that the vicar had a fancy woman at a village near here?" asked the wife. "You don't suppose it's this Emma, do you?"

I eyed her for a while as she went back to reading. She was becoming properly interested in new explanations of the murder at the very moment we'd been stopped from investigating them. I fished in my pocket for my silver watch: six o'clock.

Hugh Lambert had twenty-six hours to live.

I looked out of the window. This would be a hot day, but not sunny. In the grey light, the mathematical garden looked just mathematical, and not at all beautiful, and the stone pond from this height appeared over-crowded with great, aimlessly floating goldfish. Each checkmated the other: they were all in a fix because someone had too much money. I looked up, towards the woods. Was John Lambert hiding there? Of course, I wanted him found. He had been black-mailing Britain, but somehow I couldn't help thinking that Britain was Usher and the Chief more than it was me. By the very fact of knowing the danger the country faced, they became men who had more to lose *from* that danger. It was wrong-headed of me, I knew, but I felt that I would rather see Hugh Lambert spared the noose than his brother found.

I'd thought that John Lambert was going to lay name to the killer. Instead, he'd proposed to trade the whole country for his brother's life.

At eight o'clock the manservant came with coffee and bread rolls, and the poor bloke didn't know where to look. The night before we'd been guests of the house; now we were its prisoners. After breakfast, we swapped over: the wife looked out of the window, and I looked again at the papers of Hugh Lambert. After a few false starts, owing to his bad handwriting, I struck:

It is perfectly possible to catch a rabbit by hand if you approach it downwind, and it is perfectly possible to release it subsequently. I have taught young Mervyn the trick of the first but not the habit of the second. I know that he sells rabbits to the carter, who takes them to the butchers of the other Adenwolds, and I know he sells moleskins to the blacksmith Ainsty, and that he once sold a job lot of them to Hamer, who distributed them amongst the plumbers of Malton in return for considerable profit. Moleskins are ideal for cleaning the joints of freshly soldered pipes, unfortunately for the moles.

I have taught the boy to draw these creatures, in the hope of curing his habit of snaring them, but his addiction to killing rabbits rivals, I fear, that of father. Mervyn practically lives in the woods, but I am aware that he makes a special point of lurking there when father is out after rabbits, knowing very well that the pleasure for father is all in the killing and not in the acquisition of meat, and that Tom, father's lumbering old spaniel, misses half the corpses in any case.

"Here's something," I said, calling across to the wife. She read it over and looked up, worried, just as a knock came at the door.

It was Usher. Cooper, still in his dust-coat, was behind him. We would be allowed to go, but we must consent to be chaperoned by Cooper until John Lambert was brought in. A full search was evidently now under way. As we left the room, Usher practically bowed to the wife, taking credit for a decision that I suspected had been forced on him by the Chief, but she swept past him without a word, for he was back to being gallant.

The wife went on ahead, I walked in the middle, Cooper lagged behind silently; and that was how we crossed the lawn and approached the path through the woods. It hadn't been settled that we'd go that way — it just fell out like that. The day was sticky and grey; the clouds rolled like smoke over the fire of the sun. As the light came and went, so did the shadows of the decorative trees.

As we entered the woods, the wife for some reason turned a new way, and we came by the railway line and the telegraph poles. The cut in the wires that we'd seen already lay in the other direction, and the present ones were intact as far as could be made out, but I knew there must be an interruption somewhere. As we walked on, parallel to the tracks, I took out my silver watch. Ten o'clock. In five minutes the "down" train would come by, very likely having by-passed the station like the train of the evening before. There was no point in asking Cooper about any of this. He had a fine head of silver hair and black eyebrows, a combination that seemed to dictate silence. I also knew that he'd taken strong exception to the wife and me on the strength of the conversation he'd overheard between us outside the yellow room. My persuasion was that he thought us a pair of mischief-makers rather than traitors, but still his dislike was obvious.

The man was a sort of grey angel of death. He would keep me from discovering the truth about the shooting of Sir George, and so he would bring Hugh Lambert — an innocent man, as I was increasingly certain — to his doom.

But as it turned out, we shook Cooper off with no bother at all.

At just gone ten, he hailed us from behind.

"Hold on there," he shouted. "I'm off behind a tree."

He stepped away from the path a little and made water as I heard the first spots of rain on the leaves overhead; he'd seemed to bring it on by pissing. As Cooper stepped away from the path I took off my cap, which was prickling my head. The wife leant against a tree up ahead, kicking the trunk with her boot-heel.

The rhythm of her kicking was gradually drowned out by that of the 10.05, which was upon us a moment later. It had not stopped at the station but unlike the train of the night before, was coming on at a moderate pace, as though picking its way through the trees.

"Look out there!" the wife suddenly yelled, and Cooper stepped out from behind his tree with his hands on his fly buttons.

"There's a man just leapt up onto that train," said the wife. "I believe it was John Lambert."

She'd had the same view of the train as I'd had, and no such event had occurred, but Cooper was flying again, white coat-tails streaming behind him. He could just about keep up with the high coaches, but he measured his pace until he was level with the guard's van, which offered hand-holds. The guard was leaning out and looking down at him as he ran, as though admiring an athletic prodigy. But Cooper was screaming at the guard to stand back so that he could make his leap, and just as the train was picking up its pace, he did so.

It was a good leap, and he gained the handholds without difficulty, but one of his legs swung out, and clattered into a stout-looking tree branch. The guard pulled him into the van a moment later, and the train retreated from view, leaving great peacefulness and freedom, and the sound of dripping rain.

I eyed the wife.

"Well, you might have *thought* you saw something," I said. "It *might* have been an honest mistake."

"I don't think you'd have any difficulty persuading Usher that a woman had made a mistake," she said.

The rain came on, making the sound of many small creeping animals.

"What now?" I said.

"Mervyn?" she said.

I nodded: "His place in the woods — the set-up."

We found the clearing, and the boy was there, amid the river sound, the fallen trees and the rusting foresters' machinery. Raindrops came down at intervals, widely spaced, and the boy was placing what looked like small sticks on a fire. He stepped back from the flames as we came up. His shotgun lay on the ground, with the bill-hook hard by.

He wore breeches, and a coat that looked like moleskin. His head seemed small under the mass of his hair. Any man of middle years would have given worlds for hair like that. He said nothing as we approached.

"Caught a fish, Mervyn?" I enquired, for he'd given that as the reason for his fires.

"I *en't*," he said.

"Then what are you burning?"

The wife hung back; Mervyn Handley looked at the fire, and I could see very well what he was about. He was trying to work himself up to a lie, but he could not do it.

"Bones," he said.

The white sticks in the flames *were* bones.

"Dead birds if you ask me," I said, looking into the flames, "and disappearing fast."

I looked at Mervyn, and he gave a brief nod before looking away.

"Pheasant?" I said.

"Moorhen," said Mervyn. "Moorhen and kestrel."

"Bagged 'em with that, did you?" I said, with a glance at the shotgun.

"I wouldn't shoot a kestrel," he said. "*Couldn't.*"

"Too fast, I suppose," I said, "and they fly too high?"

"Not that one," said Mervyn, nodding down at the flames, which had now all-but consumed the bones. "'Alf-dead to begin with, he were."

"What happened, Mervyn?" put in the wife.

"Kestrel attacked the moorhen . . . Never would've done it if he hadn't been half-starved . . . Pair of 'em scrapped in air, then they come down together like a stone."

The kestrel was "he"; the moorhen "it".

"As they fought, they'd forgotten to fly," said the wife.

"That's it," said Mervyn, looking at her.

"And you kept the bones," I said.

"Aye," said Mervyn.

". . . Until now, anyhow," I said, and he made no answer to that. "Why until now?" I asked, after a beat of silence.

"Wanted shot of 'em," he said, moving his hair away from his eyes.

There came another fast, scuffling sound from the woods, and Mervyn Handley crouched down and took up his shotgun. I found myself taking a step back. He was armed, I was not. And what sort of kid was this anyway? The scuffling sound came again, louder this time. A rabbit flew into the clearing, and it was running for its life even before Mervyn levelled the rifle, took aim and blasted. A great flash of flame came from the gun; the rabbit somersaulted twice in the air and lay still. But Handley made no move towards it. Instead, he continued to eye me directly and levelly, as if to say, "Now look."

"What do you know about the killing of Sir George, Mervyn?" I asked him, as something scuttled in terror through the trees.

"Nowt," he replied, and I was certain that I had finally driven him to a lie.

We walked back fast from the woods, without quite knowing why. The rain had stopped, and we came by the cricket pitch just as it was lit by a flash of sun. We gained the second green, and approached the hedge-tunnel, but we had to wait as the second charabanc of the week-end came into view. It contained the coppers from Scarborough. Most of them smoked, as did the motor, which was driven by a man who looked to be concentrating harder than he ought.

We walked on up the hedge-tunnel and past the station, which was silent and empty.

"Who needs trains when a motor's available?" asked the wife, and I wondered whether it would ever come that there were *road* police to go alongside the railway force.

The Angel was fairly bustling, and as I stepped towards the bar — where Mr Handley was serving — I heard one fellow say, "Will's been on cracking form in the nets," and realised that at least one cricket team was in, even though nobody had yet put on their whites. I also spied Woodcock and the signalman in the corner. Both wore rough suits, and twisted greasy neckers, and both might have been waiting to appear before the magistrates at any police court in the country. Of course, there was no question of me seeing Woodcock without him seeing *me* and he lifted up his glass in a sarcastic sort of way, saying, "Journalist!"

Of the Reverend Martin Ridley there was no sign, even though I had the idea that he was the keenest cricketer of the lot. He would no doubt be preparing for the game by drinking wine of a better vintage than was offered by The Angel.

The wife was craning to see all around the bar. She wanted to find Mrs Handley, I knew, and to talk to her about Mervyn.

"Rain's holding off, boys," said one of the cricketers, and his remark for some reason made me feel anxious. I put my hand in my inside pocket, and brought out the letters I'd taken from the Hall. I looked each one over quickly, before passing it on to the wife. They were written by Hugh Lambert, either to the man Paul, or to John Lambert. They'd been sent from London hotels or a house in Bayswater, London W. The dates were 1907 and 1908 — well in advance of the murder. They were about poems and parties; and some were about nature and country matters. As I was reading, I heard the wife say, "These are some of Hugh Lambert's letters, Mrs Handley. Jim borrowed them from the Hall."

The wife passed a couple of the letters across to Mrs Handley, who looked them over for a while. Then she handed the bundle back to Lydia, lifted the bar flap and moved towards the front door of the pub, saying, "I've something to show you."

She came back a minute later, pushing her way through the cricketers, and holding a paper — another letter by the looks of it. She passed it first to Lydia, who read it over quickly before handing it to me. Well, after

260

all the Mayfair hotels the address did come as a shock, for this dated from the time after his arrest for murder:

"His Majesty's Prison Wandsworth, Heathfield Road, London S." The letter was addressed to Mrs Handley. It began with thanks for a letter of hers, and "all the news of The Angel". Hugh Lambert then fell to talking about the prison:

There is a warder here called Parkhurst, which causes me to wonder whether there is a warder in Parkhurst Prison called Wandsworth. The man seems doubly displaced because he also bears a remarkably close resemblance to Dawlish, the chaplain at my old college. But he is much nicer than Dawlish.

As you can already tell, this place is doing peculiar things to my mind, but I am otherwise perfectly content. Everything is wonderfully concentrated, and you have the whole world here in its distilled essence. The sparrows in the yard do duty for the Adenwold country-side; a cigarette after supper (or "tea") is an evening in the bar of the Ritz, and as for "prisoners' association" — well, that's a chapter from a Dickens novel. Please send my best regards to your husband, and tell Mervyn to look for a robin's nest in the old plum tree in the graveyard. There are two holes in the trunk at the start of the branches. When I saw it last, the north-facing one was occupied by the family of robins; the other (west facing) was occupied by a family of flycatchers, and the robin parents fed the flycatchers and vice versa, which I found charming. Enclosed are two sketches for Mervyn. The first is a robin and a flycatcher side by side, the second (as I do hope you can tell) is of a mole. I don't know why. Perhaps, in my present situation, I should turn mole. Do tell Mervyn, by the way, that if a mole were the size of a man he would create a tunnel his own width and thirty-seven miles long after a typical night's work.

I handed the letter back to Mrs Handley, and she was on the edge of tears.

"The drawings are at the framers in Malton," she said. "I'm going to put them up in place of the fish pictures."

(You'd have thought wall space came at a premium in The Angel, whereas in fact the fish pictures were the only ones in the place.)

"We saw Mervyn in the woods just now," I said. "He was burning bird bones: a kestrel and a moorhen."

The wife was frowning at me, but I'd checked Mrs Handley's tears at any rate.

"The kestrel attacked the moorhen, and they came down together," she said. "It happened out at the back here. Our Mervyn came racing in to tell me while I was talking to Master Hugh. We all went out to see, and Hugh looked down at these two birds and he said something like 'That's father and I'. Mervyn heard it quite distinctly, and when the police were first here asking all their questions I was daft enough to let on.

Well, they had Mervyn in — took me and him by train to York, and asked us that many questions. The boy was in tears from the moment we left to the moment we came back — I've never seen him in such a state."

"He told us he'd never travelled by train," I said.

"He never has *since*," said Mrs Handley. "Put him off for life, that trip did."

"That's why you never went to Scarborough," said the wife, and Mrs Handley said, "Yes. It was a consideration."

"Was his statement put in?" I said. "Was he called as a witness?"

Mrs Handley shook her head. "It never came to that," she said.

I noticed there was a small glass of wine on the bar in front of her. I had never seen her drink before.

"Mrs Handley," I asked her, "do you really think that Master Hugh is a murderer?"

She just drained her glass, and said, "Do you want some dinner?"

We went over to a table and ate some cheese and cold meats while crowded in by the cricketers. At one point, they were so arranged that I saw a clear channel through them, and station master Hardy was at the end of it, sitting at a table in the "public". He looked red-faced, perhaps on account of his suit, which looked very constricting. Every so often, one of the strapping cricketers would go over and place an empty pint glass on his table, and each time I glimpsed Hardy there were more and more glasses containing sticky dregs under his nose. It wasn't so much that the cricketers were not mannerly, or that they were drunk, it was just that they didn't seem to notice him at all.

When Mrs Handley came to collect the plates, I asked whether Mr Gifford had pitched up.

"Now, where he's gone I don't know," she said, with a distracted look.

Well, I would not tell her what little I knew on that score. But I did let on that John Lambert had gone missing from the Hall. (It couldn't hurt to mention it; the fact would soon be common knowledge with all those coppers in the district looking for him.)

Then the wife said, "Where's our bicyclist, Mrs Handley?"

"I've no idea, I'm sure," she said.

"Has he booked out?" asked the wife.

"He has not."

"When was he *due* to book out?"

"No date's been given. He's paid for yesterday and he's paid for today, and he can keep doing that as long as he likes as far as I'm concerned. His bicycle's gone, though, you might have noticed."

"But it's punctured," said the wife.

"Well," said Mrs Handley, "I saw him pushing it off into Clover Wood not one hour since."

CHAPTER
TWENTY-EIGHT

We stood outside the front of The Angel looking at the soft grey-ness of the sky, the great trees bright green against it. The rainbow was half there and half not, like the memory of a dream, and seeming to carry the message: this is not what you'd call the perfect summer's day but it's beautiful in its way, you know.

Two chimes floated up from the village.

"Hugh Lambert has eighteen hours left alive," I said.

"And what about your investigation?" asked the wife.

"In the first place . . ." I said.

"I think time's too short for 'in the first place'," said the wife.

". . . You don't think Hugh Lambert murdered his father," I said, "and nor do I."

"Mervyn's the key to it, wouldn't you say?" asked the wife — and it wasn't quite like her to be asking questions in this way. As a rule she didn't give tuppence what I thought. Instead, she was giving me a chance to say what she herself couldn't.

Just then, the blurred voice of Mr Handley came from behind us.

"Where *is* that boy?" he said. "He's late for his bloody dinner."

He held a pewter of ale in his hand, and because of this and the natural impairment of his speech, it was impossible to know how worried he might be. I turned to him and said, "We'll keep our eyes skinned."

He turned and went back inside his pub. We watched him do it, and the wife said, "I do wonder about that bicyclist, you know."

He'd always been a special study of the wife's, and this was down to the shocking business of seeing him stab his own tyre. All bicyclists were martyrs to rough roads: their machines were too flimsy and were forever getting crocked, and the bicyclists were forever moaning about it. To see the damage self-inflicted put the whole thing on its head.

"Clover Wood is that way," I said, pointing directly over-opposite.

This time, I found a track rather than crashing on through the undergrowth, and I led the wife along it. Wherever the path divided, we took the wider route, but these would become narrow after a while, and we'd end in a jam of trees and thorn bushes. We pressed on through narrow gaps until we did at last strike another good-sized track. It was lined with tall everlastings of a very dark green, and by rights ought to have led to a blank-faced tomb or cemetery. In fact it led to a perfectly round clearing: a Piccadilly Circus of the woods with a fallen log in its centre, two people sitting on the log and two bicycles on the ground hard by. I knew that one bicycle would be punctured, the other not. We were about fifty yards short of the couple, who were the bicyclist from The Angel and a young woman

I'd never set eyes on before. Their voices carried along the track, and I motioned the wife into a gap between two of the everlastings. I stepped in after her, and watched the couple.

The fellow's arm was around the waist of the young woman. It rested there rather guiltily — that arm knew it was taking a liberty — and the conversation went stiffly.

"It is a very happy chance that you came along, Dora," the fellow said.

"But I don't have a puncture repair outfit," said the woman.

"Even so," said the bicyclist.

("That's very magnanimous of him," whispered the wife, as a silence fell between the two on the tree trunk.)

"There's practically everything *but* a puncture repair outfit in my saddle-bag," the young woman eventually said.

"I'll take it into the blacksmith's again tomorrow," said the man. "I tried him yesterday but he wasn't about."

"Do blacksmiths fix punctures?" asked his companion. "After all, I'd have thought it was a rather delicate operation and *they're* all fires and hammers."

"He might be able to fettle up a couple of tyre levers," the fellow said.

"Why do you need a tyre lever?"

"For levering off the tyre. It's very hard to get the modern Dunlops over the wheel rim without one."

"Oh."

And they sat silent once again.

("He'll lose all feeling in that arm of his," I whispered to the wife.)

"I don't suppose that you find bicycles very interesting as a topic of conversation," the bicyclist said, after a further minute.

"Well," said the young woman, "I'd rather ride them than talk about them."

"That goes for so many things, don't you find?" asked the bicyclist, who immediately coloured up. He was getting nowhere fast with his spooning.

"You see, my original plan," he went on, "as I think you knew, was to make for Helmsley after spending just Friday night at The Angel. It was only the condition of the machine that made me hang on here."

"I come along this track most Sundays about this time," Dora said with a sort of sigh.

You don't want them sighing at this stage, I thought. But the fellow answered her sigh with a sigh of his own, followed by the remark: "Well, no fear of an interruption here."

And somehow that did the trick, for after an interval of staring forward in silence they both turned towards each other and began kissing, which they continued to do as the wife crept off the way we'd come with me following, and as the Adenwold church bells began striking three.

CHAPTER
TWENTY-NINE

Come five o'clock, we were watching the cricket game.

I stood on the boundary by the three poplars; the wife, being restless, was making a circuit of the ground. I was thinking about how, coming out of the woods, we'd struck two of the coppers in the search party. I'd asked them whether they'd come upon any scent of "their quarry", and one of the two had said, "The quarry? That's over yonder, en't it?" which had made me think John Lambert might yet escape them.

We'd just given up a hunt of our own: for young Mervyn. Our best hope seemed to be to find him and hustle him into saying what he knew, but Mervyn was not at his set-up and had evidently not returned to The Angel, for we'd come across Mrs Handley who'd told us that she was also searching for him. She had not been over-anxious, though: the boy was allowed the run of the woods and fields, and would often tramp off to East or West Adenwold and stay out all day.

The cricket game was being played against a great wall of grey sky that was darkening by the minute, and which made the players' whites seem to glow. A woman I'd never seen before stood by the pavilion twirling a lacy parasol, and I thought: *That'll have to do duty as an umbrella before long.* A second charabanc had brought the second team (the two motors were now drawn up alongside the pavilion), and she must have come in with them.

The first innings had ended after a shockingly short period of time, and the Reverend Ridley was giving directions to his team, who — having batted and scored thirty-six — were now about to go out and field.

The pep talk concluded, some of the players performed physical jerks as they strode out, for all the world as if they were about to do something strenuous. There might have been raindrops already flying, or it might just have been the colour of the sky that made me think so.

The players were now all arranged.

A fast bowler ran up and, reaching the wicket, leapt and pedalled his legs as though cycling — seeming, as he rose, to make the shape of a sea-horse in the air. He landed running; the ball flew past the batsman, who turned and watched it rise into the hands of the wicket keeper, who, having caught it, chucked it to another fielder and gave the batsman the evil eye for a while.

Then it all started again.

The wife was now at my shoulder on the boundary.

I asked her: "Did you hear what the vicar was saying?"

"Something to someone about not sending a lot down on the leg side to Pepper. He said they'd be absolutely slaughtered if Pepper got a lot to leg. He'd only have to start glancing at their legs, and they'd all be finished."

270

"I expect Pepper's the man in bat just now," I said. "What are the teams called, do you know?"

"The Enemies and the Friends," the wife said, in a vague sort of way.

"No," I said, "I don't think you can have that right."

The wife, pointing at the umpire, asked, "Why is the referee wearing two hats? It's not sunny and he's wearing two sun hats."

"That's exactly *why* he's wearing two," I said.

A third ball was bowled. The wicket keeper failed to stop it, and he looked down at his white boots as if he'd never seen them before while another fellow went into the woods to collect the ball.

"The umpire might end up wearing any number of hats and woollens," I said. "The players give him whatever they don't need."

Another ball was bowled, and the batsman stopped it dead. He did the same again twice more, and then there was a general collapse into chaos as everyone began walking long distances in different directions.

"What's going on now?" said the wife, sounding quite alarmed.

"End of the over," I said.

At the end of the disturbance another bowler stood ready, but the wife was still interested in the umpire.

"He's the man in charge of the game?"

"He is."

"How can he command any respect if he's wearing two hats?"

"I suppose he must rely on force of character."

271

I turned towards the wife, but she was walking away again along the boundary.

"Hold still," I called, for another ball was about to be bowled.

"Why?" she called, turning about.

"You shouldn't move behind the bowler's arm," I said. "It's distracting."

"How can I distract him if I'm behind him and being perfectly quiet?"

"It distracts the *batsman*."

"What rot," the wife said, and she set off again.

Well, we were just lingering out the hot, grey afternoon, wasting the time, I could not influence the wife in the slightest degree, let alone prevent one death and solve the mystery of another. For want of anything better to do I counted the men on the fielding side, going clockwise from the vicar, who stood only a little way from my boundary position. Having counted them once, I did so again.

I could make them only ten.

I began pacing the boundary, as though I might discover another player by viewing the game from a different angle. I had not seen one of them make off during the game. Had they arrived at the ground as ten? But no, the vicar wouldn't have stood for that.

. . . It was just that I was that bloody *tired*. I started counting again as another ball was bowled, and the batsman smashed it for six into the woods. The fielder nearest to me put his hands on his hips and said, "Oh my eye."

272

One by one, most of the fielding players disappeared into the edge of the woods. The ball was lost. The two batsmen met in the middle of the pitch for a confab, and the wicket keeper took one of his gloves off and examined his hand, which was evidently just as fascinating as his boots. The wife came wandering up to me again.

"What's happened now?"

"They've lost the ball."

She rolled her eyes.

One of the fielders, on the border of the woods, was looking agitated and calling to the others, but it wasn't until the two batsmen broke off their talk that I knew something was up. I half-ran, half-walked across the pitch, and when I came to the edge of the woods, I saw the players gathered around some object. I could not at first make it out, for they surrounded it, and it lay in long grass. I pushed my way through, and saw in the grass a dead dog. Half its head was perfect, and the other half was not there.

"Shotgun," said one of the cricketers, eyeing me.

The dog was a terrier — Mervyn's, name of Alfred.

CHAPTER
THIRTY

When the players went back onto the pitch, I counted a full complement of eleven fielders.

"I'm sure there was one less before the dog was found," I said to the wife, and at that instant the sky darkened yet further, and the rain started again. The players at first walked towards the pavilion, but as the rain came faster they began to run.

"I don't think there's anything for it but to get out into the woods and look for Mervyn," I said as, five minutes later, we made our way under the rain back towards the second village green of Adenwold. "I'll borrow an oilskin from the pub."

"We'll be soaked through if we walk in this," she said. "Let's sit in the church."

But it turned out that the Reverend Ridley kept the door locked; so we sat on the two bench seats in the porch, and talked over what had happened and what might happen. At twenty to six, we heard the bolts being released on the inside of the church door, and it swung open to reveal a face I could not at first place: it was Moffat, the amiable man who kept the baker's shop. He had entered the church by another door. Some muttering between him and the wife revealed him to be a reader at the church or a helper of some sort, or there again perhaps standing in for the verger, who was in Scarborough. At any rate, he passed us hymn books, and showed us to a front pew. Evening Prayer was in the offing.

The baker went away to ring the bell, and I thought of the other bell — the one that would be ringing in Durham gaol in fourteen hours' time. The church had a medical smell — incense — and was filled with a kind of silvery rain-light. I wondered who would come to the service, since most of the village was in Scarborough. The answer was disclosed over the next five minutes: the baker's daughter came, and two of the tiny old ladies we'd seen outside the almshouses. They sat at the back, smiling with their faraway eyes. The manservant from the Hall came, and with him the maid who'd assisted him at the party. It occurred to me that they might be married. The manservant smiled a little at me, embarrassed no doubt at having been my gaoler. As the clock was striking six, some of the cricketers came in: big men trying to look smaller as they eased along the pews.

The Reverend Ridley made his entrance at just gone six. He wore a black cassock, and his red head and black body seemed to belong to two different people; the prayer book was tiny in his hand, but it soon became obvious that he hardly needed to look at it. He knew the ropes; he really was a vicar after all. It was a plain, short service: no music, just the vicar, the prayer book and Bible readings from the baker. He did them very well, and I thought: *That's what the fellow's really about.* He was a church-goer first and a baker second.

When the vicar blessed us all, I had an idea we were approaching the end of proceedings, and it was at this point that I heard the scrape of the door opening.

I turned about, half-expecting to see John Lambert, but it was Mervyn Handley who stood there. He held his shotgun by his side, like a staff. The baker immediately rose and went towards him saying, very calmly as it seemed to me, "You can't bring that in here, Mervyn Handley."

The vicar had paused in his reading. He was eyeing the boy.

"Where *can* I put it, then?" I heard Mervyn ask in a sulky voice.

"In the umbrella stand in the porch," said the baker.

Well, it was the country-side after all. Every man jack was armed. A shotgun in an umbrella stand might be nothing out of the common here. Mervyn went out and came back in, but when he saw me, he coloured up and looked around, as if contemplating a breakaway.

"What's he doing in here?" I whispered to the wife. "He's Catholic."

"I've an idea," said the wife.

The Reverend Ridley finished off the service, and the wife stood up fast and followed Mervyn through the door and into the porch, where he was removing his shotgun from the umbrella stand. The other church-goers were giving him a wide berth.

"Don't you think it would be better if you gave us the gun?" Lydia asked the boy.

276

"No," he said.

"You don't need to go to church to talk to God, you know," the wife ran on. "And you don't need to go for forgiveness."

The boy kept silence.

We were out into the churchyard now. The rain had stopped; it was only dripping off the trees. A flare of sunlight came through the clouds and the wife said to Mervyn: "If you really want to be forgiven, and you really do repent — well then, you already *are* forgiven."

". . . Because I don't much care for goin' to church," said the boy.

"Not many do," I said.

Another silence.

"It's dead boring," I put in.

"Oh, don't listen to him," said the wife.

"I en't," said the boy, and he looked at Lydia as though on the point of further speech.

"If you know anything about the murder that happened here, you must let on," I said. "Master Hugh has only fifteen hours left to live."

At which he turned on his heel.

"Where are you off now?" I called after him.

"Look for me dog," he said.

"No, Mervyn!" called Lydia, hurrying after him.

I looked across to the vicarage. A woman stood at the garden gate. The Reverend Ridley approached her. She was pretty, in a white dress, and she twirled what was either a parasol or a dainty umbrella. It was the woman who'd been watching the cricket. Ridley wore his cricketing clothes with his cassock slung over his arm.

He went quickly up to the woman, and kissed her on the mouth, which put paid to the twirling of the parasol. He then took her quickly indoors.

I turned about to see Lydia standing at the gate of the churchyard and speaking again to Mervyn. Beyond them on the road was the carter, Will Hamer. I hurried up to him, hearing Lydia say to Mervyn, "You're to come back with us to The Angel."

"Did you bring that woman here?" I asked Hamer.

"Well now," he said, "I'm not supposed to let on."

"What's her name?"

He grinned down at me with a look of great happiness.

"Is it Emma?" I said. "Was she the governess at the Hall?"

"*You* know what o'clock it is, don't you?" he said, and the grin gave way to laughter.

The vicar and the woman — Emma, as it seemed — were crossing the churchyard, closing on Will Hamer's rulley. The vicar carried a bag. "May I speak to you about the murder of Sir George Lambert?" I asked, as he approached.

"Certainly not," he said, in a mild enough tone as he and the woman climbed up onto the bench beside Hamer.

"I'm a policeman," I said, as Hamer turned his wagon, and only then did I remember to fish for my warrant card, but Hamer's "men" (the donkey and the old horse) had a turn of speed in them after all, and they'd disappeared into the hedge-tunnel by the time I'd got it out.

★ ★ ★

We took the boy to his mother, who only seemed about as relieved as if some fairly insignificant missing object had been turned up. We then took tea of bread, cheese and rhubarb tart with the Handleys in the saloon bar (which was otherwise deserted) and as we ate I watched the boy. He said nothing concerning either John Lambert or Hugh Lambert, even though John was the main subject of the conversation: Mrs Handley put the boy's disappearance down to his being upset over the forthcoming execution, and I let that go. She was right in essence, anyhow.

Mervyn was back to his old helpful ways, giving a hand to his mother as she laid out the table, but he was agitated over something, and I didn't think it was his missing dog. Evidently it — like him — was habituated to long rambles in the woods, but could be relied on to turn up in time for its grub, which was made up of the day's leftovers and was generally served up to it at about eight, before it settled down for its kip. I would not for the present tell Mervyn its fate. That would only put him further into his shell.

The clock in the bar said a quarter after seven when we finished the tea. Draining off the dregs of my teacup, I said, "I'm off back into the woods," and nobody appeared to find this very surprising, since that was where the hunt for John Lambert was being largely conducted.

"I'll sit here and keep Mrs Handley company," said Lydia, by which she meant that she would sit with the boy as well, in case he should speak up. I had no doubt that she'd seek the aid of his mother in persuading him to talk.

The latest downpour had stopped for the present, and a kind of airless, wet-wood smell came floating through the open windows; but I was sure we hadn't seen the end of the rain, so I turned to Mr Handley, who had been supping John Smith's ale while the rest of us drank tea, and asked whether he had an oilskin about the place. He made some reply that was much longer than yes or no, and at the end of it, he stood up and quit the room.

"He has an old ulster," said Mrs Handley, turning towards me, and it was the first time she had translated, so to say, on behalf of her husband. She knew very well the difficulty everybody had in understanding him, and I wondered whether it made her ashamed of him. She never seemed to make conversation with her husband, and yet she was an intelligent woman. She would *want* to talk, and that was no doubt where Master Hugh had come in.

Mr Handley came back with the coat. It had dried leaves in the bottom of its deep pockets, and smelt of old wood fires. I wondered whether it was a left-over of his farming days. He would be much better suited to farming than running a pub; he wouldn't have to talk as much, and there wouldn't be John Smith's ale always to hand. Mr Handley showed me a special pocket in the ulster, and the gist of what he said was that any object placed in there would be kept perfectly dry no matter what. As if to prove this he brought out from behind the bar a packet of Woodbines and a box of Vestas, and he stowed them in the pocket, indicating that I might smoke as many as I liked, gratis. As he leant over me I smelt the ale on his breath, which brought to mind a question.

I asked whether Hardy, the station master, had been as drunk as he'd seemed that afternoon, and Mr Handley replied (as I eventually worked out): "He was goin' some, aye."

I asked, "Is that out-of-the-usual for him?" but couldn't make out the answer.

I entered the woods once again by the path directly across from The Angel. It hardly mattered where I went in since I didn't know what I was looking for, but only that everything bad in Adenwold started and finished in the woods. There was grey daylight over the fields but it was dusk in the woods, and I was soon lost. The air was stirless and damp; there was not a breath to breathe, and I was far too hot in the ulster. It put me in a bath of sweat.

I came after a while to a straight track bordered by evergreens, but this one didn't lead to the Piccadilly Circus of the woods. I kept imagining that I'd struck the railway line, which would give me my bearings, but it refused to appear however much I crossed and recrossed in the ferns, nettles and brambles.

As I heard the chimes for eight o'clock, I was in a district of giant trees, where the largest of the lot had toppled over onto some of its fellows and was held up leaning, like a drunk. There then came a while sitting on a low branch, smoking one of Mr Handley's Woodbines, thinking hard about the Reverend Ridley and listening for human sounds. But I heard only the birds ascending to and descending from the treetops, from which drops of a light rain swirled down spiral-wise.

It was getting on for nine before I gave it up, and began looking for a way out, which brought me, half-dazed, to the first village green, and the silent cottages and stores. Crossing the station yard in my clammy coat, I walked onto the "up" platform.

Here I made out the figure of the station master moving in the station house behind lace curtains, and I heard the clatter of pots. Hardy was a bachelor of course, and it appeared that he had no servant, and was making his own tea. I walked along to the waiting room, where the great black horsehair bench faced the dead fireplace. A picture on the wall showed "The Ruins of Rievaulx Abbey", and a horseless cart sat in the middle of these ruins, as though to pile on the misery. The walls were bare and white, and I pictured in my mind's eye Hugh Lambert in his cell. I stepped out of the waiting room, and looked at the platform clock: 9.20. Well, very likely the condemned man *had* done it — and it suddenly struck me that young Mervyn might be seeking forgiveness not for himself but for Master Hugh. By going to church he might be trying to put a word in for his friend, keep him from the fires of hell.

Another possibility was that Mervyn himself had shot Sir George Lambert, and this neither I nor the wife had felt able to put into words.

I was ambling up the narrow road that led back to The Angel when I heard voices coming around the corner. It was the Chief and Captain Usher. Now this might be ticklish. We'd seen off Cooper so easily that I'd put him from my mind completely. Yet here were his governors.

The Chief wore a waterproof; Usher carried a tightly rolled umbrella. As we closed, I tried to return the Chief's gaze without looking at his nose, which was still not right. They both looked wearied out.

I gave them good evening.

"Not so good for Cooper," said Usher.

"He chased a fellow onto the train," I said. ". . . Thought it was John Lambert."

A beat of silence.

"I don't suppose it *was*," I ran on.

"That's not really any of your business, is it, Stringer?" said Usher.

He was being cagey as usual, but there was no doubt that John Lambert was still at liberty.

"Might I ask about friend Cooper, then?" I said. "I saw him clatter his leg."

"Nasty bruise, that's all," said the Chief. "I dare say you've been searching for Lambert yourself, in spite of instructions."

Instructions, not orders. The Chief was on my side over this, but it was necessary for him to disguise the fact.

"I've just been dangling about, really," I said. "I watched a bit of the cricket game this afternoon."

"And what happened there?" said the Chief, folding his arms.

"First side in got fifty-two — no, more like thirty-six. They weren't up to much, anyhow. The second lot were on about three, maybe four, when the ball was lost. Then rain stopped play."

"I wish I'd been there to see it myself," said the Chief.

Usher was looking at his watch.

"We ought to be pressing on, Chief Inspector," he said.

"Could I ask one last question, sir?" I asked Usher, and we eyed each other levelly. "Is it known for an absolute fact that Hugh Lambert is . . . that *way?*"

"We've no hard evidence . . . thank God," said Usher.

I nodded to the pair of them, and carried on up to The Angel as the chimes came for nine-thirty.

CHAPTER
THIRTY-ONE

I heard no stir from The Angel as I came up to it, and I saw no light at our window. I went through the front door, climbed the stairs and knocked with a light knuckle on the door. No answer. I pushed the door open. The half-closed curtains dusked the room, which smelt of lamp oil and lavender. The wife lay under the covers in her night-dress, and I took her at first to be fast asleep, but I knew she could not be in the circumstances and, as I entered the room, she rose and propped her head on her arm.

"The boy?" I said.

"Nothing doing," she said.

"I'm just off down for a pint," I said, and I went downstairs, and pushed through the door that gave onto the two bars.

Mr Handley was there alone, surrounded by the green-shaded oil lamps and looking at the fireless grate with his usual pewter of ale in his hand. He nodded at me before returning his gaze to the grate, saying something that was most likely, "I'm wondering whether to light it."

The air was still close, and the windows all open. It was light that was wanted more than heat, but Mr Handley next said (I think), "I'm minded to do it."

I asked him if he'd pour me a pint first, and as he did so I asked him the whereabouts of his wife. "Turned in," he replied, in his blurred voice.

"Mervyn?" I said.

"Aye, him an' all," said Mr Handley.

"Any sign of the dog?" I asked — just to see what he'd say.

Mr Handley shook his head, saying something like: "That bugger stops out all hours ... law unto his bloody self."

"What about the bicyclist?" I said. "Is he in bed too?"

"Reckon so," said Mr Handley, and I felt like asking whether he was quite sure he hadn't drugged the lot of them for the sake of a quiet life.

"Still hot, en't it?" I said, presently.

"It is that, aye," said Mr Handley, who, having drawn us a couple of pints, was kneeling at the grate and making paper faggots with back editions of The Yorkshire Post.

"Always like this of a Sunday evening, is it?" I asked him.

"Aye, dead loss," he said.

"You'd rather be farming, I expect," I said.

"I liked that line of work," he said. "I liked a ... when I worked."

I couldn't make out the middle word. It was short, sounded like "ewe".

"A what?" I said. "A few?"

"A view," he answered, rising from the grate.

Behind him, blue smoke rolled fast over the coals of the fire.

"You lost the farm on account of Sir George," I said.

"That's it," said Mr Handley with a sigh; but then he stirred himself to a joke, which I heard quite distinctly: "God giveth and God taketh away."

"The pub must be a kind of prison for you," I said, "after life on a farm, I mean."

"Aye," said Mr Handley, but I didn't believe he meant it, for he then said something very like: "I'm looking to take in hand a York house."

"Did I have that right, Mr Handley?" I said. "You want to take on a York pub?"

He nodded.

"Any particular one?"

"Grapes," he boomed, "— on Toft Green."

"I know it," I said. "Hard by the new railway offices. Very popular spot and a regular gold mine, I should think, what with . . ."

But I did not want to speak further of the Grapes, which was a success — I now recalled — mainly on account of its landlord, a little, bright-eyed bloke who talked ten-to-the-dozen with the railway clerks, who used the place as a home from home. Chattered like a bloody monkey, the fellow did, and it was impossible to imagine Mr Handley in his place.

"I've had a tip the present fellow's moving on, and the tenancy's coming up," Mr Handley said, "and I do fancy it."

He took a long go on his pint, put down the pewter and grinned at me.

287

"The living's high in York, en't it?" he said.

I considered the question. The place had its gentry, of course, and it had its workhouse and its people for ever on the *verge* of the workhouse, but it was mainly full of respectable sorts like me. In my days in London I'd been something else: not quite respectable, a junior railwayman darted in engine grease, living in a world of my own, believing that the be-all-and-end-all of life was highspeed trips on the main line. My ambitions had started and finished with the footplate of a locomotive. It had been a sort of dream existence, and ever since then I had been trying to make my way in the real world, and not making it fast enough. I was only the Chief's lapdog, and the Chief was only Usher's. We were both too small to influence events of any importance, and that is what the week-end had proved

But Mr Handley was talking hopefully of York.

As he spoke, I noticed that the six green oil lamps that lit the inter-connected bars of The Angel were surrounded by moths and that there were also many daddy-long-legs bouncing up and down the walls. The kindling in the fire was seething as the flames took hold, and it dawned on me that there was another sound coming from beyond the opened windows, a sort of sizzling. Mr Handley was watching me and smiling as he saw me noticing the rain, but there was also a questioning look to his face, and it seemed that he had just asked me something about my own life — touching on some wide and philosophical matter requiring speech stretching late into the night.

Putting Hugh Lambert from my mind, I began telling Handley of my days firing, taking him on several journeys, fairly closely described: winding under the fearfully over-crowded signal gantries of the south London suburbs on the way to the great Necropolis of Surrey; racing across the Lancashire Fylde in another hot season with the windmills to left and right turning their arms over like bowlers at cricket. Next minute, the poor bloke was being shunted under the grey February skies of Dover onto the stone pier with the steamer for France rocking and waiting . . . And each time with trouble in prospect.

He told a few things of his own, and it was just the landlord and me sailing on the brown sea of pints of Smith's towards midnight. At Mr Handley's request, I'd long since stopped offering money for my pints; he had taken to me like a brother.

It was quite wrong to take the man for a lunatic, as most of his customers probably did. His voice rose and fell in all the right places; it was melodic in its low, rumbling way, and I had no doubt that he made perfect sense for all that he put away between six and eight pints of Smith's in the two and a half hours that I sat up with him.

I was back in the bedroom as the clock struck midnight, undressing by the light of a candle stub. I fell straightaway asleep, but woke at the chime of three, and walked along the corridor to the jakes where I pissed for what seemed like about half an hour. Returning to bed, I dreamed of a train formed of a locomotive pulling a line of carriages that somehow became brake vans that were all finally revealed as cricket pavilions. The train wound its way through pretty country-side, slipping the pavilions here and there as required by teams of cricketers who stood waiting at line-side locations. The slipping of the pavilions went off perfectly, and the cricketers were delighted to have them, but somebody somewhere raised a voice of objection, and it was a woman speaking out even though there'd been no women involved in the giving and receiving of the pavilions.

I turned over in bed, and the wife was sitting up.

She was talking to Mervyn, who stood in the doorway.

"It's four o'clock, Mervyn," the wife was saying to the boy.

I too sat up, and the boy glanced at me and then looked away, his eyes roving about the room as though the purpose of his visit had been to inspect it.

"Mervyn," I said, "they've shot your dog."

"*Who?*" he said, quickly.

"That's just what I want to know."

He stood silent. In spite of his question, he knew who'd done it.

"Mervyn," I said, "Master Hugh will be hung at eight o'clock."

"I'll not speak to you," he said, "but I'll speak to your missus."

Swiftly and silently, as though she'd known all along that it would fall to her to hear out the boy, Lydia climbed out of bed and, taking the boy's hand, led him into the corridor — and whatever was said didn't take long for she was back within a matter of seconds.

CHAPTER
THIRTY-TWO

I dare say we ought to've woken Mr and Mrs Handley rather than making off at just gone four-thirty in the morning with their son in tow and the rain streaming down. But whereas the difficulty before had been to make Mervyn Handley speak, the difficulty now was stopping him.

"It were all over the telegram not sent," he kept saying, as we walked past the row of low, bent cottages that stood black against the greyness of the dawn.

"And it was the porter, Woodcock, who Sir George asked to send it?" I asked again, although I thought I had this clear.

"It were up to 'im, aye," said Mervyn. "It were 'is job, only he'd booked off for t' day, an' 'e wouldn't do it."

"And he cheeked Sir George?"

"I should just think 'e did, aye. Give 'im a right mouthful."

"But this is all hearsay?" I said, as we passed in front of the cottages.

"You what?" said Mervyn.

A thin line of smoke went up contrary to the rain from one of the chimneys.

292

"You know of this," I said, "but you never saw it."

"I saw what come next," said the boy. "Not likely to forget it, either."

"Let's be right now," I shouted over the rain. "Sir George threatened to write —"

The boy nodded eagerly, saying, "Letter of complaint, like."

"Where to?"

"Railway brass at York."

"Did he mean to complain about Woodcock or Hardy?"

"Why, *both*," said Mervyn.

"Hardy," I said, ". . . had he got across Sir George before?"

"No," said Mervyn. "You en't listening. *Woodcock* 'ad. Woodcock would always give trouble, and Hardy wouldn't do owt agin 'im."

"Because he was scared of him."

"Scared? I'll say 'e was."

"And Hardy was more scared of this Woodcock than he was of Sir George," put in the wife.

We were now crossing the station yard. The trees thrashed under the rain, and the station looked like nothing more than a camp in the woods. It had been important to have the boy's story clear by the time we reached it, and this had meant he should come along with us, but I did not want a child put in the way of what might happen next.

"Look, you mustn't come up," I said.

So he remained in the yard under the slanting rain, with the wife standing beside him, and not quite knowing — from the looks of things — whether to take his hand.

I walked on until I gained the platform boards of the "up". The tracks and signals, and the rattling sign reading "Waiting Room", seemed nothing but a bluff. One light burned low in the roaring greyness — it spilled through the booking office doorway. I walked up to it, and Hardy was there in full station master's uniform, watching the spread of tiny tin soldiers and scratching his head. As I looked on, he leant forward and swiftly changed the position of some of the men. In 1884, the British square had broken, and the station master was setting that to rights again. He made his move, and stood back. Our eyes met.

"You murdered Sir George Lambert," I said.

He looked at me with curiosity — in a daze at having been dragged from Africa back to Adenwold.

"You murdered Sir George Lambert," I said again, holding up my warrant card this time. "You went to see him at the Hall over the matter of a telegram. I don't know what the telegram was about. It hardly matters. He'd wanted it sent, and your porter, Woodcock, wouldn't do it. Sir George called you up to the Hall. He was drinking, getting ready to go out shooting rabbits, and he was in a rage, having been arguing with his son. You thought you'd be well in with him since he'd taken so strongly against the previous bloke in your job, but he'd had bother with Woodcock before, and he wanted you to stand him down. He was giving you a hot time of it. You made out you'd do it but you knew you hadn't the nerve. Then I'd say *this* happened

294

. . . You took a shotgun from the Hall. There was no shortage of them there. You went into the woods and called to Sir George when you saw him alone. You fired on him. You were wearing gloves at the time. You then came on Hugh Lambert, lying drunk in the woods, and you left the shotgun by his side."

Hardy continued to study the soldiers.

"They walked through a fire of light, these men," he said, looking up from the leaden figures. ". . . I read that in a book about them."

I saw the alphabetic dial of the ABC machine behind him. That was the contraption by which Sir George had wanted his message sent — most of the small stations on the North Eastern had them. They were simple to operate and required very little training, unlike the Morse system of telegraphy. There had been no telephone in the Hall until lately. Sir George had been dependent on the station for sending messages.

But now the wires were down, and in nearly three hours' time Master Hugh would be executed for Hardy's crime unless a message was sent.

". . . A fire of light," Hardy said again. Then, rapidly, "Who do you have your story from?"

"The boy," I said. "Mervyn Handley. He was in the woods — he practically *lives* in the bloody woods — and he saw you fire. You know very well that he did. You saw him yourself."

"Oh well," said the station master, with an intake of breath, "I don't say it isn't right."

"He was scared of speaking out. He was no doubt threatened."

"Not by me," said Hardy. "I'm not the type to threaten."

"You're more the type to *be* threatened," I said.

"I have my *own* boy," said Hardy.

"You have a son?"

"Here," said Hardy, and his fat finger shook as he pointed at one of the figures on the board: the drummer boy. "He was the hardest to paint, you know."

"Why?" I said, although I was thinking of the cut wires. Was it possible that the Chief and Usher had restored them?

"Oh," said Hardy. "Well . . . because he's the smallest."

No, I thought, *the Chief and Usher would not have restored the connection, with John Lambert still at large and threatening to communicate with foreign agents.*

I eyed Hardy.

"Did you hear us talking in the woods to Mervyn this morning? Did you shoot his dog?"

He shook his head, which set his cheeks wobbling.

"Why do you have these soldiers?"

"To set an example," he said. "Help me play a brave man's part."

He sighed.

"To bring me up to —"

"A confession?" I put in. "Well, you've left it rather late, but will you own to it now? The boy will stand to what he saw in court, you know."

(Would he really? I hadn't put the question to Mervyn, and he evidently went in terror of police and courts.)

"I'd have been on the stones, you see," said Hardy. "Sir George said I was helpless to manage, and that I ought to go."

296

Hardy moved as he spoke — wobbled a little way to the left — giving me a view of the clock on the wall. Five to five.

"A man like that can get what he wants, and he meant to have me dismissed no matter what." Hardy breathed a shuddering breath: "And I couldn't stand Woodcock down — there was never any question of it. He'd made himself a devil to me as things were."

"And he came to know you'd done it?"

"Oh, he *knew*," said Hardy.

"You told him yourself, I shouldn't wonder — thinking to put the frighteners on him, make out that he'd get the same treatment . . . Only you were under his thumb from then on."

I advanced a little way into the booking office.

Hardy was at the wall cabinet.

"I'll come along with you," he said, "but let me find my greatcoat."

He opened the door, turned and there was a rifle in his hand.

"Oh," he said, facing me, as though surprised to find himself holding the thing. "This is the same as the lads have." He indicated the board with a nod of his head. "It's a Martini-Henry."

The gun looked ridiculous compared to the inch-long ones on the display — just as if Hardy's gun was over-sized rather than the others being *under*. But he levelled it at me, and his fat hands weren't shaking as he did so, either. I listened to the rain, which seemed to come down with hysterical heaving breaths — a whole summer's worth falling all at once. Why had I not brought Mervyn's shotgun out of The Angel? An evil voice came from the doorway behind me.

"In a fix now, en't you, copper?"

Woodcock. He'd come down from his crib in the signal box. I ought to've known he'd be somewhere about. I'd seen him in the pub earlier and there'd been no train to take him away. Still under the gun, I half-turned to him. He was making some motion with his hand in the region of his fly-hole.

"What's your game?" I asked, at which Hardy gasped out, "No talking now."

"What's my game?" repeated Woodcock. "I'm scratching me fucking love apples — any objection?"

There was a beat of silence.

"I swear there's fucking fleas in that bench," Woodcock said.

He'd perhaps been kipping in the waiting room then, not the signal box.

"Didn't think you were a journalist," he said. "*They're* quite clever."

I said, "Lambert hangs at eight."

"Here," said Woodcock, "do you know why the trains ran through? Why were the wires cut?"

I made no answer.

"In the end," said Woodcock, "I just thought I'd see how it fell out. I'm in the clear anyhow."

"The boy knows you were in on it," I said, ". . . covering up a murder. That's why you shot his dog — warn him off. How do you know *he* won't speak against you?"

I indicated Hardy.

Silence in the booking office.

"Now look here . . ." I began again, but Woodcock cut me off, saying, "Shut it, I'm thinking."

Another beat of silence, and then Woodcock looked at me as if to say: *I've made my decision.*

He took his hands out of his pockets, and began moving forward, coming past me, advancing on Hardy.

"Give that over, you soft bugger," he said.

Hardy stared at him for a moment, then handed him the rifle just as though he'd been mesmerised. There was now a good deal of shuffling of boots on the wooden floor as Woodcock took Hardy's position before the clock, and Hardy — wheezing away — skirted the military display and eased out into the rain, with Woodcock calling after him: "That's right, clear off, you double-gutted bastard."

Woodcock put the shooter on me.

"It *is* loaded, you know," he said. "Old Father Hardy kept it ready at all times. Know why? He meant to blow his own lamp out, only he couldn't screw himself up to it, so he was in a bind: too scared to live and too scared to die. The wonder is that he ever pulled the bloody trigger in the first place. Do you know what I think?"

"I don't give a fuck what you think."

"I reckon he was canned."

Woodcock turned and, still keeping the shooter on me, opened the cupboard from which it came. I had a clearer view of it this time, and saw small tools, paint pots, coils of wire, company manuals of various kinds and a shelf given over to bottles of spirits.

"An innocent man'll be dead not three hours from now," I said.

"Innocent," said Woodcock. "Now that's putting it a bit strong. Wasn't friend Lambert a bit of a . . ."

"What?"

He hesitated.

". . . Down in London, like. It *is* a crime, you know."

Still keeping the gun levelled at me, he reached into the cupboard, and brought down one of the spirit bottles. He pitched it across to me.

"After you," he said.

I unscrewed the cap, and took a belt. It might have been whisky, might have been rum; I don't touch spirits as a rule.

"Here we are," said Woodcock, "two railway blokes who like a bit of a drink. If we can't come to an understanding I don't know what . . . Just put the bottle on the table, if that's quite all right."

I did so. There was no sound for a moment but the ticking of the clock, and the seething of the rain.

"*You* want Lambert to be spared the noose, so you need to get a wire off sharpish — only the lines are down so you're a bit stumped. *I* want *you* to leave me out of account when you come to write up this whole bloody business."

"You mean you'll help me send a wire in return for immunity?"

"You've got the drop on it just nicely."

"What about Hardy? He's the guilty man, and you've sent him on his way."

"Where's he going to go, you fucking bonehead?"

300

I looked again at the clock. The hands seemed to be making leaps. Ten after five.

"Straight now," said Woodcock. "Do we have an agreement?"

"If you put that shooter down," I said.

But Woodcock continued to eye me. He seemed to be weighing the matter.

"I reckon you're the type that keeps a promise," he said, "— a good little company man."

He reached into the cupboard and pitched across one of the books, grinning and saying, "Here, cop hold."

The title of the book was *North Eastern Railway: Rules and Regulations for Traffic Department Staff.*

"Swear on that," said Woodcock, before turning away from me, and pointing the long gun at the ABC machine. He was aiming not at the two dials, but at the edge of the wooden base of the thing. He fired once, and I thought my eardrums had split; then he yanked at the lever under the handle, and took aim again at the other side of the base, saying, "You might want to stop your ears, mate."

He shot again, and the wood of the counter and the wood of the base of the machine had split, but the ABC machine was now free. Woodcock had shot away the two screws that moored it to the counter.

CHAPTER
THIRTY-THREE

We were crashing through the woods in the grey dawn, with the rain spilling down at irregular intervals from above, as if the tree canopies held so many broken pipes.

I carried the ABC machine — which was an armful in itself — and a storm lantern taken from the booking office. Woodcock held the battery for the ABC and two long loops of wire. We'd left Hardy's rifle in the station, although I'd pocketed the cartridges.

It seemed that I really did have an agreement with Woodcock, and that he meant to stick to it. Who'd got the best of this deal? Woodcock was fairly cute, and I was pretty sure he had. For one thing, I ought by rights to have made the stipulation that he would turn King's Evidence against Hardy. But I was not trained up in telegraphy; I knew that I would not be able to set up the ABC so that it worked in its new position. Accordingly, I had no bargaining power to speak of.

As we'd come out of the station, I'd not seen the wife in the yard (or Mervyn or Hardy), but I assumed that Lydia had taken the boy back to The Angel, and that Hardy had made off. He would be run in eventually, though, even if his woodcut had to appear in the *Police*

Gazette every week for the next year. Woodcock was a little way ahead of me. Every time he pushed a branch aside, it sprang back and gave me a fresh soaking.

"Why wouldn't you send a wire for Sir George?" I asked him.

"Couldn't be arsed," he called back. "My work stops when I book off — if not before."

We were sweeping fast through knee-high gorse and bracken, keeping our heads low to avoid the black branches.

"Who are you going to send to?" called Woodcock.

"Well, it won't reach long distance, will it?"

"Signal's piss weak," called Woodcock. "Only goes along the branch."

"I'll send the message to Pilmoor," I said. "That's on the main line, and they'll have a good connection for London. The chap there can send it on."

I pictured Pilmoor station — two skimpy wooden platforms shaken to buggery every time an express flew by. In theory my message could be sent there within five minutes of a connection being established, and it would only take that long again for Pilmoor to transmit to London. The question was whether they could send it direct to the Home Office . . . or would they have to go through some London exchange? We came to a wide clearing, which turned out to be a wide pond — all stagnant and clogged with weeds; not the one I'd struck before. It looked grey in the dawn-light, and was surrounded by tall everlastings, like a gathering of giants.

"Where's *this*?" I said.

"It's left from here," said Woodcock, and we skirted the water by a path littered with fallen trees, from which other trees were sprouting like signals on gantries. Sometimes we went over, sometimes under.

"I know the bloke at Pilmoor," said Woodcock, "— telegraph clerk, I mean."

"They do run to one, do they? What's he like?"

"He's a cunt."

Presently, we came to the edge of the woods, and there we stood before a scene of disaster: the empty stretch of railway line, the fallen cable and the hissing rain. We moved beyond the breakage, heading westerly, as I supposed. Two poles beyond the collapse, Woodcock pointed to the ABC and said, "Plant it here."

I set the machine down by the track ballast.

"You off up?" he said, indicating the pole. "Or am I?"

As he spoke, he was attaching the long wires to the back of the ABC. I hadn't quite thought it through, but of course our wires would have to be tied onto the overhead cable.

"You do it," I said, and he was up the pole like a bloody monkey on a stick with the wires in his teeth.

I leant over the storm lantern to protect the wick from the rain, and took out a box of matches. I struck the first, and it was blown out — not by the falling rain but by the warm wind the rain made. The same thing happened to the second, but I got the lamp lit at the third go. I then moved it close to the ABC, and looked at the two dials. One was the communicator, and the other was the indicator — sometimes called the receiver. The two dials were like overcrowded clock faces. On each were set out the numbers from o to 9, the letters of the alphabet and all the punctuation marks and other symbols. It was only the English language, but it looked brain-wracking enough just then. I drew out my pocket watch and lowered it towards the glimmering lantern: ten to six.

"All set?" I called up to Woodcock.

His shout came through the rain.

"Hold your fucking horses!"

He was fifteen foot above me, leaning out from the top of the pole, and scraping at one of the telegraph wires with a pocket knife. I looked again at the ABC. It was like a portable grave, with the one dial (the communicator) lying flat and the other (the indicator or receiver) raised vertical like a little tombstone. Around the outside of the communicator dial were golden keys, one for each letter, number or punctuation mark. You pressed the key you wanted, the handle flew to it and that was it sent. I found myself mentally picking out the letters for J-O-H-N-L-A-M-B-E-R-T. Where the hell was he? I had no notion, but in the darkness of the storm, it was very easy to believe that he'd come to grief. I looked at my silver watch again: six, dead on.

"What's up?" I called to Woodcock.

"All this . . . green shit on the wires," he said.

Verdigris. That's what it was called, and the connection wouldn't be made until it was removed. Woodcock was certainly putting his guts into the job, leaning out far from the top of the pole like the high-flying man in the circus as he reaches out for the swinging trapeze.

"Worked out your bloody message?" he called down.

"Lambert innocent," I called up. "Do not hang . . . forward directly to Home Office, London."

(There would be no difficulty in reaching the Home Office, I decided. Any telegraph clerk would have it in his directory.)

Woodcock, still at his wire-scraping, called out something I couldn't catch.

"Come again?" I called up.

"*Please* do not hang!" he shouted down. "Remember to ask nicely!"

He was a cold-hearted little bastard, and that was fact. It was five after six.

Woodcock was now tying our two wires to one of the six carried out from the pole. Christ knew how he could tell which was the right one. Then he was down from the pole, and pulling at the trailing ends of the wires he'd tied onto the ones above. Crouching low, and working by the light of the storm lamp, he connected them somehow to the back of the ABC, and then took the battery out of his top-coat pocket, which he tied on by two smaller wires. As soon as the connection was made there came a blue flash, which I took at first for our little bit of electricity. But then came the boom of the thunder, and the rain doubled its speed. Woodcock was crouching on the bank of slimy track ballast, eyeing me and trying to light a fag.

I glanced at my watch: 6.25.

"Never mind that," said Woodcock. "Hand over your pocket-book."

"Eh? Why?"

"Because I need bread, you silly sod. How much do you have in it?"

"Nothing doing, pal," I said, at which he stood up.

"I'm taking a big risk by sending this message," he said. "It puts me right in the bloody line of fire."

"I've given you a fair spin," I said. "You're off the hook; we have an agreement."

"I'm clearing out in any case," he said. "Meantime, I might or might not work this doings for you. It all depends on you handing over your gold."

"Forget it, mate," I said.

"All right then, I'm off, and I don't much fancy your chances with that thing."

He climbed the track ballast and stepped over the rails and into the field beyond. The lightning came again, and Woodcock was suddenly a hundred yards further on, walking with his hands in his pockets through cut corn under the roaring rain. There came another bang of thunder, and out of this seemed to grow another, more regular noise — the beating of an engine.

The first Monday train. I hadn't bargained on that. Would it stop at the station? The week-end was over now, after all. If it did stop, then Hardy might board it and ride away to freedom. It would look queer, the station master getting on the train; it would be like the *station* getting on it, but who'd lift a finger to stop him? Everything was going to pot. I ought to have brought the Chief in again, even if that meant involving that pill Usher. The engine drew out of the woods, and came on. The rain made a haze above the carriage roofs; and it made a waterfall as it rolled down the carriage sides. *Will Woodcock still be in sight by the time this has passed?* I wondered.

He was, but only just — a small black shape on the far side of the field in the milky light. I looked down at the ABC — at the white dials glowing in the lamplight. It was all connected up, but those dials seemed to have sprouted a few more foreign-looking signs and symbols since the last time. Woodcock had got me so far, but he wasn't the sort to do people favours — his heart just wasn't in it. It struck me that, in pushing his luck in the way he had been, Woodcock had been asking me a sort of question. I took out my watch, and the hands seemed treacherous.

Six thirty-three.

I scrambled up the bank and sprinted over the tracks and across the field towards Woodcock. He turned about and watched as I gained on him. I came to a halt at two yards' distance, with the rain making a curtain of water between us.

"Fancy a scrap?" I said.

I got a good one in the very moment he nodded his head. Another silent flash came just then, and it showed me Woodcock bringing his fists up in a way he'd no doubt wanted to be doing ever since he'd clapped eyes on me, but our set-to did not last long, and it was over before the thunder boom that belonged to that particular lightning bolt came rolling around. We both happened to be down on the corn stubble at that point, and Woodcock, standing up, said, "Have it your way," and began trailing back in the direction of the tracks and the ABC.

As he walked, he lit another cigarette, and began muttering to himself. When he got back to the ABC (which was soaked but, I trusted, well sealed) and its faintly glowing companion the storm lantern, he immediately crouched down and set about winding the handle on the front of the wooden case.

"What's this in aid of?" I asked him.

"I've put the switch to 'Alarm'," said Woodcock, "and I'm turning ten times to give ten rings."

"I can't hear anything."

"No," he said, "but they can."

"You sure?"

"Nope."

"Why ten? It seems a bloody lot."

"That's the code for Pilmoor — tenth stop on the branch, en't it?" "They *would* count it from fucking Malton and not the other way. What's *our* code?"

"Six bells."

I looked at the time. Six-forty. Lambert would be with the priest now. The High Sheriff of Durham would be taking coffee with the governor of the gaol, and being reminded of the correct form. When he stopped winding, Woodcock turned a switch and stepped back, saying: "Off you go, then."

I looked at my watch, and for the first time I could do so without straining: ten to seven. I didn't need the lantern to see the dials in the clearing light, but still the rain thundered down. I looked at the necklace of gold keys around the indicator dial. You pressed the key according to the letter or number you wanted to send; the pointer flew to it, and at that instant the circuit was broken, and you pressed the next letter, winding the handle to fire that one off, and so on.

I pressed the key for "F", and began.

My message, of which I was not over-proud, was: F-O-R-W-A-R-D-T-O-H-O-M-E-O-F-F-I-C-E-L-O-N-D-O-N-L-A-M-B-E-R-T-I-N-N-O-C-E-N-T-M-U-S-T-N-O-T-H-A-N-G-A-C-K-N-O-W-L-E-D-G-E-S-T-R-I-N-G-E-R-Y-O-R-K-R-A-I-L-W-A-Y-P-O-L-I-C-E-A-D-E-N-W-O-L-D.

I had finished with a full stop. That was the icing on the cherry, so to say, but I had not bothered with spaces between the words.

"Like to lay on the drama, don't you?" said Woodcock, who'd been looking on from behind. I made no reply to that, and Woodcock came forward and once more turned a switch on the machine. We would now await the acknowledgement.

Two minutes to seven by my watch.

A further three minutes went by, and no sound came from the ABC. It was just a lump of bloody wood; you might as well expect a tree to talk. My eye ran up the wires connecting the thing to the cables above, and it all looked about as scientific as washing on a line.

Woodcock said, "Exciting, en't it?" and just as he spoke, the machine gave a ring, and then another five, which seemed like a miracle, not least because I couldn't immediately see any bell. A second later, the needle on the indicator dial began flying.

Craning forward, I watched the letters as they were signified. The first was "I", and the whole message ran as follows:

"I-N-N-O-C-E-N-T-O-F-W-H-A-T-?"

He'd even put the fucking question mark in.

"I told you he was a cunt," said Woodcock, and he was up the telegraph pole directly, adding, "Reckon the signal's come and gone, and come again. He's only had the first part of it. Even that clot would know it was murder if he'd got the bit about the hanging. I'll take down the wires, and we'll set up further along."

"You're saying it's the verdigris?" I called up the pole.

"Eh?" said Woodcock.

"The green shit!" I said.

"That's it, mate!" called Woodcock.

It was five after seven.

"I can't afford to shift," I said. "There's no time. Can you not just scrape a bit more off?"

"Makes no odds to me," he called down, and I wondered if that was really true. He was leaning and scraping once again, anyhow.

"Green shit," he was saying as he came down, "that's what it's called in the manual, I believe."

Two minutes later, I re-sent, as Woodcock lit another cigarette. (He was a great hand at smoking in the rain.) The lightning had stopped, and the rain was slowing now. Woodcock set the machine to let us hear back from Pilmoor; then I blew out the lamp and paced up

311

and down by the railway line. Hugh Lambert would be making ready to leave the condemned cell. A handshake from the warder who'd stopped up half the night with him. That warder would be a hard-arsed character, but dignified with it.

The six bells came after five minutes, and the pointer jumped first to "R", and then:

E-C-I-E-V-E-D.

"Can't spell," said Woodcock from behind.

The pointer kept on moving, as Woodcock ran on: "Christ, you'd think he'd be able to spell 'received' in *his* job."

"Shut up, will you?" I said.

"You *watch* the needle, you bonehead," said Woodcock, "you don't *listen* to it."

The remainder of the message ran:

. . . W-I-L-L F-W-D-H-O-M-E O-F-F-I-C-E.

"He's wasted another minute telling us that," said Woodcock, as the pointer fell back to zero for the final time. "I'm off, anyhow," he added, and he turned a switch on the ABC, and began sauntering away towards the trees.

"*Where* are you off?" I called after him.

He half-turned and said, "We have an agreement, mind," at which he entered the woods, and was gone from sight. He was on his way — I would discover later — to steal thirty pounds from the safe in the booking office at Adenwold station, and then to disappear.

I sat by the tracks contemplating the ABC.

Was my business with it concluded? I didn't fancy lingering beside it in case it rang again, followed by some further query or contradiction from Pilmoor. Come to that, I didn't even know if Woodcock had left the switch open to receive. But I felt duty bound to sit by the thing, and I did so until the rain had quite stopped, the sun was raying down and the Adenwold chimes of eight had floated faintly across the drying field towards me.

In the silence that followed, I lay back and closed my eyes. When I opened them, the sky had washed itself light blue. A bumble bee bounced into view, and I heard the call of a wood pigeon, a steady, urging-on sound. It seemed to keep time with a regular noise from the woods, a tramping of feet. I looked up, and thought for a moment I saw Hugh Lambert all in white, breaking free of the woods, but it was not Hugh. It was of course John, changed from his evening suit into the clothes in which I'd first met him. The sunlight flashed upon his spectacles. He put his hand up to them, and stood at the border of the woods, watching. I rose to my feet, and saw, from the corner of my eye, another man advancing to my left. He too wore white, and he limped. It was Cooper in his dust-coat. He held a shotgun, but somehow I dismissed that from my mind. He *would* hold a shotgun. John Lambert — who carried no weapon — was the one to pay attention to. I called out his name. He was looking at the ABC, head tilting in wonder as his eyes roved up and down the wire joining it to the telegraph lines.

"Is the connection made?" he said, and he began to advance.

"It is," I said, "and I trust that your brother has been saved."

Cambridge man, first-class degree and brilliant intellect, yet he looked baffled; and when Cooper's shot hit him in the chest, the look of bafflement increased, and kept on increasing as he slowly collapsed. I looked towards Cooper, and he had the gun trained on me, weighing up the wisdom of a second shot.

PART FOUR

Tuesday, 7 November, 1911

CHAPTER
THIRTY-FOUR

We walked along Whitehall in the rain. The black cabs came on and on like one long funeral. Tiny trees along the pavements; the buildings were grey cliffs and every man held an umbrella except for the Chief and me, and the two policemen in capes who happened at that moment to be lumbering along beside us like carthorses. We passed the entrance to Downing Street — one tradesman's van was parked a little way along it with a white horse in the shafts.

"Do you suppose Mr Asquith's at home?" I said.

The Chief made no answer, but looked at his watch.

"We've an hour to kill," he said.

The letters on the side of the van read: "Williams of Pimlico".

I said to the Chief, "You'd think they'd put 'Williams of Pimlico: Suppliers of Bread to the Prime Minister'."

"Full of good ideas, you are," said the Chief.

He stopped and eyed me for a moment before adding, by way of making amends, "The Tories wouldn't buy the bread if it was a Liberal prime minister and the Liberals wouldn't buy if it was a Tory."

"Expect not," I said.

"Shall we take a pint?" said the Chief.

The pub was like a tiny baronial hall, with shields on the wall, and criss-crossed with high beams; and it reeked of past-food. As the rain streamed down the windows, and the Chief bought two pints on expenses, the man at the next table was talking about India. "Do you see yourself going out there?" he kept asking the woman he was with. It was pretty bloody obvious enough that he wanted her to go out there, so why didn't he just say so? Another fellow, steaming on the same bench as me, said to a man standing before him in a coat with a fur collar: "For the first time in years I've been able to do a bit of shooting," and as he spoke, the pub was filled with the sound of the Westminster bells, which were so deep-toned they might have been inside your head.

"Care for another?" the man at the table asked the woman.

"I don't know," she said. "Do you?"

"Well, I know I don't fancy going out in *that*," the man said, contemplating the streaming windows.

Why must he go round the houses so? He put me in mind of the Adenwold bicyclist. The lengths that fellow had gone to just to get a fuck! He'd even made a show of taking the bloody machine to the blacksmith's to get the wheel fixed. As if anybody had been interested! Well, *I* had been, and the wife, too; she'd always suspected him, just as though one bicyclist might prove as important in the whole business as the combined forces of the state.

The Chief was saying something about the fellow we were going to see — Major somebody or other. His name came in two parts: Henderson-Richards or some such hedging of bets. I imagined him as a man who couldn't decide between Henderson and Richards, who considered them both good names and had determined to have the best of both worlds.

He was in the Special Police, or army intelligence, or both. It was the office for muffling-up, anyhow, and our meeting with him would mark the end of the business that had begun with the transfer of Hugh Lambert at York. It would all be laid to rest, and with no undue ceremony beyond my own name being put to a paper.

My name evidently counted for something in this — otherwise, why would they have called me down to London for the signing (even if it had taken them three months to get round to it), and that with a special first class travel warrant and with the Chief as chaperone?

"Take another?" asked the Chief, draining his glass and watching me over the top of it.

He was altered in his approach towards me since the Adenwold events — more watchful. I'd brought off something big, after all: Hugh Lambert had been released and pardoned, if that was the term. Usher had fixed it all after talking to Hardy and Mervyn — this in spite of his strongly held opinions against men of Hugh Lambert's type. Lambert had evidently had a handshake from the governor of Durham gaol, a letter from the governor of Armley and an armful of money and a rail pass into the bargain.

This last he'd used to come up to York station in the middle of August.

As before, old man Wright and I had been the only ones in the office. Wright had a scar on his forehead — nothing to the Chief's scars but very noticeable all the same. He'd slipped and fallen on his July week-end in Scarborough — taken a tumble down the steps from the Marine Parade to the beach. I couldn't help thinking it was his own fault for having talked it up so much in advance.

Also as before, it was a day of unbreathable heat on Platform Four, and the sparrow had been outside the door, for I'd had my snap in front of me as on that earlier occasion. But this time Hugh Lambert had practically trodden on the poor thing — didn't give it a glance. He'd marched up to me and put out his hand, and I was that shocked to see him that I forgot to stand. Old Wright did so, however, and *sharpish*, as if he'd seen a ghost, for he'd heard all about Hugh Lambert.

"I owe you my life, Detective Stringer," Lambert said, and he sounded none too happy about it.

"I'm sorry for what happened to your brother," I said. "I called to him at the wrong time. They thought the machine was being used to communicate on his behalf. It was just a . . . bit of a mix-up."

"A mix-up," he repeated, and he evidently didn't think much of that way of putting it.

He then stood and eyed me for a while, looking down on me — I couldn't help thinking — in more ways than one. He wore a boxy suit that didn't suit him and he looked more out-of-sorts than he had before, but in a new way. After an interval of silence, he turned on his heel and quit the office.

Even Wright was put out on my behalf.

"That was a bit rich," he said, coming up to me quickly as though I'd just been struck a blow. ". . . After what you did for him."

Well, what had I done? I'd killed his brother, or as good as. Hugh Lambert's own life was somehow of no account to him and this, according to the wife in our many hours' conversation on the point, was a consequence of his father's treatment of him. Because of the way he was, his father had undermined him (it was the wife's word), and undermined he'd *stayed*.

This was the wife's big theory: this business of the undermining. As for his brother's death, this — according to Lydia — was none of my doing. It was Cooper who'd pulled the trigger. It was all out of my hands. I'd done my level best and should be proud.

I'd had this from the Chief as well, but with something added: I could tell the Chief was pleased by what I'd brought about. It had solved the problem of John Lambert, a man with all the mobilisation plans in his head, and a man who'd proved himself not to be trusted.

But what kept me awake at night was this: Hugh Lambert had told me in the police office that his brother would be in danger from people who would be in Adenwold "over the week-end", and because of what he'd told me, I had become one of the people. I was one of the "they"; in fact, I was the very man.

The strangeness, the ghostliness of it . . .

As the Chief waited at the bar, a fellow came darting in out of the rain clutching some papers in a paste-board envelope, and he handed them to a bloke holding a glass of ale, who said, "Thanks, pal."

"No, thank *you*," said the other.

The one who'd received the papers was looking at the other fellow's bowler, which was quite soaked.

"You'll need a new one now," he said, and the man with the wet hat laughed.

These two were government officials; they were engaged in conducting the business of the state, and seemed very happy about it — or not *vexed* by it, at least.

Wet hat dived back out into the rain, and the Chief was joined at the bar by the man who'd been sitting next to me, and this fellow had left his newspaper on the bench. From where I sat, I read the date: Tuesday, 7 November, 1911. The paper lay folded to reveal an article on the weather. Not the present weather — the dark clouds and warmish rain — but that of the late summer, which had broken all records and remained just as much a talking point in the papers as all the endless strikes and revolts among the workers. "Cuckoos and chaffinches were heard singing in September," I read, picking up the paper, "and chiffchaffs late into October . . . There have been curious approximations to the habit of nature in more torrid climates." The man whose paper this was did not seem to be buying a drink, but was talking loudly to another bloke at the bar and, as I looked on, he said, equally loudly, "Well, I'm going to the lavatory now."

That meant I could look a little further into his newspaper.

322

I turned to the foreign pages and read the heading: "The New Franco-German Treaties". They'd just been signed, or were just about to be. Germany would leave off hounding the French in Morocco, and in return would get Spanish Guinea with no objections. Taken all together, Germany had carried her point; or maybe the French had. Even the *Times* man didn't seem to know. Underneath the report was something further about France. The heading read: "A Proposal For the Extension of State Control Over the Railways of France".

I folded the paper and replaced it as the Chief returned with the drinks, and something about the way he put them down on the tables — a little carelessly, and with a slight spillage — told me we'd both end the day canned.

The War Office was just the other side of Downing Street — very handily placed for prime ministers wanting to start wars. The doors of it were guarded by ordinary coppers, who nodded at us as we went in. One of them gave me a particular look — not unfriendly — and I wondered whether he thought I was going in to collect a medal: a reward for all the sleepless nights.

The feature of Henderson-Richards's office was a large and beautiful fireplace, which he was standing beside as we were shown in. There was a good blaze going, and he leant against the corner of the mantel-shelf watching it. He was a thin man with long hair that fell down over half his face like a grey curtain, and he wore the softest and lightest shoes, which made no noise as he walked towards us and shook our hands. He was not what I'd expected.

There were two seats ready for us before Henderson-Richards's desk, and a single document on the desk. But he returned to the fireplace in order to address us.

"I trust you gentlemen had a satisfactory journey down from Yorkshire?"

You'd have thought that Yorkshire was a foreign country, but he spoke pleasantly enough.

"The broad-acred county . . ." he said, smiling and lolling against the mantel-piece. "Quite a week-end you had of it, back in July, Detective Sergeant Stringer."

He was still smiling, but I thought: *He's glad about what happened as well, and he has the confidence to show it.*

"You've read my report, sir?" I asked him, which clashed with the Chief saying, "Detective Sergeant Stringer was a little over-hasty in some of his actions, sir, but he is an excellent man as a general rule."

We both continued to look forward — towards the desk of Henderson-Richards rather than towards the man himself, but I was thinking of the Chief as a sort of beer-smelling, tobacco-stained knight in shining armour.

Henderson-Richards now walked over, sat in his desk chair and addressed me directly, saying:

"It doesn't fall to everyone to save a man's life, Detective Stringer."

(*Or to cause a death*, I thought.)

"Is there anything you'd like to ask me?" he enquired.

324

"Yes," I said. "What's become of Hardy?"

"Didn't you know?" said Henderson-Richards. "Hardy is in Bootham, the York mental hospital."

That was a turn-up. Still, his confession had been believed, and that was the main thing.

"Will he be charged with any crime?"

"Not fit," said Henderson-Richards, shaking his head.

"What about the porter, Woodcock?" I said. "Have the police laid hands on him?"

"Woodcock!" said Henderson-Richards, suddenly galvanised. "What a dark horse he was! What couldn't he have achieved with a man he respected over him?"

He was evidently expecting an answer to this out-of-the-way question.

"Well," I said, "what *would* he have achieved? What would have been the opportunities open to him? Station master of some hole-in-the-corner place?"

I was coming out pretty strongly for Woodcock. Well, he'd been straight enough in his own way.

A beat of silence; then I repeated my question: "Do you know his whereabouts?"

"No," said Henderson-Richards.

"As to Gifford . . ." I said. "It was Cooper who . . . He'd somehow had sight of Gifford's German documents, and he'd put two and two together and made . . ."

Henderson-Richards was giving me such a blank look that I quite feared for his health.

". . . five," I said.

Henderson-Richards was frowning, shaking his head.

"Is he all right?" I said. "Gifford, I mean?"

"Quite," said Henderson-Richards.

He said it sharply. The upper classes said "Quite" in that way when they meant shut up.

"Cooper," I said. "Has he been disciplined for . . ."

"What?" said Henderson-Richards. "Who?"

Again he spoke sharply, but like an actor.

I got the message: Cooper did not exist.

"John Lambert hadn't made contact with anybody, had he?" I said. "I mean, the mobilisation secrets were not disclosed?"

"That's a secret that will not be disclosed," said the Chief, but he looked pleased enough as he leant forwards and smartly swivelled the paper towards me. I saw something like: "The officer shall keep secret any information of a confidential nature obtained by him by reason of . . ."

"Sign at the bottom, please," said Henderson-Richards.

I fished for my fountain pen, and Henderson-Richards sat back and half-smiled towards the Chief in a way that stayed in my mind throughout the railway journey back to York, as I sat in the first-class compartment with the Chief, and then later on in the dining car, and then in the compartment again as the sky darkened and the rain flew against the windows. I thought I now had everything pretty clear, although Gifford remained a bit of a mystery to me. The Chief knew all, of course; or nearly all. I had begun to think differently now of his absences from the office, his distracted way of talking. He was in on a whole lot of

326

things he could never tell me about, and I wondered whether this was partly a question of age. Would I be in on a lot of unmentionable things when I was approaching retirement? I hoped so. It was important to take secrets with you when you died.

At York, the wife was waiting with Harry. I gave him the funny paper I'd bought for him at King's Cross, and gave his cap a shove, which is my usual way of saying hello.

Lydia kissed me, and we made for the footbridge, with the Chief walking behind.

"Want to speak about it?" she asked.

"Not over-much," I said, as we climbed the footbridge steps.

A long "up" train was rolling along beneath the bridge.

"Thanks for asking," I called over the racket, "but I've signed the paper, and I'll say no more about the matter."

"Well, I'm very glad to hear it, Jim," said the wife, half-turning towards me and giving a grin.